Aspen Pulp

Patrick Hasburgh

Aspen Pulp

THOMAS DUNNE BOOKS
St. Martin's Minotaur
New York

THOMAS DUNNE BOOKS.
An imprint of St. Martin's Press.

www.minotaurbooks.com

Library of Congress Cataloging-in-Publication Data

Hasburgh, Patrick.
    Aspen pulp / Patrick Hasburgh.—1st ed.
      p. cm.
    ISBN 0-312-33183-5
    EAN 978-0312-33183-2
    1. Private investigator—Colorado—Aspen—Fiction. 2. Missing persons—Fiction. 3. Aspen (Colo.)—Fiction. 4. Ski resorts—Fiction. I. Title.

PS3608.A7897A87 2004
813'.6—dc22

2004048176

First Edition: December 2004

10 9 8 7 6 5 4 3 2 1

To my wife, Cheri,
who led me out of the darkness that I led her into,
and for Jensen Grace,
who was waiting for us in the light

A note to the reader

Numerous events in this book may bear similarity to those of my life, but the scenarios and happenings are solely a work of fiction. I have drawn freely from the imagination and adhered only loosely to a vague pattern of personal experience, providence, and calamity. In spite of occasional references to actual places, real events, or existing persons, *Aspen Pulp* is a work of complete fantasy. In the book, as in my life, I have pursued parody and jest in lieu of common sense and literacy.

Nobody is going to save your ass but yourself.

—Charles Bukowski

Aspen Pulp

Chapter One

"**Remember when** this town was a work-free drug place?" Herman asked.

The Swiss expat slammed back a shot of tequila and then flinched as if the smelly yellow liquid had ignited a cerebral aneurism.

"If you can remember those days, you weren't here," I said.

It was about nine in the morning, late in the politically whacked summer of 2003, and the Big Easy's dishwasher was just finishing the nightshift, chanting what sounded like Spanglish reggae into the dreadlocks of a kitchen mop. But the Rasta wetback was making enough sense to serenade me back to 1975. That's when I was the Big Easy pearl diver and that low-ceiling firetrap was the coolest joint in Aspen. I got ten dollars a night and all the beer I could drink.

The Easy kitchen had been set up to feed silver miners beans and franks during the boom of the 1880s, and more than a century later it took all night and a case of Coors to chip out the lobster bisque from the cast-iron pots. You'd think the owner would spring for a new Maytag, but he's on death row for putting his wife through ten years of mental cruelty and then a wood chipper.

"Now you get tested all the time," Herman said. "Life's nothing but a lousy test."

"A snap quiz," I said, recalling that I had recently inebriated another birthday.

Herman Thayer had been in Aspen since he almost won the World Pro Skiing Championship in the mid-seventies, losing three years in a row to a former Olympian whose name sounded like something you spread on small pieces of triangular toast. He always had more wins than the Frenchman but lost on points because he'd either finish first or not finish. Herman had yet to learn that life's a marathon, not a sprint.

"I hate the French," he said, glancing at the TV behind the bar as a FOX morning news anchor slapped around a Parisian apologist over France's Mesopotamian ambiguities. "They'll do anything to win."

"Except fight," I said. "But what can you expect from a country where half the population cuts cheese for a living."

"Yeah, well, if it wasn't for the Frogs I'd be living in Starwood."

Herman tossed down another shot in a way that whiplashed the grim remains of his blonde hair into a transparent pompadour, and I flashed on how handsome he used to be before the booze and the coke twisted him into a punchline. The locals called him the Night Mayor because he never slept. He could win fifty grand in a giant slalom against the best in the world after snorting through a rack of eight balls on a seventy-two-hour binge. But people don't respect that kind of talent anymore.

"You could've bought John Denver's house," I said.

Aspen's country boy was now thanking God personally after he turned his airplane into a submarine off the coast of Santa Barbara.

"I think it went for just under six million," I continued, "but it had a solar-powered security system and an endangered species petting zoo."

"I had money once," Herman said. "It's a pain in the ass."

Starwood was where the rich people in Aspen lived if they found Red Mountain too crowded or too expensive. I found all of Aspen too crowded and too expensive, but so were good public golf courses and sushi bars. In spite of the tawdry press and aging rock-starian excess, this sky-high hamlet is still one of the last great places on earth. That was why I had crawled back into town.

"You working today?" I asked, motioning to the bartender that maybe Herman had had enough breakfast.

But the keep poured him another shot and slid it down the bar.

"I'm always working," Herman said. "Like a fucking peasant."

"We're all peasants," I said.

"Not you, Jake," Herman slurped, lopping off his tequila shot. "You're a hot-shit Hollywood sellout."

"Everybody's got his price, Hermy. I just know exactly what mine is."

"Yeah, thirty pieces of silver," Herman said, like someone who had read a book or two. "And don't call me Hermy. I hate that."

The racer-chaser chicks used to call him Germy Hermy back when he was banging them two at a time. He was Aspen's own Typhoid Mary, but at least the snowmeister never passed around anything fatal.

"Let me buy you a real drink," Herman said, hand-signaling the bartender like a deaf-mute at a spelling bee. "I got a tab here."

"I'm trying not to drink anything real," I said, swizzle-sticking a packet of sugar into my Diet Coke and taking a sip. "At least not before the market opens."

"The Farmer's Market in Carbondale? They're open. I was down there already, buying paint."

Herman taught skiing in the winter and painted houses in the summer, and the co-op in Carbondale was a long way from almost medaling in the downhill at the Sapporo Olympics. But the square-headed kamikaze hit a tree at about a hundred miles an hour, so maybe it was okay for him to be drinking at eight in the morning. Herman spent ten months in a body cast before he was thrown off the Suisse ski team for dealing his leftover Percocets. I have never heard of anybody who ever had any *leftover* Percocets. But that's when Herman decided to come to the United States and turn pro.

"The stock market," I said, thinking that a toddy might taste better than the carcinogenic concoction I was drinking and remembering how my portfolio had been circling the drain ever since George Junior curiously bushwhacked the election and Osama bin Laden powdered the World Trade Center into a trillion tons of talcum.

That our cheerleader-in-chief and his madrassas of dissemblers had the Third World's cheap seats cheering for Saddam's side during the second half of the Gulf War also forebodes what else might happen when genetically connected Skull & Boners skip political science class. But don't get me started on Bill Clinton, either. We should have sewn that monkey puncher into a giant condom and dropped him off the Chappaquiddick Bridge. Bubba put procuring pudgy delights before principle, an unpardonable sin when one signs up to run the big white hut.

"So how's business?" I said, trying to hang a U-turn away from one of my political tangents.

"Better than the stock market," Herman said, licking salt off the back of his hand. "I'm painting a Victorian on West Smuggler. Thing's eight hundred forty square feet and just sold for a million two."

"You can't buy that kind of craftsmanship anymore," I said, half right.

"It's a mail-order shit box," he said, completely right.

A gang of self-righteous trust-funders and no-growth terrorists protected the ghettos of Aspen from the carpetbaggers' backhoe, but only after previously allowing themselves to scrape off some shanties and put up mausoleums of their own. Most of the buildings the Historical Society goes to war over were picked out of a JCPenney catalogue before it was hung on the inside of an outhouse and used for toilet paper.

"We got assholes who think anything built before American Bandstand is historically significant," Herman said.

I nodded and stirred some ice. My ears were chirping like a choir of crippled crickets at a faith healing contest.

"Why the fuck you put sugar in Diet Coke?" he asked.

It wasn't the first time I'd heard the question.

"There's eighteen tablespoons of sugar in a regular Coke," I said. "Booze metabolizes into about the same amount. I'm easing out of the Jones by cutting down on the sweets."

"What are you, in rehab?"

"Not anymore," I said.

I'd done a two-month jolt in an outpatient program at St. John's in Santa Monica back when my final television series was cancelled after the first episode. It was an industry record and, unfortunately, my best work.

"It doesn't stick," Herman said.

"You have a brilliant grasp of the obvious," I said, looking at his empty shot glass. "Hold on to it tightly."

"C'mon, have a drink," he said. "It won't kill you."

"*Hasn't* killed me," I said. "There's a difference."

The red circles around Herman's eyes made him look like an Elton John knockoff without the mink bangs and the Bolivian powder puff, but when you slapped him on the shoulder it still felt like you were hitting the corner of a mailbox.

"Pretend I'm in training for the Olympics," I said. "The liver healing events."

"I was in the Olympics once," Herman said. "It was a pain in the ass."

Rehab was also a pain in the ass. It wasn't like I didn't come down with a touch of the Stolichnayan flu more than the next guy. I just couldn't stand the Calvinism of the twelve-steppers. It was like I was witnessing the birth of a new religion. You couldn't hang out with people who still did drugs or drank, which narrowed my circle of close friends considerably. And they wanted you to tell the truth all the time, which widened my circle of enemies. You had to keep all your agreements and "work the program." In Hollywood, AA meetings were like Broadway productions, and everybody was working the room instead of the program.

The speakers probably had their own PR flacks, and when they told their personal tales of alcoholic woe and humiliation, it sounded suspiciously like they were pitching a movie idea to the development execs at Paramount. How many years sober you had was like listing your film credits, and a fatal car wreck with a felony DWI was almost as good as winning an Academy Award.

I never had more than sixty days sober in a row, and I sounded like Carry Nation when I did. The only thing they let you do was smoke, and it was the only thing I was really trying to quit.

So I stopped drinking on my own. I was a little better at it than Darryl Strawberry, but apparently not as good at it as the president, a guy who was sometimes too smacked to fly in the Texas Air National Guard but not quite smacked enough to go to AA meetings. George W. and I are what're known as dry drunks: drinkers who trade Wild Turkey for cold turkey and dare to tread the tightrope of sobriety without a net. But people get the government they deserve.

"So Herman, you going to teach skiing again this winter?" I said, straight-arming another blitzing political tangent as if it was a linebacker who had slipped a block.

"What else am I gonna do, work for Sears?"

"Why not," I said. "They'd probably pay you a fortune to be a greeter at Target."

But I may as well have blown my brilliant wisecrack through a dog whistle.

"All I gotta do is pass the ski school piss test," Herman shrugged. "I got popped for skiing on THC at the last Winter Fest. I was being festive for Christ's sake."

"Maybe it's time to give it up," I said.

"Skiing?"

"Festivities."

I was trying not to be judgmental for the obvious reasons.

"And be a writer like you, Jake?" Herman said. *"Nein danke."*

"I'm a writer like you're a painter, Herman." I said. "I just did it for the money and because it sounded cool when I was trying to get some ski bunny into the sack. After a while I had to actually start writing or they would've arrested me for date rape."

"Painting houses never got anybody laid," he said, like he knew.

Herman stuck his tongue through a paper napkin and made a hole. He did it again and then put the napkin over his eyes as if he were wearing goggles.

"I know what it's like to be upside down in an Olympic downhill," he said. "But the idiots in this town don't ski if the sun isn't shining."

"No shit," I said, like I was pledging for Herman's own personal peanut gallery. "If assholes could fly, the place would be an airport."

Our observations were maybe alcoholically acute, and the deculturing of Aspen was probably something we could have whined about all day. But I had to get out of the Big Easy before I started kissing Bloody Mary and it would suddenly be Thursday somewhere and I'd be trying to buy a Porsche Turbo with a busted credit card.

I put a twenty on the bar.

"It's good to be back," I said.

"Don't kid yourself."

Herman aimed his kaleidoscopic eyes at the center of my forehead and gently touched my hand.

"You can't stand in the same river twice, Jake," he said like a man who had gotten to know James Crumley in the can.

"I know," I said. "But you can get your feet wet."

Chapter Two

I turned left out of the Big Easy and headed down Hyman Avenue toward the mall that is a patchwork of nineteenth-century clay bricks the city council bought from St. Louis back in the summer of 1976. Why the council covered the downtown core with antique bricks is still a mystery to most of the locals. The four-block area is closed to cars, it's impossible to rollerblade without breaking your neck, and it's against the law to ride a bicycle. But I guess they wanted to retrofit some St. Louis charm into Aspen.

The silver miners from Leadville, who survived crossing the Continental Divide during the spring of 1880, called Aspen "Ute City" because it was in the middle of Ute Indian territory. This didn't make the noble Ute happier hunters, and they endeavored to take as many scalps as possible while pillaging the mining camps and molesting the white women. But those skirmishes would prove to be merely rigged games of sticks and stones against blue-eyed technologies, and the miners chewed up the red man, spinning them into cigar store props and poverty while claim-jumping their way over the Rockies.

There are thirty-two miles of bankrupt mine tunnels spider-webbing through the mountains surrounding Aspen, but back in the boom, a silver strike the size of a bedroom could produce a half a million dollars in quick cash. Now that same amount of insider funny-money couldn't buy a studio loft in Aspen's famously insane real estate market.

The population swelled to twelve thousand until the rush went bust in 1893 after the US Treasury decided to ditch the silver standard and leverage gold bullion against billions of pieces of green paper. But for a few good years, Ute City was fat with cash, landmarking its easy money with the elegant Wheeler Opera House and the dignified Hotel Jerome, both spectacular architectural visions of the time. Quaint Victorians and saloons stood shoulder to shoulder with stone churches and bordellos, competing for the wet kiss of the cowboy's grubstake. Today, Aspen is a hodgepodge of magnificent Queen Anne restorations and tacky 1970s chintz. It looks like the guy who designed Pioneer Town had a nervous breakdown.

The Independence Lodge was an Old West rooming house where cowboys and miners and then ski bums could flake out and sleep off a hangover for a few dollars a night. When I first arrived in town, the Independence was still operating as a flophouse with a grog shop conveniently located on the ground floor. Most recently, the pricey storefront was a Banana Republic, and the tiny rooms where miners once shook dreams and silver from their pans and serious skiers passed around joints and planned first descents were now filled with stacks of wool slacks and cotton golf shirts.

I spent my first night at the Independence back when I hitch-hiked into town in the fall of 1971. I had escaped the steel plants of Lackawanna, New York, to become a ski instructor on Aspen Mountain. I love Aspen. All of my changes have been here, and it was the once-cool cachet of the Aspen ski instructor that allowed me to con my way into show business and a twenty-year Hollywood binge.

I lit a cigarette and sat down on an overwrought-iron bus bench in the middle of the mall, next to a faux mountain stream that was really a storm sewer, across from one of the few locally owned stores, Interesting Irwin's. When the sewer ditch was first put in, I saw a guy who was probably from Manhattan down on his hands and knees, drinking the brown water. He was telling his two mortified kids that it was okay to drink the water because it was running in a clear mountain stream. They're probably still in therapy, but I know what it's like to be thirsty.

Interesting Irwin's was an antique gun shop selling Sharps buffalo rifles, hand-tooled cowboy belts, and Western collectables. Billy the Kid probably only used one gun in his brief career as a psychotic gunslinger and miscreant, but Irwin always seemed to have at least two or three of his "old" ones for sale. The rich people in this town will buy anything: a house on Red Mountain for nineteen million dollars or a bindle of coke from a Mexican dishwasher.

But at least the Latinos are contributing to our capitalistic conundrum; what the hell was *I* going to do with my dwindling days on the planet? I had survived to the station in life that is euphemistically referred to as middle age, but the chances were slim that I'd live to be a hundred and six. Even if I was inclined to go to the gym and lay off the carbohydrates, there was no way I could repair the damage from thirty years of bacchanalian excess. I was fifty-three and looked it. In dog years I was a mummy.

I was also broke—although living the left-wing lie that hopes the quagmiry liberation of the we-thought-they'd-be-so-happy Iraqis and ruling-class tax cuts will continue to butcher the bear that had been feasting at the Wall Street café. I swear to God, if I ever get rich again I'll take every needy kid I know to Toys-Я-Us and regularly write five-digit donations to Ethiopian hospital funds. I had probably made ten million dollars in Hollywood, but I'd spent ninety percent of it on fast cars, beautiful women, NASDAQ long shots and white drugs. Then I wasted what was left.

A new Saab pulled up across from the Popcorn Wagon, catty-corner to the Wheeler Opera House. Behind the wheel of the Swedish steed was a rookie cop whose obvious affection for his service revolver rivaled the love a ten-year-old boy might have for a Daisy BB gun. But it's hard to get experienced law enforcement officers in town, because the forty-two grand a year they make is less than a nanny's salary. As a result, the police work can be slipshod and improvisational, which is okay because most of the crime in Aspen is drug-related, except when a student council president decides to knock over a grocery store to get back at his divorcing parents, or a little princess shoplifts a pair of sable slippers. Aspen High might have more kids on probation than Def Jam Records.

The officer's name was Ernie Grubbs, and I knew him from when he had stopped me at a sobriety check on Cemetery Lane my first week back in town. I'd told Ernie I hadn't been drinking, but he'd run me through the roadside gymnastics anyway. I remembered he'd been impressed that I could walk backwards and recite my ABCs while holding one finger on my nose and the middle one of my other hand right in the center of his face. Ernie got out of his patrol car and sauntered toward me, his Butch Cassidy a little too butch.

"Chief Rick get ahold of you?" he said with a twang that took a few points away from an IQ that didn't have many to spare.

Chief Rick was Richard Rankin, Aspen's Chief of Police.

"No," I said, keeping an eye on his gun hand. "What did I do?"

"Nothing I know of," he said. "But there's plenty of time."

"You just think there's plenty of time," I said. "When I was nineteen I thought so, too."

"I'm twenty-five," he said.

"Give it a chance," I said.

He did look a hell of a lot younger than twenty-five, but I keep thinking that airline pilots look like ninth graders, so maybe I was off base.

"Well, he's looking for you."

"Tell him to call me."

"He's the chief. It's not my job to tell him anything."

"Write him a note on the back of a parking ticket and stick it on his windshield," I said, pretty proud of myself.

"That's illegal," Ernie said.

I couldn't figure out if Ernie was stupid or just humorless.

"I saw one of your TV shows on Nickelodeon last night," he said. "The one with the cop and the private detective?"

"They all have a cop and a private detective," I said.

"Yeah, well, this one was the one that wasn't very good."

"That isn't the mission of television, Ernie," I said. "I just tried to make the cop stuff real, which is hard to do, as you know."

Ernie checked the slant of his holster.

"You started drinking again yet?" he said.

"Not yet."

"Yeah, well, when you do, don't drive."

"I can't. The bank repossessed my car."

"It's the economy," Ernie said. "That illegal Mexican labor's bankrupting the whole country."

"But the president is giving them green cards if they'll enlist. Join the army, learn English."

"That wasn't his idea," Ernie said. "Bush is a good man."

"So's his dad."

"Got that right," he said. "It's the Texas blood."

"Don't mess with Texas," I said, recalling the bumper sticker politics of the Lone Star State.

I could have busted Ernie's bubble and told him that the Bush blood was as blue as a button-down Oxford. But it looked like I was going to be on the shut-up-and-listen end of the conversation.

"So who came up with the green-card-give-away idea then," I asked, cracking wise just below Ernie's radar.

"Probably Hillary," he said. "And now she's a senator for fucking Christ Almighty."

"Actually I think it's because she got more votes than Rick Lazio, but you never know with that family."

I hadn't had this much fun since I'd freelanced an episode of *Cheers* back when I was on the Paramount lot.

"Doesn't matter," he said. "She and Bubba will be doing hard time once it gets found out about the drugs they were flying into the secret airports they built in Arkansas. They were using seven-four-sevens loaded wall to wall with blow. It's where they got all that money."

"They built secret airports in Arkansas?" I said.

"Back when Clinton was governor," Ernie said.

"How come nobody knew about it?" I said. "I mean, except for guys like you."

"They had a stealth system and radar-jamming devices," he said, as if I had my head up my ass for asking. "The place was state of the art."

"Where'd they get all that?"

"From the Jews."

"Silly me," I said. "You don't think that had anything to do with the Twin Towers, do you?"

"Not directly," Ernie said, glaring at me.

September 11th was sacred ground, and there was an unwritten rule that both the left and the right wouldn't polarize the tragedy into a political football. But I could see that Ernie was dying to tell me that, at the very least, Roger Clinton had sold used flight simulators to the Saudis, or that the hand-grenade-haired Chelsea was a retro fan of Cat Stevens, the "Peace Train" songster who changed his stage name to Yusuf Islam and now composes jingles for jihad.

"When you were a ski instructor, you pulled some shit around here," Ernie said.

"It was part of the job description."

"And took some drugs."

"But only the ones I couldn't sell."

"I know all about that. I ran your package in the cold case files they got down in the basement at HQ. Wheeler, Jacob Jensen: DOB nine eighteen fifty, white male. Aspen leaf tattooed on the inside of left forearm."

Ernie pulled up my sleeve and checked the aspen leaf tattoo just to make sure he had the right guy.

"Why the hell did you tattoo that there?" he asked.

"Because if I'd put it anywhere else, it'd be a maple leaf by now."

But apparently Ernie's stomach was still too tight for him to get my point.

"It's what we call an identifying characteristic," he said, sounding like he had written a few prime-time cop shows of his own, "and part of how I knowed you was you."

"You must have gone through Quantico."

"Where?" he said.

"FBI School," I said. "In Maryland."

"I got my GED in the Marine Corps. They had an MP program."

Then Ernie stared at me in a way that made me uncomfortable.

"Just watch the drinking," he said.

Ernie swaggered back to his fifty-thousand-dollar patrol car. But I guess the police department has to compete for respect in a town full of Hummers.

"Hey, Ernie, you like that car?"

"Nah, makes me look like a Democrat," Ernie said, peeling off.

A smarter man might have been concerned about why this young cop was so interested in how much I was drinking and what I did more than a quarter of a century ago. But I was just happy not to be jammed in traffic at the corner of Wilshire and Little Santa Monica in front of the CAA bunker designed by I. M. Pei—or play.

I looked at the stainless steel Rolex that I had traded down to from the solid gold President I used to wear, losing ten grand in the deal but ending up with twenty-six hundred dollars for rent money. It was almost 6:30. I was getting hungry, and maybe even a little thirstier than I knew I should be.

Chapter Three

I took Ernie's advice and started watching my drinking immediately, sitting at the hand-carved bar of the Rude Goose and stroking a longneck bottle of beer. If I'd worn a six-shooter I would've had to leave it in my saddlebag, according to the scripture painted on an authentic Gay Nineties mirror that doubled the number of bottles on the top shelf, as well as the hang-on hippie bartender with the wispy gray ponytail braided down his back. The Goose has been the home of hard-drinking cowboys for over one hundred years, and even though my bottle of brew was non-alcoholic, I felt low-down and ornery.

Happy Hour used to be a ritual at the Goose, but now most of the locals who chilled out at the bar after a hard day at work or on the slopes live down valley in affordable housing. Only thirty-five percent of Aspen's workforce lives in town—which means a lot of people in Aspen have a lot of time on their hands. I was one of them. And that time allowed me the luxury of pondering why the hell young Ernie was so damned interested in me.

Back in the seventies I'd been arrested for dealing pot with one of my ski instructor buddies named Tim Lackey, but I was never convicted, because Tim refused to testify against me. He was a standup guy, and as a result, he stood in jail for six years for money laundering and tax evasion.

The Feds never got Tim on the drug charge, and thank God for all of us they didn't have RICO back then. The Racketeer Influenced and Corrupt Organization Act is what finally put Teflon Don John Gotti behind bars until he died a slow death from head cancer, which could have been his karma for disappearing the milkman who accidentally ran over his kid. But Tim and I were basically just amateur bud merchants running from the corrupt influences of college, so I think the drug busters gave us a break.

I got to blow my share of the marijuana money we had stashed in an abandoned mineshaft in the Zaugg Dump on the west side of Aspen Mountain during a five-day binge in Las Vegas, while Lackey was being escorted to the House Of Many Doors for seventy-two months. The Dump is the mine tailings of a claim staked by a German immigrant named Billy Zaugg back in 1881, and the steep piles of mud and rock make for some of the most treacherous Double Black Diamond terrain on the mountain.

I lost three hundred grand at the craps tables in Lost Wages, Nevada, Hollywood's sister city of human wreckage. I was twenty-eight years old and probably the only guy who had ever double-downed with tens playing blackjack at the MGM Grand. I gambled my last thousand dollars at a change machine in the Las Vegas airport and couldn't grasp why I was still even after six hours. But I was on my way to make a fortune in show business, so it didn't matter. Five years later, I spilled that much when I was a fixture at the Monkey Bar in Beverly Hills.

Tim got out of prison and got sober and now is one of the best skiers in town, an out-of-bounds monster on the steep and deep in the backcountry when it snows big. The rumor is he's living off a wad of the drug dough the Feds never found. But I know this isn't true and I still owe him a hundred and fifty large for his half of our leafy green grubstake. Lackey and I were going to open a helicopter skiing operation in Alaska and be deep powder guides. But it was mostly just coke talk punctuated with I-love-you-mans. I've seen him a couple times over the last few years, and he's never asked me about the money. Like I said, Tim Lackey is a standup guy.

Police Chief Rick Rankin entered the Rude Goose and scanned the place with the trained eye of a professional law enforcement officer. After about twenty seconds he could see that I was the only one in the place and walked toward me. Rick was volleyball-tall and underwear-model handsome and could probably still strip for tips at bachelorette parties. He eased down on the barstool to my right and waited for me to speak first. I indulged him.

"You get my note?" I said.

"What note?"

"There wasn't one written on the back of a parking ticket on the windshield of your car?"

"I'm the chief of police—I don't get parking tickets."

I'd met Rick when he was loading chairlifts at Snowmass and I was teaching little rich kids how to ski, back when both of us were trying to ass-kiss our way off the mountain. He had a cute and friendly nickname for just about every local he knew, and he knew just about everybody. I liked to call him Sammy Glick.

Rick handed out roses to the ladies on Valentine's Day and had a biscuit at the ready for every sled dog in town. He volunteered for the fire department and picked up trash in the town park. So when Big Rick Rankin tossed his hat into the ring to become chief of police, he was a shoe in.

"How you doing, Mogul Man?" Rick asked, regarding the longneck bottle of beer in front of me a little too carefully.

I wasn't sure if he called me Mogul Man because of the way I used to ski the moguls or because I took off to Hollywood. But it was a nickname I could live with.

"No complaints," I shrugged, taking a swig and showing him the bottle's G-rated label. "But Ernie told me you were looking for me."

"At least he got that one right," Rick said.

"Give him a chance," I said. "He's new."

"Ernie isn't the sharpest shovel in the shithouse."

As a television writer on waivers from the bigs, I always enjoyed Rick's delicate command of the English language. He made Chris Rock sound like Jerry Falwell.

"What are you drinking?"

"Nothing fun," Rick said. "City council wants everybody to lay off the party favors. PR campaign for this season is that Aspen's a drug-free workplace so the tourists won't have to worry about their ski instructor being loaded."

"Herman Thayer said those exact same words to me this morning," I said. "But in a slightly different order."

"Where'd you see Germy Hermy?" he asked.

I had forgotten that it was Chief Rankin and not the racer chasers that bestowed the Germy moniker on Herman. I smiled at the implications.

"The Big Easy. He was doing shots for breakfast."

"And what were you doing?"

"Reminiscing," I said. "Okay if I buy you a drink?"

Rick never wore a uniform or carried a gun, so it was hard to tell when he was on duty. Tonight he was wearing a silk cowboy shirt with a string tie, suede leather pants, crocodile boots, and a good-guy white Stetson about the size of a yawning swan.

"If it's a Patron," he said.

"How about a Cuervo?"

"Life's too short to drink cheap tequila."

Tequila was pretty much all the same swill, so I tried to avoid treating marginal friends to the ten-dollar shots. I motioned to the bartender's reflection, pointed to the tequila on the lower shelf, and signaled for a double with two fingers. But he might have thought I was flipping him the peace sign.

"You still looking for work?" Rick said.

I nodded, but insincerely.

"Although I don't have a car," I said. "The bank took mine back under the lemon credit law."

"Ruthless bastards," he said.

For a cop, Rick couldn't tell when a clown was kidding.

"I'll sell you my kid's," he said. "He's off being a freshman at CU."

"I have eighty-six dollars."

"You can pay me off by the month. My old lady wants it out of the backyard."

"What kind is it?" I said, like a beggar trying to choose.

"A Chevy," he said. "I may have some work for that Hollywood hack skill-set of yours. But you're going to need wheels."

"It come with a tank of gas?"

"You want to be a smart-ass or you want to make some money?"

"That's always been a tough choice for me."

"I'll say," he said. "Laura Keller wants to talk to you."

"Laura Keller?"

"You got to remember her, right?"

I remembered Laura Keller, and I was probably one of the few local guys in town who hadn't given her his Jimmy in a snowdrift after she stumbled out of the Caribou Club.

"Kinda," I said.

But the more I thought about it, the better I remembered her, which is more than I can say for most of the women I haven't slept with, and even many of the ones I have.

"But her name's not Keller anymore," Rick said. "It's Post or Kellogg or some name like that. She married a guy whose great grandfather invented shredded wheat or something."

"Metamucil?"

But Rick wasn't as much fun to play with as Ernie Grubbs, and he wouldn't hit the ball back.

"They moved into Rupert Murdoch's old palace up in Starwood."

"So she's loaded now," I said.

"And rich, too." Rick said. "I can't believe she's still alive."

"How does she look?"

"Like she finished first in a facelift contest," he said, "perpetually amazed."

"If she's already amazed, why does she want to talk to me?"

"Laura's kid took off and someone needs to find the little brat," Rick said. "She asked me first, but I'm too busy to chase after some idiot teenager who splits for two months every couple of weeks. Her talking to you about it was my idea."

Rick downed his shot of Cuervo and bit into a slice of lime.

"And you need a job."

"I was thinking about teaching creative writing," I said.

"That's funny," he said, as if I was kidding. "C'mon, isn't this what they used to do on the *Rockford Files* every week?"

"Jim Rockford was really James Garner," I said. "And he had stuntmen and story editors to bail him out."

"You got me to bail you out," he said, trying to make it sound like he actually meant it. "Just pretend it's the same catch-the-bad-guy crap that used to puke out of your typewriter."

The bartender must have misinterpreted my hand signal for Rick's double and had placed two shots of Cuervo on the bar—one shot in front of Rick and one shot in front of me. My shot was still full. I tried not to stare at it, and Rick tried not to stare at me.

"You could probably get away with drinking that," he said. "You look like you're doing okay."

I didn't know if Rick was giving me a vote of confidence or a slight nudge off the wagon's fender. We both shrugged.

"Anyway, that's the gig," he said. "You decide to give it a run, Laura wants you up there tomorrow morning to work out the details. But it's all got to be real quiet because she's high society now."

Rick climbed off his stool and shot his cuffs as if he was about to conduct an orchestra, nodding to the bar mirror like someone who liked what he saw. The poor man was obviously suffering from acquired situational narcissism, an affliction one catches from always thinking he is the most important person in the room. There is no known cure, but the Bill O'Reilly Foundation is raising research funds.

"Think about it," he said, and walked out the door.

I was alone in the Rude Goose with a full shot of tequila in front of me. The hippie bartender was busy rinsing glasses with his back to the bar. I could take a drink and nobody would be the wiser. I picked up the shot and ran the index finger of my right hand around the rim. The cheap tequila was golden brown and smelled like heaven in a Tijuana whorehouse. I had been in this position before and knew the drill. I saved up sober days like so many dollar bills in a personal savings account and then spent them all on a big binge.

But for some reason I poured the tequila into the bar sink and banged out the swinging doors of the Rude Goose and into the cold Colorado night. To my last day I will never know the reason why.

Chapter Four

I was heading down Cemetery Lane and across the Slaughter-house Bridge to McClain Flats, driving toward Starwood. It was early morning, and I was freezing my ass off as handfuls of hard snowflakes stung my face like sharp rice at an angry wedding. Rick's kid's Chevy didn't have a top and it wasn't even really a Chevy. It was a 1969 Corvette, the one that looks like a slice of Kraft cheese melted over a roller skate, the kind of car you bought when you got out of the Navy. My buddy, the police chief, said the 'Vette was a "collector's item," and that I was lucky to pay him only a hundred a month for the privilege of driving it—a grievance collector maybe. The Corvette needed a rebuild and a brake job. But I needed wheels, and beggars can't be choosers no matter how willing we are to get down on our knees.

I had found a *John Denver's Greatest Hits* tape filling a hole in the Corvette's fiberglass above an AA "One Day at a Time" license bracket housing the rear plate. But it must have dated back to the original owner, because Denver didn't rap about ho's and pimps like the white college kids, and I doubted Rick's kid was "in the program." I hammered the antique tape into the dash and thanked God eight-tracks went the way of platform shoes—the cartridge was about as sleek as a trash dumpster. But John's voice still sounded warm and familiar through the one functional speaker, in spite of the fact it sometimes made him sound like he was singing through a kazoo.

I turned right on Trentaz Drive and drove up the last step to Starwood, looking southwest to the Elk Range, a fortress of jagged peaks surrounding the fourteen-thousand-foot summits of Mount Daly and Capitol Peak. I have never forgotten what these mountains looked like, but whenever I saw them again it was like I was seeing them for the first time. Musicologists might not rank Denver as an important artist, but he worked just fine for me this morning as he sang about a guy who left home for the Rocky Mountains.

The last time I was in Starwood I had a dental hygienist from Portland naked in Spider Sabich's chest-deep bathtub. What started out as a deep powder lesson had snowballed into a three-day exchange of body fluids and sexual preferences, but that was when the ski racer's bathtub was still a public domain—before Claudine Longet put a bullet into Spider's belly. The shooting was the first glimpse most of the locals had of Aspen's dark side. Since I had been out of town it had gotten considerably darker.

I pulled up to the same Starwood gate that welcomes His Royal Highness Prince Bandar Bin Sultan home to his fifty-thousand-square-foot Aspen cabin, the gas pump perk where the ideologically elastic House of Saud sometimes hides out to sheik their considerable booty during Ramadan or the latest Wahhabi bomb-a-thon.

"Jake Wheeler for the Laura used-to-be Keller residence," I said, smiling self-consciously at a young Latino in a security uniform. "Nice looking gal with a tight face."

He checked down his list, stealing a look at my cheddar cheese–colored Corvette.

"Nice car," he said, and meant it.

"Thanks," I said. "I just got out of the Navy."

"Three sixteen Deutschendorf Drive. Go past the tennis courts on your left and the horse pastures on the right," he said. "The place with the statues. You can't miss it."

"*Gracias,*" I said, using up most of my Spanish.

I put the Corvette into first, eased out the clutch and unimpressively bucked away in a cloud of blue smoke. I wound up Starwood Drive and marveled at the conspicuous wealth. The houses were the size of private mental institutions, trickling with creeks and wildflower gardens, bright gazebos, and aspen groves. Most of these trophy homes sat empty except for a few weeks in the summer and the Christmas holidays. The county's housing shortage could probably be solved in a heartbeat if these people would rent out their spare bedrooms. But if wishes were horses beggars would ride, and I was driving a borrowed Corvette.

John Denver was kazooing that "it's a long way home to Starwood in Aspen," and he was right. I felt like I was back in Beverly Hills, and all this money was making me nervous. I turned the Corvette into the wide circular drive of 316 Deutschendorf and parked between a twelve-foot-tall rogue grizzly forged in bronze and a gigantic bull moose pounded out of copper. Whoever built this place must have been a huge Teddy Roosevelt fan, because Starwood is the habitat of elk and black bear. The grizzlies and moose live up in Jackson Hole with Harrison Ford.

I got out of the Corvette and walked toward the house. I was wearing faded Gap Loose Fit jeans that didn't fit as loosely as advertised, a rugby-style Polo pullover, and a brown calfskin duster I'd bought in London when I was on a tear and making big dough. I felt like Keith Richards when I wore it, but I still wanted to make a good impression. A caretaker was hand scrubbing the inlaid tile of a driveway mural that depicted a huge mallard duck. The caretaker wore a white smock and a Chinese peasant hat. The duck appeared to be holding a golf club.

"Make sure that thing doesn't leak any oil," the caretaker said, snubbing my ride without even bothering to give it a closer look.

"Don't worry," I said. "There's no oil in it."

I walked to the solid oak-and-Tiffany front doors shrouded by a ten-foot span of Texas longhorns that hung over the doublewide arches of the entryway like a guillotine. The handgrips were fashioned out of authentic eagle claws crushing fake snake heads, and the doormat could pass for endangered rhino hide and probably was. I looked for a donkey tail to tug but had to settle for a doorbell button made from an old Dad's Root Beer bottle cap. I pushed Dad's button, something I was once an expert at, and instantly I could hear the University Of Alabama fight song playing somewhere deep inside the house.

"Ms. Laura told me you could go right in," the caretaker said—obviously as embarrassed as I was about the Crimson Tiding doorbell.

"Does Ms. Laura have a last name?" I asked.

But the caretaker didn't answer me and just kept scrubbing his duck.

Chapter Five

As I entered Rupert Murdoch's former digs, it was immediately clear to me why the Australian media magnate dumped it. Even for a dish monger who made his bones on Fleet Street before oozing into the US as the publisher of the *New York Post* and the say-so behind the al Jazeera–like Fox News, the place was in your face and tasteless. I hiked over a gangway that had been scavenged from a whaling boat, crossing a swimming pool in the center of a uniquely chilling living room crammed with harpoons and what I guessed to be tools used to harvest blubber.

I headed toward the sound of a television tuned to the Weather Channel that was probably coming from a kitchen. There was a study on my left, walled with bookcases of "classic" action movie videos guarded by a life-sized cutout of Tiger Woods and a middle-aged, pear-shaped man I didn't recognize. The man was wearing a Crimson Tide football helmet and looked ridiculous; Tiger was holding a golf club and didn't.

Laura was sitting at a white marble table in the pure white

kitchen. She was wearing a sheer white silk robe and oversized Jackie Kennedy sunglasses. I couldn't blame her for the sunglasses; the room was a little bright. Laura was drinking a glass of tomato juice and biting off tiny bits of a carrot she held in the same hand as the glass. There was a half-full bottle of Stoli Crystal next to the sink. The bottle was open, so I presumed that the glass of juice was in reality a Bloody Mary.

"Hi, Jake," Laura said. "Thanks for stopping by."

Her smile was so easily familiar that I thought maybe she was trying to remember if we'd ever slept together, and she wanted to keep it informal if we had.

"Nice to see you, Laura," I said.

"Cool duster," she said, nodding at my Keith Richard knock-off. "Can I get you a Bloody Mary?"

"Actually, how about a virgin?"

Laura laughed so hard and fast that it caught me off guard. It was a good laugh, and she looked much better when she did it, her face less amazed and more natural.

"You must be new," she said.

Apparently Laura didn't remember me. That was probably a good thing, but for the moment I was crushed. I had always thought I made lasting impressions. She poured me a straight glass of tomato juice and handed it to me, bending from the waist so I could see her amazingly round breasts. I felt Jimmy flinch and turned my head slightly sideways, trying not to stare. Laura's eyes were wide and catlike; she had high cheekbones and a perfectly round mouth that probably wasn't very good for making square deals. The facelift didn't matter. This was still a great-looking woman.

"Nice place you have here," I said.

There was an awkward silence, and I noticed that behind Laura on a pure white sandstone counter there was a white porcelain soap dish with a white paper bindle sticking out from underneath a white Cuisinart.

"Rick told me that you wanted to maybe talk to me about me maybe helping you find your daughter," I said.

My sentence ran a little long because I was trying to find my bearings. Laura's silk robe had slipped open a couple more inches from both ends, and I could now see that she was as waxed and polished as a Maserati and probably just as high maintenance. She uncrossed her delicate feet, wiggling perfectly manicured toes that had little Aspen leafs hand-painted on the nails.

"*Step*daughter," Laura corrected me. "I'm not old enough to have a daughter Tinker's age."

"One of the Never Never Land perks, no doubt."

"Rick warned me that you can be an asshole."

"What other people think of me is none of my business," I said, repeating the only decent advice I'd ever heard in an AA meeting. "How old is Ms. Bell?"

"Seventeen going on thirty-eight," Laura said. "And if I knew I was going to inherit Heidi Fleiss, I would have given this marriage a lot more thought."

"Your stepdaughter is a hooker?"

"I was being theatrical."

The competition must be killing Laura, I thought.

"Whom does she hang out with?" I asked, like a private investigator pretending to be an English professor.

"I wouldn't have the faintest idea. We stopped talking at the wedding reception."

A tall black man with incredibly muscular legs entered the kitchen. He wore a tank top and running shorts, track flats and wraparound sunglasses. He moved wordlessly to the refrigerator, opened it and gracefully drank an entire quart of Gatorade in about two seconds. If this guy was Laura's husband, his great grandfather must have invented buckwheat, not shredded wheat. He leaned over and kissed Laura on the cheek.

"You going to need a ride into town?" he said.

"I'm fine, sweetheart," she said.

The track star glanced at the Weather Channel on a white Sony monitor, then turned it off and left the room.

"Who was that?"

"Dat be Byron," she said like Brer Rabbit, and probably testing my PC.

"Husband?"

"Surrogate," Laura said. "Hubby's in Alabama."

"Hubby Tinker's dad?"

"Genetically."

"What's he doing down in 'Bama?"

"Watching football," she said. "He spends the whole season down there."

"Absence makes the heart grow fonder," I said.

"Or go yonder," she said. "Charles gives his alma mater a million dollars a year, so they let him pretend he's an assistant coach."

I moved to the sandstone counter and pulled the soap dish out from underneath the Cuisinart. The bindle was open, and there was a small mound of powdered cocaine piled in the fold. I took my little finger and dabbed the tiniest possible dollop on my gums.

"I'm ready for my root canal," I said.

"My husband likes me thin."

"And nervous," I said. "Maybe he should get a poodle."

I dumped what was left of the blow into the sink.

"We have to be careful with the maid," I said.

"The maid is my supplier."

"And I thought it was hard to get decent help these days."

"The last thing I need is a lecture from some Hollywood burnout."

I was touched. Laura did remember me after all.

"Rick told me you knew something about police work and private detectives," Laura said. "I didn't want to go to a professional."

"Then I'm your man," I said.

"I'll pay you two hundred dollars a day plus expenses," Laura said, taking a deep drink from her Bloody Mary. "And if you fuck this up, I'll have you killed."

"Sounds reasonable," I said. "Do you have any pictures of Tinker, or would you rather describe her to me from the wonderful memories you two share?"

But Laura just opened a kitchen drawer and took out an envelope of photographs.

"I found these hidden in her ski boot," Laura said.

She counted out fifteen crisp one-hundred-dollar bills that looked like they were just printed up down in the basement, stuck them in the envelope and handed it to me.

"We're done now," Laura said. "You can leave."

I walked out the front doors of Laura's private mental institution and toward the Corvette. It had been washed and polished. The track star was sitting on the hood.

"What are you doing here, man?" he said, not friendly.

"Helping out Ms. Laura, man," I said, friendly as a fat white guy can be.

I was going to ask Byron if he was the person who washed my car and thank him if he was. But when he stood up, I changed my mind.

"I'm giving her all the help she needs," he said.

"And that's gotta be a big job," I said. "But I'll bet you're great at it."

I offered Byron my hand but he just glared at me and then jogged off. I climbed into the Corvette and coaxed the engine to start, chugging over the golfing duck and out the wide circular drive.

I had my first job in two years.

Chapter Six

I hit the horn as I squealed the Corvette through the Starwood gate, but it didn't blare so I just saluted. I felt good, the fifteen hundred bucks in my pocket feeling better than the ten thousand I once raked in weekly ever felt. And I didn't have to shell out half of it to Uncle Sam and my agents, lawyers, and business managers; it was all mine.

Instead of going back into town, I looped through a roundabout and headed up toward the Maroon Bells, passing Aspen Highlands Ski Area on my left. I drove by a herd of coiffed llamas and shampooed caribou grazing at the T-Lazy-7 Ranch and wound up the six miles to the jagged twin peaks, dodging the occasional rollerblader streaking downhill in a racing tuck. As I gained altitude, the Aspen leaves began to ignite in tight patches of red and gold. Winter was coming.

I parked the Corvette behind a public restroom intended to blend into the Rocky Mountain terrain, but which actually ended up looking like a giant outhouse designed by Barney Rubble. The large fake rocks reminded me of what Stonehenge might resemble if it was turned into a 7-Eleven. The air was cold and thin as I climbed out of the Corvette and walked down a steep path toward Maroon Lake, sucking for oxygen like a broken bilge pump. I reached for a cigarette, thinking a smoke would help me expand my lungs, but the red box of Marlboros was empty.

I got down on my hands and knees and slurped a long cool drink out of the ice-blue water, scattering a school of cutthroat trout. I looked up at the permanent snowfields just below the peaks of the Maroon Bells and then scanned the floodplain of sagebrush and wildflowers. The Corvette was the only car in the parking lot. I was alone.

I sat down on a tree stump and pulled Laura's envelope out of my jacket. I counted the cash and then jammed it back into my jeans. The photographs of Tinker were the kind taken with a digital camera and printed out on a home printer. The quality was remarkably good, and made me glad I had sold my stock in Kodak.

In the first photograph, Tinker was wearing a soaking wet T-shirt and a thong bikini bottom. She was standing on a rocky shore and leaning against a windsurfer. I recognized the body of water in the background as Ruedi Reservoir, twenty miles northwest of Aspen. Ruedi was the beachhead for water sports in the Roaring Fork Valley—although even in midsummer the water barely warmed to fifty degrees. That probably explained the rosebuds peaking underneath Tinker's wet T-shirt. The next photograph was pretty much like the first one except Tinker wasn't wearing the wet T-shirt. She was naked from the waist up.

Tinker may only have been seventeen, but she was clearly an outstanding filly, even in a field as fast as Aspen's. She had the body of a Las Vegas semi-pro and the smile of a homecoming queen. The contrast immediately began causing me a conflict of interest, but Jimmy didn't flinch and I felt proud of myself.

The third picture was taken indoors. Tinker was on a double bed that looked like it couldn't make the cut at a Motel 6. There were a cheap clock radio and lamp on one bedside table and an open bottle of 151 Rum next to an extravagant pile of South

American motivation on the other. Tinker was completely naked and appeared to be pleasuring herself with what looked like a Nokia cellular phone. I wasn't as proud of myself as I had been a moment before.

The photographs got worse or better from there, depending on one's proclivities, or perversities. The next three were of Tinker and an older man. The man was balding but had the fit build of a cyclist—though he had to be in good condition, because in one photograph he was holding a naked Tinker upside down while she apparently checked her gag reflex. I wondered who was taking the pictures.

There were two more photos of Tinker and another man, who was much younger. The pictures were taken in the same cheap room and probably at the same time. The mystery of who the photographer was in the first batch of pictures may have been solved. The young man was probably in his late teens and could pass as Tinker's prom date. But I couldn't imagine a girl as experienced as this ever bothering to go to a prom. Tinker had a tiny mongoose tattooed just under a bellybutton ring. But it wasn't the only ring she wore.

The last photograph was of the three of them. The young man and the baldheaded cyclist were attempting to plug every orifice Tinker made available, and most of them were. I wondered again who was taking the photographs. I felt sick to my stomach. Jimmy had flinched only once and then shriveled up and hid. I couldn't blame him.

Aspen is notorious for out-of-control kids, and only a few summers ago a gang of ski-masked bandits robbed the movie theater and pistol-whipped a street mime for his tip jar. At first everybody blamed the Mexicans, but the gang turned out to be boys and girls from some of Aspen's most prominent families.

But it must be difficult for young people to define themselves in a town so short on adult role models, where Dad won't give up skiing the steeps and Mom still yanks home one-night stands from the Caribou Club. It's probably why these kids acted out—pushing the envelope of dangerous behavior as far as they could

in an attempt to notify the world that they had arrived at the edge
of the childhood rye and were ready to jump off. But Tinker was
a young girl in even deeper trouble than Aspen's post-adolescent
standard, and I was a television writer, not a shrink or a cop or a
private dick.

A car suddenly backfired, and I just about had a heart attack.
I dropped the photographs and turned toward the parking lot. But
there wasn't another car in sight. The next backfire was accompa-
nied by bark exploding off of the tree stump I was sitting on. I had
dubbed enough shows on Hollywood sound stages to know what
TV gunfire sounded like, and I quickly discovered it sounded exactly the same in real life as the third shot ricocheted off a boulder
and whistled past my ear.

I grabbed the photographs and sprinted toward the safety of
the topless Corvette as fast as my fat legs could carry me inside the
confining—but fashion-plate cool—calfskin duster. The parking
lot was only maybe four hundred yards away but looked like it
was in another country. I felt like I was moving in slow motion—
as if I was in the recurring dream I used to have in high school
about running down the halls in my underwear.

A bullet tore through the collar of my coat and I could feel the
hot sting of a powder burn on my cheek, but it snapped me out of
my high school nightmare and I concentrated on saving my ass—
juking toward the Corvette as bullets blasted holes the size of coffee cups into the plastic rocks of the Flintstone shithouse.

I piled into the Corvette without opening the door, and my
jackhammering hand could hardly hold the ignition key, but I finally started the motor and wheeled the Corvette around in a
smoking donut—except that it was the tailpipe that was smoking,
not the tires. I metaled the pedal and waited for the big Detroit
V8 to cough up its stuff as a bullet blew off the rearview mirror. I
heard someone scream but then realized it was the high, strangled
pitch of my own voice. I'd had no idea I was such a coward.

Finally the Corvette gravitated down Maroon Creek Road,
sideswiping aspen trees as my heart attempted to catapult itself
onto the dash. I cursed red meat and cholesterol and promised

God if He let me live I would never eat anything but nuts and berries. I had written this scene a hundred times and was humiliated that I was as terrified as I was, in the reality of it. There was nothing funny about gunfire and murder, and I made a mental note to take out a full-page ad in the trades to make my amends.

Then Ernie Grubbs casually pulled up alongside me in his Saab, lights flashing and siren wailing.

"Pull over," he said through a PA system mounted in the grill.

There was no way I was going to stop. I had no idea who was trying to kill me, but I immediately put Ernie at the top of a very short list.

He cut the Saab over in front of me and locked up all four wheels. I had no choice but to stand on the brake pedal, but it went straight to the floor, so I swerved around the Saab and then vaulted over a ditch and into the pastures of the T-Lazy-7 Ranch. The Corvette spun to a stop in a cloud of llama dung.

Ernie slid out of his patrol car, his gun hand hanging loose over his service revolver.

"Someone is trying to kill me," I said.

"Just get out of the car real nice and slow," Ernie said. "I'll put the bracelets on you so you can calm down."

I got out of the car and Ernie slipped the cuffs on my wrists, I was leaking sweat.

"When did you have that last drink, Mr. Wheeler?" Ernie asked, like my former AA sponsor at my first meeting.

"I wasn't drinking," I said. "Someone tried to kill me."

"*You* were trying to kill you," he said, clever as hell. "It's called the DTs."

Ernie gently led me to the rear door of the Saab and protected my head just like they do on television as he pushed me into the back seat. He closed the door, and I could see that the handles had been removed on the inside in case I tried to make an escape.

Chapter Seven

Aspen Police Headquarters is located in the basement of the Pitkin County Court House, a turn-of-the-eighteenth-century office building on Main Street a block east of the Hotel Jerome. It is dank and creaky and smells like a gym bag, but at least the jail is famous. Theodore Bundy spent some time here in the mid-seventies before he escaped from the legal library on the second floor. Apparently Ted had charmed the ladies who worked in the office in spite of the fact he was awaiting trial for raping and murdering a nurse who was on a ski vacation in Snowmass in 1971. They gave him the run of the place. When he saw his chance, Teddy jumped out the window and disappeared into the mountains. I could never figure out what impressed the women of Aspen. I always told them I wanted to be a writer and tried to look astute. Rape and murder never occurred to me. Bundy was eventually recaptured down in Florida and took a ride on Old Sparky for the murder of two coeds at Florida State.

I was warming my biggest cheeks on a steam heat register that was about as comfortable as the tree stump up at Maroon Lake. Ernie had removed my handcuffs and was leaning against the hallway wall outside a string of police offices, pretending to read the *Aspen Times*. But he may have only been looking for his name in print.

"Let me know if you need any help with the big words," I said, trying to get back on his good side.

But he didn't answer me.

"Can I have a cup of coffee?" I asked.

"No," he said, without taking his finger off the sentence he was staring at.

"Why not?"

"Contaminates the urine sample."

Ernie looked at me. I could tell he was happy.

"I knew you'd get in trouble sooner or later," he said.

"A broken clock is right twice a day," I said. "Don't be so impressed with yourself."

Chief Rick came down the hall and signaled me toward his office at the far corner of the basement. He was wearing tan Patagonia hiking shorts, a blue fleece vest, Chaco sandals and a red turtleneck. A pair of high-altitude sunglasses with black leather blinders held his hair in place like a tiara. He looked like a guy auditioning for a Land Cruiser commercial. I didn't particularly like Rick's wardrobe, but for a guy on a city salary, he certainly had a very full closet.

"C'mon, Mogul," he said, like I was suddenly a pain in his ass.

I got up and walked after Rick. Ernie followed close behind like a prison bull who was expecting me to pull out a sharpened spoon and make a break for it.

"Not you, Grubbs," Rick said. "Just me and the stuntman."

"But it's my collar, Chief," Ernie said, looking like he was about to stamp his feet.

"Jake isn't a *collar,* you banana. He's working special assignment for me."

I smiled at Ernie like a man with friends in high places.

"Cream and sugar," I said.

And then I followed Chief Rick into his office hoping Ernie wouldn't shoot me in the back.

Chapter Eight

It was obvious that Rick's office hadn't been remodeled since about 1901. There was a spittoon next to a roll-top desk with an accompanying bentwood chair that looked as if it was designed to keep sweaters from shrinking, and in one corner a large standing clock that read eight-nineteen had an advertisement for a stomach tonic painted on the dial. I checked my watch and it was 5:47. One of us was wrong.

One wall of the office was covered in framed photographs from floor to ceiling, virtually every inch. There were photos of Rick and John Denver, Rick and Jill St. John, Rick and President Clinton, Rick and Jack Nicholson, Rick and Dick Cheney, Rick and the once-much-richer Ken Lay, Rick and Ted Kennedy, and, of course, a much younger Rick with the finally condemned and executed Ted Bundy.

There were dozens of others, and in every one of them Rick was standing at attention in his police dress blues wearing white gloves, spit-polished shoes with spats, and razor-creased pants with a red stripe running down the outside of each leg. His right hand was in the exact same spot on everybody's left shoulder in each photograph. It was like Rick was the celebrity and the famous people were really just yokels standing next to his cardboard likeness for a fake photo-op at the county fair.

I had never seen Rick wearing a uniform, and he looked like a Nazi with a Beatles haircut. But there was one photo of him and Stephen Hawking where Rick was down on one knee next to the physicist's wheelchair. He actually looked humble, his right hand reaching up to the favored spot on the crippled genius's left shoulder.

Rick's wall of fame reminded me of a writer I knew in Hollywood who had papered his entire office with his writing credits—dozens of "written by" and "story by" credits freezed-framed from mediocre TV shows and B-movies. The really sad thing was that the guy couldn't write home for money, and I had always thought that if he really needed to see his name all the time, it would've been less embarrassing if he'd just stolen a peek at his driver's license. But fame is the ugliest drug of all and, once you're addicted, the hardest to kick. Johnny Carson was the only guy who ever survived the cure, I think.

Rick took a seat in the sweater stretcher behind the rolltop and pointed me to a hard stool in front of his desk. It looked like the kind used for a witness stand. I sat down.

"Ernie told me you tried to outrun him in the 'Vette?"

"That shit box couldn't outrun a shopping cart," I said. "I was trying to get away from Maroon Lake."

"What were you doing up there?"

"I had to take a prehistoric dump and wanted to use Barney Rubble's crapper."

"Don't fuck around with me, Mogul," Rick said. "This is serious."

"No shit," I said. "Someone tried to kill me."

"Nobody tried to kill you."

"You weren't there."

"Is there a reason someone would be trying to kill you?"

"Not that I know of."

Rick picked up a palm-sized silver nugget he used as a paperweight and tossed it from one hand to the other.

"Were you drinking?" Rick asked, looking me straight in the face.

"I retired from drinking," I said. "With the title."

Rick tossed me the nugget.

"Were you wearing that duster when this whoever it was for some unknown reason tried to kill you?" Rick said in a cocky way that made me want to slap the shit out of him.

"I didn't have time to change on the way over here. Ernie had me in handcuffs."

"So you were wearing that coat?"

"It's got a bullet hole in the collar to prove it," I said, tossing the nugget back.

Rick started to laugh.

"You been out of the high country too long, boy," he said.

"I was almost out of it forever," I said, fingering the bullet hole in the duster's collar.

"You know," Rick said, still laughing, "it ought to be against the law to wear brown leather coats this time of year."

"Fill me in," I said, wondering just what the hell he meant.

"It is elk season, you chucklehead. At three hundred yards you probably look just like a trophy for Christ sake."

Rick was really laughing now.

"Were you wearing an antler hat, too?" he said, just about busting a gut.

"You're saying someone thought I was an elk?"

"Absolutely."

"That's ridiculous," I said. "Someone fired off about fifty rounds. I had to run my ass off."

"Elks run."

"But they don't drive. The rearview mirror was shot off my car."

"Look," he said, "you got some once-a-year hunter from Chicago sucking down beer all day long in an elk blind. He's drunk. He's tired. He wants to go home. You're pretty big, wearing brown leather. Looks like you could be an elk to me."

"Elk season isn't until October," I said.

"That's rifle elk season. This is black powder elk season. In two weeks it's bow and arrow elk season."

Black powder season was a short, late-summer window of hunting for the purist elk slayers. Hunters had to use black powder and antique rifles, usually muzzleloaders or Sharps buffalo guns. The devotees dressed up like Davy Crockett, and every once in a while I'd see one of these nuts in fringed buckskin loading up on supplies in City Market.

"It's the best hunting there is. I'm going myself this weekend," Rick said.

I tried to imagine Chief Rick in a coonskin cap. It wasn't hard.

"Guy probably had a Sharps. I'm surprised he missed you—they're good to about a thousand yards."

This wasn't making much sense, but it was making a little, and Rick can be a very convincing guy. After all, he used to be a chairlift attendant, and now he's the chief of police posing in pictures with Dick Cheney.

"How'd it go up at Laura's?" Rick asked.

"Okay," I said. "She's paying me two hundred a day to find her kid."

"You don't have to find her, you know."

"I don't?"

"This kid takes off all the time, sometimes for months. If you find her, you put yourself out of a job. Two hundred a day is nice work in the off season."

"I have to try, at least," I said.

"C'mon, O.J. made a career out of not finding the real killers and Greta Van Susteren got rich off the Modesto cops not finding Laci Peterson."

"They found her," I said.

"Floating to the surface isn't finding," Rick said.

"Okay, how about Elizabeth Smart?"

"Doesn't count, she eloped. And remember, you have up to a year to send a gift."

"That part wasn't in the movie," I said.

"C'mon, Jake, not finding people is a goddamn cottage industry in this country, for Christ sake. They're like weapons of mass destruction."

I was about to change Rick's mind about my not trying to find Tinker by showing him the photographs when an ungracefully aging earth mother entered the office. Ernie must have bribed her into bringing me my coffee, but I couldn't blame him. He didn't have very much dignity to lose, and my relationship with Rick was gouging into what he had. Cosmic Mom was wearing a hemp shift, braids, and beaded-leather moccasins, and no doubt was a Pitkin County protected species. She looked familiar to me. But everyone in this town my age looked familiar; I just hoped that I had never asked her to ball after smoking some Peruvian red.

"No cream, or sugar," she said, handing me my coffee. "I won't allow it."

"Thanks," I said, taking the cup. "Hey, what was Ted Bundy really like?"

"A real cutie," she said, walking out the door.

Ted was into necrophilia, but at least he was a cutie. I took a sip of coffee and discovered it was tea.

"I think Tinker's in trouble, Rick," I said. "Maybe big trouble."

"Plenty of kids in Aspen are in big trouble. Their parents won't grow up."

I put my cup down on the corner of Rick's desk so I could take the photographs of Tinker out of my pocket and hand them to him. But I stopped cold when I saw a framed family photograph on his desk. It was of his wife and his daughter and someone I assumed was the Corvette's former owner, the son who had just left for Colorado U. Rick's wife was right out of central casting and looked like June Cleaver. His daughter was a cute cowgirl, probably a barrel racer and maybe fifteen. Rick's son was the naked young man in the photographs with Tinker.

"So use your head and stretch this gig out," Rick said.

But it sounded like he was talking to me from someplace underwater and I felt like I might have fainted.

"What?" I said, not quite getting the tea cup to my quaking lips.

"Guys like you won't be getting too many more breaks like this," he said. "If I were you I'd milk it."

I thought it might be better if I put down my cup, but I didn't think I could make the edge of the desk, so I just held it in both hands as if it was a sick kitten.

"I'll try," I said.

"Are you okay?" Rick asked, watching me cradle my cup.

"Yeah, fine. I just forgot what this altitude could be like on an empty stomach."

I reached into my pocket and fumbled out a hundred-dollar bill. I handed it to Rick. It calmed me down a little.

"My first payment on the Corvette," I said.

"You don't have to pay me now," Rick said.

"A deal's a *deal*," I said, louder than I wanted to. "And thanks for giving me that break with Ernie. I may have gotten a little carried away."

"Don't worry about it. He needs the practice."

I put down my cup, got up from the witness stand and left Rick's office. I climbed the stairs to the ground floor and walked down a narrow hallway covered with wanted posters and community event notices.

I couldn't breathe.

Chapter Nine

I floated out the front door of the Court House and deliberately took the chipped concrete stairs one at a time. My legs felt like they were made from mashed potatoes.

"Jesus Christ," I whispered, realizing I probably could use a drink, and maybe even a gun.

The Corvette was in police impound at the rear of the Court House, but I really needed to walk and clear my head. I headed south down Galena Street and thought about going into the Ute City Bank Bar & Grill to buy a pack of smokes from the bartender—and maybe even a drink. The Tinker-and-Rick's-kid connection was the kind of thing I couldn't keep secret for long. Rick was the guy who got me the job, and whether he wanted me to do it well or not, I couldn't lie to him. As a recovering Catholic I knew I had already committed the sin of omission. But one thing was for sure: The photographs of Rick's kid weren't going to go up on the chief's office wall anytime soon.

I was really trying not to drink, and the last thing I needed was the nervy jangle of a cigarette. So I passed on the Bar & Grill, went up to Cooper Street and turned left, walking by City Market on my right, and toward the Snow Eagle, a fifties-style motel at the corner of East End and Highway 82 that had been converted into employee housing. When I was a ski instructor I lived there for a few months before I found a decent place of my own. But back then we called it the Spread Eagle, for obvious reasons.

I let myself in the door of the ex-motel room with an add-on kitchenette and a Murphy bed. The place was about as big as the executive bathroom in my office at Universal Studios, but it was the most affordable place in town and was at least temporarily available when I rolled back into town. I had to move out the week before Thanksgiving because the ski instructors would be coming back from teaching in South America, and they had first dibs. But at least the Aspen Skiing Company was nice enough to let me stay here until then for fourteen hundred a month. The Ski Co is very humanitarian, owned by its parent company, General Dynamics, a conglomerate renowned for manufacturing napalm and nuclear subs.

The shower felt hot and good, and I stood in it until the hot water ran out—which was about two minutes. Then I broke out a new Gillette and started to shave.

"So this is what it's really like," I said to the frightened man in the cheap mirror.

I had shot and killed so many people on television, I considered myself an expert. But I wasn't. The incident up at Maroon Lake had rocked me like a bad cap of mescaline. I couldn't shake the feeling, not to mention the inherent weirdness escalating in the Tinker search now that I had digital proof that she was being done, in more ways than one, by the chief of police's favorite son and a fit and bald older man. I flicked on my ten-inch TV, and ironically *The Rockford Files* was airing on A&E. Jim Rockford was competing against Lance White, played by a very young Tom Selleck, for the Goodhew Award, a fictional version of an Oscar for private detectives. It was a classic episode, and I considered reconsidering my opinion of television writing. Stephen J. Cannell's delightful words made an impossible scenario very believable, and James Garner made getting shot at look easy. We were on the same page.

There was no doubt about it. I needed a gun.

But beyond the scripted prose of a "gangbanger's tray-eight" or a "street punk's nine-millimeter monster," I didn't know anything about guns. I never kept one around when I was in LA for the same reason Freddie Prinze shouldn't have kept one. I pulled down the Murphy bed and stretched out to watch the rest of Rockford. I might learn something from this private dick, I thought. But instead of paying attention, I fell asleep.

I woke up at ten the next morning after logging about fifteen hours of sack time. But I was probably making up for twenty years of Hollywood white nights and jaw-clenching contests. I went into the bathroom, watered the monster, and brushed my teeth. Then I pulled on a pair of old sneakers, some fresh blue jeans, my Aspen State Teachers College sweatshirt and the brightest jacket I owned. It was a crimson red crew jacket from *The Adventures of Magic Max,* a show I had worked on for ABC in the early eighties. Even an elk wouldn't have the bad taste to wear it.

There really wasn't an Aspen State Teachers College. It was just a goof some locals cooked up twenty-five years ago to sell sweatshirts and coffee mugs, because Aspen seemed so much like a college campus. It was a pretty effective goof. One time, the "faculty" of Aspen State scammed their hoax onto the AP sports wire for vanquishing the Harvard football team in overtime, and every few years some very dumb kid would show up in September for freshman orientation. They usually stayed, writing home to Mom and Dad that they were learning a lot and that college was a real fun deal. I thought that this was maybe how Police Chief Rick came to town. Ernie may have applied to Aspen State Teachers College as well, but he probably hadn't been accepted. I walked out of the Spread Eagle and headed over to City Market. I bought two apples and a bag of grapes. I have no idea what came over me.

Officer Ernie was parked across the street in his squad car as I left the market. He was watching me but I ignored him. I thought maybe I should talk to Rick about a restraining order. The guy might be a stalker—which would have been peculiar given my current sewer-level celebrity status. But I had more important things to do. I took a bite of one of my apples and ambled toward the Hyman Avenue Mall.

Chapter Ten

Interesting Irwin was looking at me, interested. The arms trader had a handlebar mustache and looked exactly like the doorman in *The Wizard of Oz,* the guy who told Dorothy about the horse of a different color.

"I'm looking for a gun," I said. "Cheap."

"I don't sell cheap guns," Interesting Irwin said, not as interested as he was when I first walked into his store and he thought he might have a chance at selling me Cochise's last ceremonial Winchester with the feathered rifle quiver. I could see a WWII Italian infantry rifle mounted over a sign that read, NEVER FIRED, ONLY DROPPED ONCE, but I wasn't sure if it was meant to be funny.

"Okay, an inexpensive gun," I apologized. "Something easy to load and easy to aim and shoot. None of that hair trigger stuff, and I want to be able to buy the bullets anywhere—like in a hardware store or at Wal-Mart."

"Maybe you should buy a gun at Wal-Mart," he said.

"Aspen doesn't have a Wal-Mart," I pointed out. "Not yet anyway. But we have a Gap."

"What kind of gun?" Irwin asked. "A buffalo gun, a nail gun, maybe a Pez gun?"

He was an inch more interested but still sounded like it was open mike night at the Asshole Saloon.

"A pistol," I said. "You know, like you can hold in one hand?"

"A one-handed pistol." He nodded seriously. "I have just the gun."

Interesting Irwin laid a rusted pistol on the counter, putting it on a fancy velvet mat. The gun looked like it had been used to hold open the door of a junkyard latrine.

"A Peacemaker, Colt .45, the gunslinger's gun of choice," he said.

"It looks kind of old," I said, "and rusted."

"It was salvaged when they raised the Merrimack," he said with a straight face.

"So it's famous?" I asked.

"Absolutely famous. Wild Bill Hickok won it off of Wyatt Earp in a card game before he gave it to Doc Holliday as a wedding present when Doc married Big Nose Kate," Irwin said. "I can't document that. But it's what the former owner told me."

"And who was that?"

"Bat Masterson's grandson," he said, without laughing.

"Oh, so it'd be like I was packing a museum."

"Exactly. But without the red velvet ropes."

Irwin was a wiseass, but who could blame him after having to sell replica Texas Ranger badges to Sly Stallone and Don Johnson as last-minute Christmas gifts for Michael Ovitz. Back when Mike was still the sheriff of Hollywood, he used to spend the High Holidays in Aspen, and if anybody from the *biz* was here, they had to shower Hollywood's messiah of the moment with frankincense and myrrh.

"How much?"

"Two hundred bucks, and I'll throw in a box of bullets," Irwin said.

"Kind of cheap, isn't it?"

"I got a Buntline Special I could sell you for a hundred and sixty grand," he said. "But Ollie North is interested in it so you got to let me know."

I hefted the Peacemaker in my right hand. It was much heavier than it looked. I held it out in front of me and aimed it at the head of a stuffed mule deer that was mounted above a vintage Esso Extra gas pump. The weight made my wrist shake, and the eight-inch barrel twitched back and forth like the needle on an LA County seismograph.

"Have you had much experience with guns?" Irwin asked.

"Only on paper," I said. "This thing ever kill anybody?"

"Not yet," he said.

Irwin gently took the pistol out of my hand, directing it away from his face.

"Wrap it up," I said, peeling off two hundred dollars like it was small change.

I walked out of Interesting Irwin's an armed man. I felt a little taller. But the five-pound Peacemaker was sagging down in my pocket and banging against my hip like a colostomy bag. My *Adventures of Magic Max* jacket wasn't designed for carrying heavy firepower. But that was probably because Max was bulletproof and could see through bricks. I could barely do a dozen sit-ups.

Chapter Eleven

I had never researched a single script I had ever written, and I doubt our television audience would argue with me about that. But I had to start finding out just what the hell was going on in this high-mountain burg. So I headed over to the Aspen library—which was more like a research center you'd find at the Scripps Institute than a public library in an aging ski town on the wane. But Aspen's property tax base was about ten billion dollars, so the town had money to burn. It's why Aspen had free buses and could afford to turn the Hyman Avenue Mall into the streets of St. Louis.

The library was empty and smelled like a new car—possibly a Volvo. There were a row of computers and a gigantic video library next to a large screening room and dozens of aisles of perfectly aligned books. The art on the wall was impressive, though appropriately oblique, and in what was more than likely a Freudian snub of the notion of public drinking fountains, I could see a cooler full of chilled Evian.

Polly Pounds was a part-time librarian who only worked in the afternoon so she could still poach first tracks on powder days. She was sitting behind a cluttered desk and reading *The Great Gatsby*—re-reading it, no doubt. I hadn't seen Polly in twenty years, but she hadn't changed a bit. I walked over to her and tapped on the book.

"Good book," I said.

"One of my favorites," Polly said, barely looking up.

"The movie sucked, though."

"They generally do," Polly said, finally looking at me. "Where you been, Jake?"

"Hollywood."

"How was it?"

"Not great."

"I'm not surprised."

"At least I got this really nice crew jacket out of the deal," I said. "But I had a piece of the back end."

"I'm happy for you."

Aspen was a place where you could not see someone since the first grade but they acted like you had run into them yesterday.

"Fifteen percent of the net profits," I said.

Net profit was a misnomer in Hollywood. The bean counters are among the most creative people in tinsel town and their job is to make sure that any excess shekels trickling toward the talent pool get charged off to private jet fuel and truffle platters for the premieres. The studios gave out fancy colored crew jackets to make up the difference.

"I need to do some research."

"What kind of research?" Polly asked.

"About the coeds of Aspen High," I said.

"You rich guys are all alike," she said, shaking her head as if I was a flasher.

The longtime local ladies of Aspen are continually pissed off that the rich guys their age seem to only chase after the younger women.

"I'm not a rich guy anymore, and I don't believe in girl-friends," I said. "I just need to find out about the kids in Aspen."

"Why?"

"I'm doing a *21 Jump Street* thing," I said.

"What's a jump street?"

Fox's first hit TV series about undercover cops in high school wasn't carried on cable in Aspen, but I didn't want to go into the particulars.

"Kind of like hall monitors, but with guns," I said. "You got any recent yearbooks or anything like that?"

After about twenty minutes Polly plopped down a stack of clippings from the *Snow Job,* the high school's student paper, and the last five years of yearbooks. I was sitting alone at a long table, finishing a complimentary cappuccino.

"Don't do anything weird with this information," she said.

"Can I smoke in here?" I asked.

But Polly didn't answer me and returned to the blue blood-letting of Gatsby. It took me a while to go through the year-books. The students all looked like pure-breeds—gorgeous kids with straight teeth and terrific hair. Rich kids are usually beau-tiful, I think, because rich boys get to marry the prettiest girls, and three generations of that produces pretty attractive gene pools.

I finally found some information on Tinker. Her last name was Mellon, and her first name was actually Tania. Tinker was a nick-name. I had always thought that Tania was a nickname, but maybe that was only when Cinque was giving it to Patty Hearst.

Tinker was a member of the Honor Society, secretary of the Drama Group, and president of the Chemistry Club. She also led Christian Bible Study meetings every Friday afternoon. Tinker played field hockey and was a statewide standout in basketball. She planned to be a psychotherapist. But I knew Tinker might ac-tually be leaning toward a career as a spokesperson for Nokia.

There was a group picture with Tinker and her classmates in French class. She was sitting in the front row as a teacher named

Richard Dupre stabbed with a pointer at a sentence written in beautiful script on a green blackboard.

I recognized the French teacher as the baldheaded bicyclist in the photographs with Tinker, a.k.a. Tania Mellon, president of the Chemistry Club and high school basketball star.

Chapter Twelve

I was sitting in the gazebo across from the Main Street Bakery and taking furtive looks at Tinker's photographs. I felt like a pedophile. There was no doubt about it. The bald man was Tinker's teacher. But I couldn't exactly walk into the principal's office and blow the creep's cover, because the other man in the group grope was the police chief's kid. I was on my own, and even looking at photos like these was against the law. It made me feel dirty. It made Jimmy feel like Janet.

The Peacemaker hung heavy in my pocket and reminded me that I didn't have a clue how to use it. But I figured I'd better learn just in case yesterday's shooter was as sober as I was—or at least as sober as I was at present. I walked over behind the County Court House and backed the Corvette out of the police impound. Ernie was just pulling in, and he rolled down the window of his Saab.

"You fill out the necessary forms to retrieve that vehicle from the impound yard?"

"No," I said.

"You better."

"Make me."

"I could."

"Like to see you try," I said, almost sticking my tongue out.

"No you wouldn't," Ernie said.

I thought I'd better up the ante before one of us threatened to tell his mom.

"Look, asshole," I said, "I don't know what your beef is with me or if it's just against the world in general because you got the short end of the stick when it came to dicks. But if you continue to fuck with me, I'll . . ."

I was suddenly at a loss for words.

"You'll what?" Ernie said, smiling as if he was Tom Sawyer and had just talked me into painting a fence.

There really wasn't much I could do, I realized.

"I'll sue you," I said, like a honcho who once had a personal attorney on retainer.

"Oh, big man," he said, like someone who couldn't afford to put his buck teeth in a retainer.

We glared at each other, and I was trying to decide if I should give him a noogie. But Ernie was a whole bunch younger than I was, so I thought better of it.

"What were you and the chief talking about that was so important?"

"That's for me to know and you to find out," I said, and drove off.

Highway 82 crosses the Continental Divide at 12,600 feet above sea level, making Independence Pass the highest paved road in the United States, originally cut in by coolie labor back in the 1880s so the Aspen silver miners could get their ore to the town of Leadville. All the rain that falls on the east side of the divide runs into the Gulf of Mexico. The rain falling on the Western Slope ends up in the Pacific. Not too many people know this, and I was wondering how I knew it. It was the kind of thing I'd told my ski classes to impress them back when I was trying to score a free lunch.

The road was twisting and narrow, with steep cliffs and giant rock overhangs. I was wheeling the Corvette pretty good. I was alone on the road, or at least I was pretty sure I was alone. I couldn't see behind me because someone had shot off my rearview mirror. But the Corvette felt sturdy and solid in my hands. Actually, it felt like a different car, but maybe I was a little bit of a different guy. I was now a member of a rare club. I had been shot at, by accident or design, and survived. It made me feel tough and formidable.

I looked high up to my left and saw a rock climber clinging virtually in thin air to a vertical granite face. It was a solo ascent, the climber appearing like a tiny praying mantis, hanging by his fingertips on the sheer rock wall. One misjudgment or an overly confident move, and the climber could plunge to his death. I thought of the Hollywood careers that have ended the same way and felt lucky.

I pulled in and parked in the Lincoln Creek parking lot that was about halfway up the pass and headed into the wilderness on a manicured path dotted with drinking fountains and porta potties. I walked about three miles into the great outdoors, enjoying the hell out of myself and stopping only to check my pulse and catch my breath.

I picked up three baseball-sized rocks and placed them a foot apart on a boulder about the size of a Buick Electra. I counted off twenty paces and looked back at the rocks. This was going to be easy, I thought, and wondered how Alexander Hamilton could have missed Aaron Burr from such a short distance. I took the Peacemaker out of my pocket and awkwardly slipped six .45-caliber bullets into the cylinder. I slapped it with the palm of my hand, trying to spin it like a gunslinger in a spaghetti western, but the cylinder didn't budge. Then I raised the Peacemaker up and out in front of me with both hands. I closed my left eye and squinted with my right, lining up the Colt's barrel on the middle of the three rocks.

"Okay, Grayson," I said to the Buick. "You've been rustling my women for too long . . . time to make your peace and meet your maker."

The origin of my pistol's moniker dawned on me just as I squeezed the trigger, and the Colt exploded with a boom louder than a jet busting the sound barrier. The gun flew out of my hands in a veil of blue smoke and fired once again when it hit the ground, almost blowing my kneecap off and putting a hole through my brand new Gap jeans.

"Holy shit," I said, breakdancing back from the Peacemaker.

I rubbed the sting out of my leg and gingerly picked up the Peacemaker, holding the barrel away from me like it was a stick covered in dog doo. This wasn't going to be as easy as I had hoped. I leveled the gun again, this time with a tighter grip and both eyes wide open, aiming at the rock on the left. I pulled the trigger. The blast was still just as loud, but I was ready for it, and the Peacemaker kicked up about a foot from where I was trying to hold it steady. The rock didn't move, but after a three-second delay I heard the .45-caliber slug ricochet off something hard a half-mile away. I hoped there weren't any picnickers in the area. I was lucky it was off season.

I emptied the cylinder at the baseball-sized rocks, but they never budged—though I did do a hell of a job trimming the aspen trees behind the boulder. I was about to reload when I heard the echo of a dirt bike. It was difficult to tell exactly where the motorcycle was coming from, but that was cleared up for me when a huge Honda exploded out of the trees about a hundred yards away. It's illegal to operate motorized vehicles off-road in the White River National Forest, but I guessed this gladiator in the fancy carbon-fiber full-body armor didn't read the sign.

I jogged to my left to get out of the bike's way, but it veered toward me. I moved to my right, and the biker corrected, aiming at me again. The Honda was only about a hundred feet away from me now, and I realized I was about to be run down. I dodged out of the way just as the dirt bike swept past, its brake lever goring through the pocket of my *Adventures of Magic Max* Jacket and spinning me around like a drunken college kid in Pamplona. Then the Honda circled and pulled a wheelie as the biker reared after me. There were no bullets left in the Peacemaker, but I decided if I waved it over my head while I ran in circles, the errant knight would see that I was the tough and formidable man I had recently become. Apparently he didn't and closed in for the kill.

Deftly sidestepping the joust, I threw the Colt with as much Little League muscle memory as I could muster, hitting his helmet dead square and knocking the Honda headcase off the bike. But the biker got up immediately—the advantage of full-body armor no doubt. Then the biker picked up the Colt and walked toward me. The wisdom of throwing one's only weapon at the enemy was immediately called into question.

"What the hell did you go do that for?" the biker said.

I recognized the voice.

"Hermy?"

Herman Thayer took off his helmet and looked at his bike.

"This better not be broken."

"Who gives a shit if it's broken?" I said. "You could've killed me."

"You just should've stood still," he said. "I was using you for a slalom pole."

Herman pulled a flask out of his armored vest and chortled down a long drink.

"You want a sip?"

"I don't know how to sip," I said.

He handed me back my Peacemaker.

"What the hell are you doing way out here with this, anyway?"

"Practicing," I said. "I'm thinking about taking up elk hunting."

"That why you're wearing that ugly jacket?"

"That's exactly why."

Herman effortlessly righted his Honda.

"You're going to need a bigger gun."

"I hope not."

I reached into the remaining pocket of my crew jacket and took out the envelope of Tinker's photographs. I handed Herman the picture of Tinker when she was still wearing the wet T-shirt and standing on the windsurfer.

"You know this girl?" I asked.

He held the photograph to the light.

"Duh," Herman said. "Who doesn't?"

"I don't."

"Tinker Mellon." Herman said. "Girl likes to eat ecstasy and ride the schnitzel."

"Have you complimented this young lady with your schnitzel?"

"Not exactly. I got so high I couldn't get it up."

"Bummer."

"Tell me," he said. "But she was crazy about the shafts."

"The *shafts?*"

"The mine shafts," Herman said. "What'd you do, forget everything that's cool about this place when you were out in Hollywood?"

"Tried to," I said, remembering the abandoned mine where Tim Lackey and I had stashed our marijuana money.

"It's how I met her. I was spelunking the tunnels under Aspen Mountain. She was maybe tripping or something, so I showed her around. She loved it down there."

"Who wouldn't?" I said.

"Why'd you want to know about her?"

"I'm opening a modeling agency."

"I used to be a model," Herman said.

"Send me your headshot," I said. "When was the last time you saw Tinker?"

"Last summer at least," Herman said, expertly kick-starting his Honda, "or maybe it was real early this summer. It's hard to remember stuff like that, exactly."

I wanted to tell Herman that this summer was already this October, but I didn't have time, because he blasted back off into the wilderness.

Mine shafts? Small world, I thought.

Chapter Thirteen

I found myself stranded at Cemetery Lane and Slaughterhouse
Bridge, waiting for the free bus to take me back into town. I had
gotten out of bed at first light to go on a run in the laceless Nike
triathlon sneakers I'd purchased after I returned from target practice. Not having to tie my sneakers was a big motivator for me,
and the new Nike was the latest in low-commitment gear.

I was wearing black running tights and a black long-sleeved
marathon jersey with a small matching cycling cap that resembled
a yarmulke with a tiny beak. I may have looked like a formidable
Israeli night-fighter, but I had overrated my aerobic ability, opti-
mistically running a mile and a half down the Rio Grande Trail
along the Roaring Fork River before staggering to a stop with
shin splints and chest pains.

The bus dropped me off three blocks from the Snow Eagle.
I had to pick up the Peacemaker and Tinker's photographs. I had
not wanted to be running and drop dead of a heart attack with
pictures of a naked schoolgirl and an antique six-gun stuffed in

the waistband of my black tights. The coroner might have thought I was a member of the British Parliament.

I took a quick shower and gulped down a bowl of Cream of Wheat but with nonfat milk instead of cream. I drove the Corvette out to the Aspen Business Center and parked next to a tall Cyclone fence that surrounded the property of the Pitkin County Department of Animal Control. Inside the fence were about a dozen dogs, mixed breeds and purebreds, performing stupid pet tricks to get my attention as I headed toward the office. Like me, they knew what it was like to be abandoned at the peak of their peeing-on-fireplugs careers, and knew that it wasn't much fun. But I already had my eye on a large malamute that was lounging by himself in the shade.

"That malamute in need of any exercise?" I said.

A teenage girl with spectacular blue eyes, orange hair, and a mortician's tan smiled at me from behind a counter inside the office. Her lip was pierced with what looked like a nut and bolt, and something that resembled a shower curtain ring clutched through her left eyebrow. Ten-penny nails penetrated her earlobes, and the links of a small chain were tattooed around her neck. She looked like she wanted to be a hardware store when she grew up.

"As much as you can give him," she said.

"Does he come with a sled?" I asked.

"No, but you'll do," she smiled. "And don't let him near anyone mean. Malamutes don't bark and sometimes Winston just bites."

"I like honesty in an animal," I said.

"Honesty is all they have," she said, believing it. "It's the people that dump them here after they get bored that are the fucking assholes."

"Do you kiss your boyfriend with that mouth?" I said.

"I can talk like this because I'm a volunteer and can't get fired," she said. "And I have a girlfriend, thank you."

She smiled at me again, wondering if I was shocked or impressed.

"Don't rub it in," I said. "And I can't get fired either."

"You're retired?"

Ouch. I didn't think I looked that old.

"On disability," I said.

"From what?"

"Hollywood," I said. "I was dissed for my ability to piss off television executives."

"You were on television?"

"I was *in* television; there's a difference."

"I hate TV."

"And I'm probably one of the reasons, darling."

"Do you know Robert Downey Jr.?"

"Not professionally."

"He did *Ally McBeal*."

"Who hasn't?"

I snapped my fingers at the malamute, but he didn't budge.

"How will Winston know I'm not mean?"

"I'll tell him," the girl said with a smile that broke my heart.

I loaded the sled dog into the Corvette and drove toward the high school. Winston looked very cool, paws on the dash, head out the T-top, and his tail told me he liked being on parole. A plastic surgeon and his personally proportioned wife, who lived in Miami but summered in Aspen, had purchased Winston from a breeder over in Conifer as an accessory for their Rocky Mountain wardrobes. But they had dropped Winston off at the pound on their way out of town. Apparently Winston had not made the impression they had hoped.

I had planned to stake out Aspen High and force an impromptu meeting with Frenchy Dupre after the bell rang, but I couldn't just hang around the schoolyard. All I needed was for Ernie Grubbs to run me in for voyeurism if I showed up during girls' gym, so I figured that walking a dog around the track behind the school was a pretty good cover. I was impressed with myself for coming up with it. Animal Control was always canvassing for dog walkers. It was a perfect arrangement, unwanted dogs walked by people with nothing better to do.

At one time in my life, all I'd wanted was a loyal dog and a good wife. But in Hollywood I could barely keep *myself* alive, much less a dog, and I never had a healthy relationship with a woman, on account of my heart being badly broken in Aspen back in the seventies. During a private ski lesson I was giving a girl from Minnesota, I'd fallen impossibly in love as only a young man can. Her name was Annie Davenport, and she was just as comfortable. An hour lesson turned into a winter of profound intimacy and commitment. But I wanted to be a writer in Hollywood, and Annie wanted to run a preschool in Minneapolis, so the relationship ended in April like a bad Harry Chapin song.

I never got over Annie, but I did learn how to drink my way through the loneliness. I was even married once, briefly, during a weekend bender in Las Vegas, to an actress who didn't know that Canada was north of the United States.

I kid you not.

Chapter Fourteen

Winston and I had walked about twenty laps around the track. I'm sure my new bud would have preferred running down elk, but it was healthier, though probably not as much fun, to keep him on dry food. I gave him a dog biscuit in the shape of a cat. It was the best I could do.

At about four o'clock we decided to head over to the faculty parking lot. I saw an old Renault station wagon with a French flag windshield decal and a "Learn French, Impress Your Waiter" bumper sticker. There was a high-tech mountain bike rack on the roof. It was a pretty good bet that this was Richard Dupre's car. I tied Winston to the driver's side door handle and sat on the hood. I felt like a cigarette but guessed from my own experiences in high school that smoking was still prohibited in school parking lots. I hadn't bought smokes for three days and was just beginning to adjust to the new and odd taste in my mouth, which was, apparently, the consequence of fresh air.

Richard Dupre exited a door at the rear of the school and

walked toward his car. He was wearing hiking shorts and clogs and a "Visualize Whirled Peas" T-shirt, so right off the bat I could tell that he had a sense of humor and practiced punch line politics. It was also clear that the faculty adhered to a pretty casual dress code—not to mention one for conduct.

"Hey, dog," Richard said, faking like he had a biscuit.

"His name's Winston," I said. "And he's a very honest dog, so keep it real."

"All animals are honest," he said.

"Honesty is all they have," I said, honoring the girl who lent me the dog.

I got off of the hood but left Winston tied to the Renault's door handle.

"Are you *Rish-arrd Due-Prey,*" I asked, reaching deep for what I'd learned from my own high school French teacher.

"Dick Dupre," he said, pronouncing his last name *Due-Pree* like the Midwesterner he was.

"Hi, Dick," I said, extending my hand. "Russell Chatham."

"The painter?" he asked, ready to fawn.

"The house painter."

For some reason the name of one of America's most under-appreciated impressionists flew into my head, and I was almost half-impressed that this perv had recognized Chatham's name. But *savoir vivre* and character have always been separate issues, not to mention languages.

"But we get confused a lot," I said.

He looked a little disappointed and started to untie Winston. Winston growled.

"Leave him there," I said.

Dick was trying to stay in his affable, good-guy teacher persona. But I could see that he was slightly off balance.

"Look, what can I do you for, Russ? I got to get to the gym."

"You look like you go to the gym. No body fat."

"Twelve percent," he said.

"Nice."

I snapped my fingers, and this time Winston heeled at my

side. The couple from Miami had obviously spent a fortune on obedience school.

"Do you know Tinker Mellon?"

Dick was really off balance now, and the blood drained from his tan face. I moved closer in case he started to list.

"Is she a student here at Aspen High?" he said, choosing density over dishonesty.

"Tinker is the natural blonde that sat in the front row of your French class," I said.

"You're a house painter?"

"Nah," I said. "I'm just a dick, Dick . . . a private dick. But one should keep his dick private, don't you think?"

I smiled. He didn't.

"Tinker's stepmom hired me to find her," I said.

"I can't help you with that."

"Don't be such a pessimist."

"Move your dog."

Dick had already dropped the affable part, and I was waiting to see just how much good guy he had left.

"Move him yourself."

He grabbed at Winston's leash just as my new best friend feinted with a show of teeth that could have taken off a hand. I handed Richard the photograph of himself holding Tinker upside down while she checked her gag reflex.

"That's a heck of a penis for a French teacher. Did you get it online?"

Dupre must have read the same spam, because he smiled slightly. I had to admit, for a statutory rapist, he didn't seem very rattled.

"Big deal," he said, and handed me back the photo.

"Tinker's underage," I said, "and one of your students. That's two big deals, actually."

He started to laugh, and the laugh sounded very real, or maybe this guy also taught drama.

"Tinker dropped out of school before these pictures were taken. Plus she's twenty-one."

"High school seniors are twenty-one these days?"

"Mostly in Detroit, but let's say Tinker's the local exception," he said.

This guy was building quite a resume: pedophile, porn star, and now a racist. But I thought it a little odd that he was turning into a wiseguy. If this had been one of my old scripts, I would have had him pissing peanuts by now.

"We could tell that to the police," I said.

"No prob," he said. "I'm sure the chief would like to see those photos of his kid."

Dupre was really starting to outflank me, so I figured it was time to show him the gun. I flashed opened my denim jacket but caught the Peacemaker by its pearl handle. The gun bounced to the pavement and the cylinder came loose, scattering six .45-caliber bullets at our feet. I tried to reach the bullets with my foot and pull them toward me. But I couldn't. If my interrogation had been a prizefight, the referee would have stopped it by now.

"What do you mean Tinker's twenty-one?" I asked.

"Twenty-one is twenty-one, genius, and you're not going to find her unless she wants you to."

"I'm pertinacious," I said, like someone thumbing through a thesaurus.

"She'll eat you alive. Those pictures weren't my idea."

"Let me guess; it was date rape?"

"Pretty close," he said. "I was high. I can't even remember that night."

"So now we're blaming the victim?"

"I'm the victim," he said, and meant it.

This guy could win an Academy Award, I thought.

"That's a nice story. How does it end?"

"You're the TV guy. You tell me."

"How did you know I was in TV?" I said, much more astonished than flattered.

"Maybe I'm an insomniac," Dupre said.

He took a half-step toward Winston and the malamute let him

know that nobody was going anywhere. I was starting to fall in love with this dog.

"Look, Tinker's dad is a degenerate sports nut," he said. "When Tinker transferred to Aspen High, he faked her birth certificate so Tinker would have a chance at making the US Ladies Basketball Team for the next Olympics."

The Dickster said this so convincingly it was hard not to believe him.

"And Tinker's got a shot at it because she looks so good playing against kids four years younger than she is," he said. "She's all-state."

"But not in good hands," I said, groaning for both of us.

Then I thought of the kid from the Dominican Republic who had disgraced the Little League World Series by pulling the same stunt, and I remembered how I hated it when high school teachers started making sense.

"Okay, so Tinker might be legal," I said. "But she's still missing."

"Or maybe at an NBA fantasy camp. Now move your dog or call the police."

Dupre held out a cell phone. I could see that it was a Nokia. I had no choice but to let him drive away.

Chapter Fifteen

"Can I keep this mutt?" I asked.

Ms. True Value was feeding her pack inside the Cyclone fence. From a distance she looked very normal, and the dogs showed her the affection anyone shows when they're hungry and somebody is handing out a free meal. We have a lot in common with animals— except that honesty thing.

"I'll have to do a background check," she said.

"You already know the worst parts," I said.

Winston curled around my feet, doing his best to show his parole officer just how happy he was.

"And I think he likes me."

"Hard to believe," she said, moving toward me but still inside the fence. "Winston treed the last two people who walked him."

"I'm a dog whisperer."

"What's your name?" she asked.

"Jacob Wheeler," I whispered. "But everyone calls me Jake, even my mom. What's yours?"

"Lynda," she said. "But everyone calls me Laser, except my mom."

"There's nothing wrong with Lynda."

"It's oppressive."

"Magnolia's oppressive," I said. "Lynda's all-American."

"Same diff," she said. "You can keep Winston for a week to see if you get along."

Laser came out of the pen and hoisted a big bag of dog meal off a wooden pallet.

"Where are you from? I mean, originally?" I asked.

"Born and raised in Aspen."

"That's unusual."

"Just another lucky winner in world roulette. It could've been Biafra."

But it was hard to tell if she meant it. This was a beautiful young woman with a bolt through her lip and a chain tattooed around her neck. I wondered what kind of statement that was against the spectacular surroundings she had been born into.

"Do you know Tinker Mellon?" I asked.

"The cunt?" she said, slinging the Queen Mother of all swear words like it was nothing more than a nickname.

"How about we just call her a bitch?"

"Why?"

"Because the First Amendment frightens me," I said.

Laser looked at me like I was the wimp I was and shook her head.

"Is your whole generation full of crap?"

"Sadly, yes," I said. "Do you know her?"

"She dated Ricky Rankin after I did."

I just about choked, but Laser didn't notice, because she was gaining speed about how pissed off she still was at Ricky.

"Or actually *when* I did," she said, "which is why I'm not dating him anymore, the shithead."

"I thought you liked girls."

"Ricky is *why* I like girls, I think."

"Probably a phase," I said. "When I was your age, I wanted to be a priest."

"I don't know," she said. "Ricky hurt me real bad."

"It was all that kneeling that changed my mind," I said, "and I could never get the hang of playing *Naked Altar Boy*."

Laser laughed, but this was the audience I used to write for, so entertaining her was pretty easy.

"His dad's the chief of police, right?" I asked.

"Yeah, and is that the fucking joke of life or what?"

"Is it?"

"Ricky is the biggest ecstasy dealer on the Western Slope, maybe the whole country."

"I thought he was a freshman at CU"

"If you're a dealer, where else would you be?" she said, like I was an idiot.

"Do you think Ricky knows where Tinker is?"

"I fucking hope not."

"But maybe?"

"Why?"

"Because her stepmom wants me to find her."

Laser looked at me suspiciously. "What does she want to do, score some X?"

"I'm a private detective."

"You told me you were a fucking TV guy," she said, the bolt turning in her lip.

"I was a TV guy," I said. "But now I have to work for a living."

"You lied," Laser said. "I fucking hate liars."

"I misrepresented myself. It's different."

"Not to me," she said. "I'm so fucking stupid sometimes." She swung the bag of dog food onto her shoulder as if it were a Gucci purse. "And I hate fucking cops."

"I'm not a cop," I said. "I'm a private detective, emphasis on private. I don't even have a license or anything."

"You need a license to be an asshole?"

"Not in Aspen."

Laser was trying not to smile.

"What's ecstasy like?" I asked.

I had pretty much worked my way through the whole medicine chest during my drug days, but I was either too old or too tired to try ecstasy when it first hit the party circuit. I couldn't remember which.

"It's a little like acid but without all the cosmic angst."

That I remembered, and not fondly, having suffered from acid indigestion ever since my first and only trip while skinny dipping in Max Yasgur's cow pond.

"But what Ricky sells is really *sextasy,* X mixed with bootlegged Viagra," she said. "It's this whole big weird erotic thing."

"Wow. Do the kids here in Aspen take a lot of it?" I asked, trying not to sound like a narc or even worse, the relentlessly understanding Dr. Phil.

"Who wouldn't take a lot of it? The guys get like this lifetime hard-on."

"I wouldn't," I said, lying maybe just a little. "It sounds dangerous."

"Not as dangerous as okey dokey coke, my parents' drug of choice," she said, and smirked. "What's yours?"

"Humility," I said. "But in very small doses."

"Don't tell me you're in the fucking *program.*"

"It's where I met Robert Downey," I said.

"I read about that in *People* magazine."

"Yeah, and I get shit-canned for not practicing anonymity," I said.

"That's bullshit. Sobriety is this big career move now," she said. "You're even supposed to talk about it on Letterman."

"That's the thirteenth step," I said.

"Do you know Ben Affleck?"

I shook my head. "But I don't think he's really a drunk. He just needs an excuse for all the shitty movies he makes."

I tried to help Laser with the bag of dog food, but she wouldn't let me.

"Tinker's probably at Burning Man."

"That freedom festival thing?"

"More like a drug dealer jamboree," Laser said, grimacing at my optimism. "I heard she was maybe going to go up there with Ricky. I went with him last year."

"Was it cool?"

"Sucked," she said. "Sony had these big screens set up all over the place, and Microsoft was puddling everybody with the next version of Windows. I passed out and sunburned my tits."

Laser clicked a lead on Winston and led him back into the pen.

"I have to think about letting you keep Winston," she said. "He's a great dog, but you could maybe be an asshole."

Laser was maybe right.

I walked back to the Corvette and noticed it was leaking antifreeze and the left rear tire was low. Round trip to Burning Man would be about a thousand miles. I wondered if we could make it.

Chapter Sixteen

I had stopped at the Snow Eagle for a knapsack of fresh clothes and what was left of the box of Peacemaker bullets. I didn't know if it would be cool to bring a gun to Burning Man, but if anyone hassled me, I would just tell them the rusty Colt was a hash pipe. The last festival of "Peace and Love" I'd been to was the first Woodstock back in August of 1969, and guns weren't part of the dress code—though I do recall the late Abbie Hoffman taking the stage in tie-dyed fatigues and trying to incite a half-million hippies to storm New York City in an attack on greed and plutocracy.

Ernie Grubbs walked up while I was topping off the Corvette's gas tank at one of the town's two stations. Regular unleaded was going for two and a quarter a gallon. But price gouging continues to be the universal theme in Aspen.

"You believe what those ragheads charge us for gas over here?" Ernie said.

"Yeah, but once we get our new Iraqi oil wells pumping it's only gonna cost about fifty cents a gallon. Like when I was your age."

"A *gallon?*"

"Like when penny candy was only a nickel," I said. "I mean, wasn't bringing back the fifties the whole point in sacking Saddam's sorry ass?"

"Well, the president said there was that human rights thing," Ernie said. "With all those mass graves and the pickpockets getting their heads cut off and stuff."

"Oh, don't be such a softy."

Ernie was wearing crisp Wrangler jeans, round-toed bull-riding boots, a snap-cuff shirt with an embroidered yoke, and a black cowboy hat with a pheasant feather band. His belt buckle was in the shape of Texas and bigger than my apartment.

"Off duty?" I asked.

"Working plainclothes," he said. "I'm never off duty."

I believed him and wondered if maybe there were cattle rustlers in the area.

"The chief went hunting, so I'm kind of in charge."

"Aspen sleeps better already," I said.

Ernie reached into the Corvette and rifled through my knapsack of clothes. Thankfully, he didn't find the gun.

"You going somewhere?"

"Laundromat," I said. "Got any extra quarters?"

"Not on what they pay me," he said. "Where's your dog?"

Ernie's obsession with me had continued, apparently. I wasn't happy that Chief Rick was out hunting, but I was suddenly thrilled I was leaving town.

"What dog?"

"That wolf you took on a walk."

"Winston's a malamute. He just looks like a wolf," I said. "And I had him on a leash, Officer."

The Aspen PD enforced the leash laws with the ruthless resolve of storm troopers, but apparently it was okay to bang the high school kids. Ernie looked around to make sure no one else was close. He moved right next to me.

"Dick Dupre is a good guy," Ernie said. "Leave him alone."

"I just wanted to brush up on my French," I said, trying not to flinch.

"You're going to brush up against some barbed wire if you don't hoof it easier around these parts."

It was a threat, but he made it sound like good country advice. I smiled at him.

"Say, when is the great white hunter coming back, anyway?"

"Depends on how lucky he is," Ernie said.

"Or how unlucky the elk are," I said.

"You just watch your drinking, Pops. I'll worry about the chief."

Pops?

The term stung me like an attack of bursitis. But before I could say anything clever, Ernie snapped the brim of his cowboy hat and swaggered off.

I watched him cross Main Street and could have sworn I heard banjos dueling in the distance.

Chapter Seventeen

The high desert was windier than a Chicago kite contest, and the tumbleweeds were dive-bombing the Corvette like blitzkrieging Christmas wreaths. It was just one of the reasons I've always tried to avoid Utah as much as possible. Not only can the Beehive State be colder than Antarctica or hot as Hades, not to mention dusty, dry, and deathly boring; it's also the home of the melodiously impaired Osmond family and it's a place that's nearly impossible to get a decent cocktail. The Mormons in the bar business have the unsaved mix their own drinks in the backroom and make them feel like they're performing illegal abortions when they do. But I did keep the Corvette's passenger seat open for the fifteen-year-old sixth wife of a middle-aged polygamist should the little woman be fleeing religious oppression and in need of an emergency deprogramming.

The line of vehicles waiting to get into Burning Man stretched about two miles into the desert. The playa was flat and cracked, and the temperature was about a hundred and twenty degrees—but it was a dry heat. The Corvette's radiator had shut down when I tried to run the air conditioner at about sunrise, so I was pushing my plastic beast slowly behind a battered school bus emblazoned with R. Crumb cartoons. Techno-rap blared from gigantic speakers tied to the roof, and it was crammed full of ravers who were probably Gen-X stockbrokers, although it was hard to tell because they were naked and covered in body paint. I thought back to Woodstock and Wavy Gravy and wondered if I should warn these kids not to take the brown acid.

A girl sunning herself on the roof of the bus had been watching me toil with the Corvette for the last two hours. For this weekend, she probably considered me an age-appropriate enemy and not a potential client, so I couldn't really expect any help. The girl was about thirty and in the real world would look like a CPA. But today she had a demon's face painted on her belly with her breasts supplying the eyes and her bellybutton, the nose. I also noticed the poor devil appeared to have a harelip.

"Is this traffic jam a bitch or what?" she said.

"Yeah, but I'm used to it," I said. "I was at Woodstock."

"Kill any Japs?"

She either had a great sense of humor or wasn't a history buff.

"No. But I saw the bombers riding shotgun in the sky turn into butterflies," I said.

The airbrushed CPA looked at me like I was from outer space, then flamed a Bic lighter over an ornate hash pipe fashioned out of a very realistic-looking dildo. At least I was hoping it was a dildo. It might have been a trophy from her first marriage.

"This is excellent hash," she said, offering me a hit with a voice that sounded like helium squeaking out of a balloon.

"Thanks. But I have a rule not to get high with anyone who was born after the Beatles broke up."

"My dad has the same rule, I think," she said, sucking on her pipe.

"How groovy," I said.

I finally arrived at the Burning Man gate and was astonished to discover that my admission to this carnival of hugs and drugs would cost me two hundred and twenty U.S. greenback smackers. The last time I had squandered this much money on entertainment and folly was when I took a Yale drama student to see *Cats* on Broadway, only to find out that I was allergic to both. Fortunately, beyond the gate, money wasn't allowed. Burning Man was a "gifting society" with a commerce based on generosity and good chi, but I figured I could fake it. I paid my toll and stepped through the entrance and was immediately roused by a man wearing cheekless leather chaps and a horned Viking hat covered in artificial fur.

"First time at Burning Man?" he asked with the tone of a drill instructor.

"No," I said. "I come here every year."

"Liar!" he said.

Immediately two topless nurses bent me over the scalding hood of the Corvette, but I couldn't scream, because one of them was attempting to pour a bottle of absinthe into my mouth. I kept it shut tight, but I was impressed by her choice of booze and wondered if she had an ex-lover who was a French poet. The crowd was chanting "liar, liar," and the Viking in the cheekfree chaps began to spank me with a rubber chicken as if I was in a Saturday morning cartoon version of *A Clockwork Orange*.

"Welcome to Burning Man," the Viking said, "a bivouac of human imagination."

"It's good to be here," I said.

I pushed the Corvette into the hot pan of a parking lot, leaving it to bake next to dozens of BMWs and Lexus SUVs. Thank God its cheese had already melted. I slipped on some gym shorts and a pair of thongs and a "Hormel Ham Invented Spam" T-shirt. I put the Peacemaker in a fanny pack and wished it squirted water. My mouth felt like a cotton kiln, and I thought I'd better find a hat to keep my brain from boiling. I rummaged under the passenger seat and found a black baseball cap, an Atomic Ski Company freebie that encouraged me to ski atomically. I put it on backwards.

The fact that I had never seen Little Ricky in clothes was going to work to my advantage. Just about every other person at Burning Man was naked or at least exposed to a large degree. The place looked like ground zero at a sunblock test. I headed toward the seventy-foot wooden man that stood, doomed and waiting, at the epicenter of a series of improvised streets jutting out from him like spokes on a lopsided wagon wheel. This was a city that would no longer exist in forty-eight hours, and it looked like it.

Thousands of brightly colored North Face tents expensively surrounded cardboard hovels and cactus lean-tos. Corporate kiosks hawking capitalism stood next to Rubbermaid outhouses, and a giant pile of plastic shit beseeched everyone to be excrementally correct.

I passed a corrugated hut called Motel 666 and was asked by a yellow-haired Asian girl wearing only a leather bombardier's helmet if I wanted to watch some lesbian pole dancers or if I might be more interested in a career selling solar-powered attaché cases. I told her I had left my kids in the car with the windows rolled up and didn't have time to fill out a job application.

During the sixties I had fiercely believed that if you were not part of the solution you were part of the problem. But the tribe at Burning Man, beyond maybe a residue of resentment for being commercially manipulated or a thin sheen of yuppie angst, appeared to be remarkably without opinion or point of view. The human heart is the only real compass we have, but so far the people here seemed to be spinning their needles in circles. By comparison, I felt like Ferdinand Magellan, in spite of my own meandering failures.

I stopped a man wearing a mirror that covered his face and asked him where I could find some water, and then realized when I did, I was actually asking my own bright red and beefy, sun-fried mug. But I think that was the point. He told me I knew all the answers already and that my thirst was good for me. It was why mankind continued in its endless journey through the universe. I had to restrain myself from kicking him in the balls.

Chapter Eighteen

I had come up goose eggs every time I'd asked someone if they knew a kid named Ricky Rankin. But I think many of the festivalites thought I was possibly a cop and kept their distance. Or maybe it was the non-kosher T-shirt that confused fake ham with Internet spam. It was nearing midnight and just a little while before the giant scarecrow would be ignited and hearts cleansed desert-wide. The temperature had dropped like an Enron 401K. I was hungry and cold.

I had spent the entire day swimming through Burning Man's human soup, and I had not seen one familiar face, although a couple of times I was virtually certain I had heard someone call my name. But when I searched for the name caller, it was like trying to pick out an eleventh-grade girlfriend at a thirty-year high-school reunion. So I thought it might have been an audio hallucination prompted by a contact high. I had experienced the same phenomenon with the sound of applause at the end of my one and only feature film.

I entered a shanty called The Primordial Stew constructed out of discarded billboards and sat down at a trashcan counter to get a bite. A waiter in grass pants put a bowl, fashioned out of a palm leaf and full of veggies, down in front of me.

"What's this?" I asked him.

"Primordial Stew," he said, of course.

"What are my chances for a cheeseburger?" I asked.

"You shouldn't put dead animals in your stomach."

"I was just testing you," I said.

I picked up the palm leaf cup and took a drink. It wasn't bad.

"What do I owe you?"

"We don't believe in money," he said, like a recent Burning Man recruit.

"I know," I said. "I read that on the back of my two hundred and twenty dollar ticket."

"You have to pay for your meal with a joke."

"Did you hear about the plastic surgeon who hung himself?" I quipped.

"What about him?" The waiter asked, slow as a post.

I walked out of the Primordial Stew and the Burning Man was burning from head to toe, his immediate world a pulsating mosh pit lit by purple and red flames. Throngs of insurance salesmen and manufacturer's reps were howling at the moon, whirling like broken gyros in a mass attempt to forget their Dilbert cubicles and work stations.

I needed to make a connection of some kind or resign myself that coming to Burning Man in search of Little Ricky Rankin was pure folly. By now, Jim Rockford would have had this case wrapped up and would be moving on to next week's high-concept episode for the Fall Sweeps. It was time to go big or go home. I tapped on the shoulder of a woman wearing a costume that was apparently supposed to be a baby seal but, in the peculiar reality of her fifteen minutes of fame, looked more like a giant white rat from a Canadian cancer experiment.

"I need to get some ecstasy," I said in my best Johnny Depp–*Jump Street* voice.

"No problem," she said.

She reached into a kangaroo pouch, took out a green tablet and handed it to me.

"This is very good," she said. "Drink plenty of water."

"Thirst is why we're here," I said. "But I was thinking about scoring some quantity."

I hadn't scored any drugs in a while, and I had never purchased more than what I needed for my own personal abuse, so I was a little new at this part.

"You know, like a lot?" I continued.

"I've got plenty," she said, handing me a handful of green tablets.

"Thanks," I said. "But I mean *a lot*. Like maybe a million hits or so, give or take. Know who I could connect with for something like that?"

"Can't help you there," she said, suspiciously eyeing my Hormel Ham T-shirt. "But don't take all those at once."

The seal disappeared back into the swarm of insanity, and I looked at the handful of green tablets in the palm of my hand. Each one of them was stamped with a perfect aspen leaf.

"*Jake,*" a voice called from the crowd.

It was the voice that had called my name earlier in the day. I turned and scanned the masses.

"It's me, Kenny. Are you Jake Wheeler? God, please be you," the voice cried.

The short hairs vibrated on the back of my neck.

"Can you hear me? Am I real?" the voice said, weak and terrified.

It was getting pretty spooky, and I pushed the handful of ecstasy as far into my pocket as I could in case its psychedelic energy was somehow arcing up to my brain. I searched the crowd again, but the smoke from Burning Man's execution obscured the swirling humanity. I was starting to freak out. Then a human form dressed in a red Danskin body suit and with a face covered in white powder swayed toward me like a homicidal apparition in a bad Roger Corman movie.

"It's me, Kenny," he said again.

I recognized the ghost's face; it was on the front half of a shit-head I knew in LA.

"Kenneth, what's the frequency?" I asked, like he was Dan Rather.

"Is it really you?"

"The one and only," I said.

"I need help."

The freaked out jerk-off in the red tights was a fading television executive named Kenneth Mandel. He was senior vice president of drama development at MGM and the asshole who had tried to single-handedly destroy what had been left of my career back when I was learning the hard lesson that in show business, luck runs in streaks. Mandel thought I was too old and untalented to be relevant for prime time, and I thought he was too stupid and arrogant to be a TV executive—even though we both embraced the incredibly low standards of current programming. But in spite of this common ground, or maybe because of it, we openly hated each other. One time I threw a spinach salad at him in the NBC commissary when he was power lunching with the late, great Brandon Tartikoff.

"You've always needed help," I said, the Good Samaritan in me struggling to not leave this wayward traveler in the ditch. "What's the problem?"

"I'm minute," he said. "Everything is so huge and I'm so minute."

"I know the feeling," I said.

"I shouldn't have taken it. But now I can't turn back the clock. I'm too small."

This guy was obviously having a hobo voyage on a very bad drug.

"Go easy," I said. "What did you swallow?"

"They said it was ecstasy."

"It doesn't look like ecstasy," I said, pointing out the irony.

Mandel was flipping out, and whatever he had taken, he'd either taken too much of it or not enough. But too much was never enough for this guy's bad taste buds.

"I should have only taken half," he said.

"That's always a good rule," I said. "Did it have a little aspen leaf on it?"

"Yeah, it did."

"You'll be fine."

"How do you know?"

"I'm an expert on aspen leaves."

I showed him my tattoo. This seemed to chill Mandel a little, but he still reached out to hold my hand. I was his only anchor to the planet Earth, and he knew it. I tried not to lord it over him.

"You're just having a bummer," I said. "Tomorrow, everything will be normal."

"I won't be like this forever?"

"Not noticeably."

"You are the most beautiful and kind man I have ever known. You are, Jacob. I mean it. I have always wanted to tell you that."

I looked at Mandel, a sad guy in whiteface who had apparently gone undercover at Burning Man in a desperate attempt to merchandise the Zeitgeist of a younger demographic. I remembered when he'd thrown me out of his office for pitching him a series about a single mom raising two Down's syndrome children. He'd told me I was "too fucking sensitive" for contemporary television and had me banished from the MGM lot. Now I felt like showing him just how insensitive I could be. But a shred of humanity must still lurk in my soul—I didn't.

"Who did you come with?" I asked.

"My assistant," he said. "But he won't leave the Fornication Station."

"It's the ecstasy," I said. "It's cut with Viagra."

"Is that why it's freaking me out?"

"If I was as big a prick as you are, it'd freak me out."

Mandel was too high to make the connection and tried to focus on his Palm Pilot.

"I have a development meeting in LA tomorrow morning," he said. "Can I go back with you?"

"I was exiled from LA," I said. "I live in Colorado now."

"I love Colorado. You're a brilliant man."

"Go wait by the entrance, and then I'll give you a ride to Salt Lake City. You can take the morning flight in from there."

"Don't leave me, Jake, please."

"I'll only be a minute. Hold my hat."

I gave him my Ski Atomically hat and then headed over to the smoldering feet of the Burning Man. I didn't want to leave any rock unturned before I returned from my first mission as a failed private eye. I was pretty good at failure, but at two-twenty-five a gallon I didn't want to waste the gas. The festival was peaking and so were the purists as they writhed in ecstasy and sweat, hundreds of the hard core reveling lockstep in a trancelike dance. A circle had formed around two dancers waltzing barefoot on the hot coals in what was a surreal but oddly beautiful ballet. The firewalkers were naked, both tall and strong men. One of the men was black and the other was white.

I recognized the taller of the two men as the track star from Laura Keller-Mellon's house in Starwood. The other man dancing in the firelight was Ricky Rankin.

Not *Little* Ricky . . . *Big* Ricky, Aspen's chief of police.

Oh, Lucy.

Chapter Nineteen

"We're out of here," I said, grabbing Kenny Mandel by the hand and yanking him toward the parking lot. "Let's go."

I was carrying two one-gallon jugs of water in each hand and a bottle of Scotch under my arm. I had traded my thirteen-hundred-dollar Rolex for some water for the Corvette's radiator, and a humanitarian at one of the Perrier-sponsored Oasis Places gifted me with a bottle of booze to help the one-time future of prime-time television come down off of his bad trip.

"Drink as much of this as you can without puking and then drink some more," I told Mandel, handing him the single malt.

"I don't drink."

"Start."

I pushed Kenny into the Corvette, filled the radiator, and got the hell out of Burning Man like it was a forest on fire and I was Bambi's mom. Mandel didn't move much on our trip to the Mormon Mecca, but every once in a while I could hear him mumble Bart Simpson's name. Kenny was a true waste product of television, and Sunday night's animated brat was probably his favorite actor. I dropped Kenny off at Salt Lake City International Airport just before dawn. I had given him a pair of sweatpants and my Hormel Ham T-shirt, but he still looked like shit, the Scotch drool having turned his whiteface into a mask of freaky streaks.

"Thanks, Jake," he said, through the tears of a clown.

Mandel tried to shoot his cuffs, but the T-shirt didn't have any.

"Nobody needs to know about all this, right?" Kenny said.

"Just *Daily Variety*," I said.

"I'm on Prozac," he said quietly, as if I was now his most trusted friend and confidant. "I don't think you're supposed to mix it with ecstasy."

Anti-depressants were the only psychoactive drugs show-biz execs could still eat regularly without hurting their careers.

"Could you give me a break?" Kenny asked.

In the final days of my swooning career, Kenny Mandel delighted in telling nearly everyone in show business that I was a "loose cannon with a drug and alcohol problem." Now I had him by the pubic hairs and he knew it.

"No one would believe me," I said. "I have the credibility of a eunuch in a paternity suit."

It was clear Mandel concurred, and he smiled his executive smile.

"But if you have any ideas, I'd *love* to hear them," he said, trying not to sound like the patronizing handy wipe he was.

"What kind of ideas are you looking for?" I said, suddenly a patriot.

Mandel put on his game face and snapped into development mode.

"Well, to give you an idea of what's currently working," he said, "I'm developing a series about an Appalachian hooker whose dead twin does good deeds while her sister does the johns."

"*Touched by an Angel,* but with an edge."

"Exactly."

"What's the title?"

"The West Virginia Monologues," Kenny said, somehow proud of himself. "Call my office and maybe you can come in and pitch an episode."

"Pitch?" I said, as if I was the evil twin and Kenny had just asked me for some free head.

"But I'll have to clear that with the exec producer, so don't get your hopes up."

"Hope is the only thing I can get up," I said, stepping on my earlier eunuch line.

"Drive carefully," Kenny said, not meaning it.

"Fly safe," I said, just as sincerely.

Chapter Twenty

I went east on I-70, passing Grand Junction, Colorado, and finally motoring through the town of Glenwood Springs. It had begun to snow, and all the way up the Roaring Fork River Valley, heavy gray clouds were socking in and shouldering against the Continental Divide like beer-laden Bronco Fans trying to get into the men's room at halftime. The first big snowstorm of the season was about to bluster. It made me smile.

I passed by Carbondale and remembered when Annie Davenport would make me bus down there with her to save money on groceries. The prices at Aspen City Market were jacked up during ski season, and Annie delighted in her role as the responsible homemaker. We were just kids playing house, but I loved living with Annie Davenport.

When I saw the lights flashing on the Colorado state trooper's chase car, I moved over to let it pass. The Corvette's speedometer hadn't worked since Gerry Ford was president, but I now drove like the man I used to honk at, so I was virtually certain I was below the speed limit.

Apparently I wasn't. The trooper's siren whooped me over to the side of the road. By now it was snowing buckets, and I must have looked like a Polar Bear Club fruitcake sitting in a topless car wearing gym shorts and a T-shirt. The trooper stepped up to the rear of the Corvette and punched the plate number into a handheld computer. She was an older gal, with shoulders that belonged on a man and a face that belonged on a Turkish coin, so I decided against winking and smiling.

"I've been following you since Carbondale," she said.

"I didn't see you. I'm sorry."

"What happened to your rearview mirror?"

"A hunting accident," I said. "How fast was I going?"

"Too fast."

"I'm sorry," I said, again.

"You're dressed a little light for this weather."

"This thing has a hell of a heater," I said.

The computer printed out a small slip of paper. She read it and then looked at me.

"This car is registered to Richard Rankin, Junior," she said.

"Yes, I know. His dad's Rick Rankin, Senior, Aspen's chief of police," I said, dropping the name like a dish. "Big Ricky is a dear friend of mine."

"He is, is he," she said, unimpressed with my china.

She looked at my driver's license and was still unimpressed. Apparently she wasn't familiar with my work.

"Have you been consuming any alcoholic beverages, Mr. Wheeler?"

Or maybe she was.

"Not in years," I said. "Did you read my license plate bracket?"

"Yes, I did."

"And what did it say?"

"One day at a time."

"And what's that?" I said, maybe a little too cute.

"An old sitcom."

The trooper reached to the floor on the passenger side and retrieved Kenny's bottle of Scotch. There were still about four fingers left in the bottle.

"Hell of a heater," she said.

"It isn't mine," I said. "Honest."

I had slid the fanny pack around into a belly pack, and I could feel the heavy handle of the Peacemaker sticking into my groin. It suddenly felt as if I was being checked for a hernia, and I coughed.

"But I'd like to mention that I am armed, Officer," I said, as lame as it sounds.

The trooper instantly pressed her 9mm squarely into the middle of my forehead.

"Out of the car!"

She flung open the door with her free hand and pushed me down onto the pavement, kicking open my legs at the ankles and flinging my fanny pack to the side of the road. It bounced, and the Peacemaker fired a shot into the front tire of the Corvette. The trooper crouched, expertly drawing down on the fanny pack as the mortally wounded Goodyear hissed its last hiss.

"It wasn't supposed to have a hair trigger," I said—even lamer.

"Shut the fuck up!" she said, sounding like *she* had one.

The big woman pulled me up by my hair and slapped me across the Corvette's fiberglass hood like a wet chamois. She was very pissed off.

"Do you have any other weapons?"

She didn't wait for an answer and jammed her hand into the right pocket of my gym shorts, pulling out the handful of little green pills emblazoned with the tiny aspen leaves.

"What are these?" she said.

"I think they might be breath mints," I said.

In seconds I was sitting in the back seat of her car and wearing handcuffs for the second time in my life and for the second time in a week. I didn't like the feeling. I was suddenly very cold, and my whole body began to shake like a paint mixer in a hardware store.

"I think I can explain all this," I said.

Chapter Twenty-One

I was sitting on the hard stool in Rick Rankin's office and staring at the photograph of Little Ricky on Big Ricky's desk. He looked like president of the Glee Club—not a drug dealer. But Terry Nichols looks like an insurance adjuster, so what did I know. The state police had ticketed the Corvette for bald tires and expired tags. I passed a breathalyzer at Aspen Valley Hospital but was charged with having an open container of alcohol while operating a motor vehicle. Felony possession of a controlled substance with intent to distribute was still pending. But apparently the old Colt wasn't a big deal. After all, Colorado was cowboy country.

Chief Rankin entered the office, tiptoeing over to a coat rack like he was walking on blistered feet as he hung up his .38 Police Special. Rick was wearing a yellow knit cap, royal blue ripstop mountaineering pants, and a mauve rock climbing jersey with a slate gray neck gaiter. He looked like he was either coming out of the closet or starring in a musical about Mount Everest.

I had never seen Rick carry a gun, but I wasn't about to ask him why he was carrying one now. I could tell he wasn't in a great mood. Rick moved to the bentwood sweater stretcher and sat down. It was clear that his feet were killing him.

"What happened to your feet?" I asked, impossibly casual.

"Fucking snowstorm. I got them frostbit."

"Did you get an elk?"

Rick shook his head and then stared at me.

"You got a hell of a sunburn," he said.

"It's the new black," I said.

Rick opened a desk drawer and took out the bottle of Scotch, the Peacemaker, and a Ziploc bag that held the little green tabs laced with insight and sex. He cleared the Colt's cylinder and tossed it at me. It hit me in the chest and fell into my lap. I grunted.

"Look, I don't give a fuck what someone does behind closed doors. But when you get busted for drugs by the state cops, it puts my dick in the toaster."

Rick poured two drinks into a couple of paper cups, almost finishing the Scotch. He offered one to me, but I shook my head, and Rick downed them both. His eyes were as shiny as Christmas tree ornaments, and he hadn't blinked since he entered the room.

"How much trouble am I in?" I asked.

"None," he said. "I told that dyke that you were working undercover for me."

"She believed you?"

"Doesn't matter. I'm chief of police."

Rick rotated his neck gaiter as if he was trying to unscrew his head. I had never seen him this wired, not even during Aspen's acid-headed glory days.

"She roughed you up pretty good. Did you like that?"

He smiled a smile I had not seen before. It gave me the creeps.

"Most fun I've had since the Boy Scouts," I said.

"I was an Eagle Scout," he said. "So was my dad."

"That kind of thing runs in the family," I said.

He opened the Ziploc bag and squinted at the tiny aspen leaves stamped on the tabs.

"This is a local brand. Where'd you get it?"

"From a dishwasher at the Goose," I said.

"José?"

"Hose B.," I said, but Rick didn't get it.

"Have you ever taken any of this stuff?"

"Not yet."

"Yeah, well be careful when you do. It's not even real ecstasy."

"It's sextasy," I said, like a spy waiting to be shagged.

"And the Viagra they're spiking it with can turn your weiner into a Crescent wrench, so make sure you're with someone you really like or you could end up slipping it in the wrong sweetheart."

Big Rick's normally weird haiku was getting even weirder than normal.

"That's probably good advice," I said, shifting in my seat.

For a second I thought Rick was going to hand me back the pills, but he spilled them back into the little plastic bag and then put it in the kidney pocket of his climbing jersey.

"When did you start packing a gun?" Rick asked.

"When I started practicing private detection," I said in a way I had never said it before.

"Looks old."

"It's historically significant."

I slipped the Colt into the fanny pack and slid it around sideways like a holster.

"How you coming with Laura's kid?"

"Going as slow as I can make it go," I said. "It's a good gig."

"She'll turn up," he said. "Maybe in a porn film."

Rick faked a laugh and then looked me straight in the eyes. I could feel my face flush but was hoping my sunburn camouflaged it.

"Tinker's a basketball star," I said. "She wants to go to the Olympics."

"Her old man wants her to go to the Olympics," he said. "Probably why she keeps running away."

"One reason, maybe."

"Whatever," he said.

Rick stood up and then walked out of the room with the delicate steps of a ballerina. I looked at the last gulp left in the Scotch bottle and, next to it, a single tab of ecstasy that Rick had obviously left for my taking. I wondered if Rick wanted me to start using again. Then I put the tab of ecstasy into my pocket and poured what was left of the Scotch into a wastepaper basket.

I flipped through Rick's Rolodex and found Laura Keller-Mellon's phone numbers. There were five of them—an 800 number, two cell phone numbers and two local numbers with a 925 exchange. I picked up the official police chief telephone and dialed 1-800-Hug-Mine, cringing appropriately.

I left word for Laura that I needed to speak to her. I didn't really need to speak to her. But she was technically my boss so I thought I'd better check in.

Chapter Twenty-two

It was still snowing heavily when I fishtailed the Corvette out of the impound yard for the second time too many in less than a week. There was already eighteen inches on the ground in town and about twice that on top of Aspen Mountain. It wasn't unusual to get a big dump in September, but this was a record-making white-out. The Corvette handled snow about as well as I handled hotel room honor bars, so I spent a good twenty minutes pinwheeling through the streets of Aspen on my way home from Big Ricky's office.

Laser and Winston were sitting on the front steps of the Snow Eagle as I porpoised the Corvette through a snow bank, expertly landing in my designated parking spot, but just a little sideways.

"What are you doing driving Ricky's car?" Laser said, a little surprised.

"I'm buying it from his old man," I said, climbing out through the T-top.

"Ricky is going to go fucking ballistic."

"I'm doing him a favor, trust me."

Laser was bundled in a greatcoat and a bright orange Elmer Fudd hat that made her look like she was a Trotskyite who directed traffic at Red Square.

"How'd you know I lived here?" I asked.

"Where else would you live?"

It wasn't that hard a guess. The Spread Eagle was the only flophouse left in town.

"I love this place," she continued. "My parents conceived me here."

"I hope it was in my room," I said. "You're a great kid."

Laser blushed, and I could see she wasn't crazy about being called a great kid.

"How's my dog?"

"Duh, it's *snowing*."

The bolt in her lip was quivering, but I didn't think it was because of the cold.

"You look a little bummed."

"I just quit my job," she said. "What'd you expect?"

"I thought you liked that job."

"They wanted me to train the dogs to be like fucking performers," she said, hugging Winston. "But Winston doesn't have to do anything he doesn't want to do."

"That's good work if you can get it," I said.

"How was Burning Man?"

"It sucked."

"Told you."

"But who told you I went there?"

"Nobody. You're just predictable. All men are."

Laser took a deep breath and looked down at her fingers sticking out of her fingerless gloves. I could see that her nails were bitten down to the quick.

"Did you see Ricky?" she said.

"No."

"He wasn't with Tinker, was he? You can tell me. I don't give a shit."

"I didn't really see anybody except for some Hollywood schmuck I hate," I said, lying just a little.

Laser got up and wiped at some tears.

"Have you ever fucking hated your life?" Laser said.

"On occasion," I said.

She kicked at a pile of snow and then blew her nose.

"Anyway, I just wanted to give you Winston. They were going to let some asshole make him pull dogsleds up in Snowmass. At least you wouldn't do that."

She handed me Winston's leash.

"I wouldn't," I said. "You look pretty sad."

"I'm very fucking sad," she said. "My life sucks."

"I'm sorry about that. But you know what?"

"What?" Laser said, as if she already knew all the answers.

"If everybody threw their troubles into the middle of the street . . . you'd want your own back," I said in an attempt to give my mother's favorite saying cliché status.

Laser looked at me like she was trying to figure out what, exactly, my mom had meant, and thinking that she might like it when she did.

"What do you think you're going to do?" I asked.

"Move to Seattle and start a band," she said. "I decided I want to be famous."

"Good living is the best revenge," I said.

"Good revenge is oxymoronic," she said, smarter than I was. "I just want to be somebody else for a while."

"I know what that's like," I said.

But she looked at me like I didn't.

"Just don't fuck up the dog."

Laser trudged off into the snowstorm, and I wondered how long it would be before I saw her on MTV. I watched her until she disappeared into a swirl of white and then snapped my fingers at Winston. He followed me up the stairs and into my apartment.

I chopped up some broccoli and onions and put it with a few handfuls of brown rice into a pan on a hot plate. I stripped off my desert duds to take a quick shower and noticed in the bathroom mirror that my ameba-shaped physique was somehow returning to a more human form. It looked like I had lost about twenty pounds.

Winston joined me in the bathroom and began to drink out of the toilet. I admired his self-sufficiency. I turned the hot water on full blast and waited for the cold trickle to turn to steam. I picked up today's edition of the *Aspen Daily News,* which was neatly folded on the back of the toilet, and began to read the headlines. Then a jolt of adrenaline ran through me when I realized that I had not picked up the paper today. I'd been too busy being arrested. Someone must have been in my apartment and put it there.

A photograph of Richard Dupre was below the fold on the front page, and the article was circled in red magic marker to make sure I wouldn't miss it. It was a single-column blurb announcing that Aspen High's favorite French teacher had left town to teach English in France and that he would be missed by all.

Convenient.

Chapter Twenty-Three

When I first heard the pounding on my apartment door, I was still in a half-dream and thought it was Joe DiMaggio downstairs in the basement of my old house in Buffalo, playing the drum solo to "Wipe Out." But it couldn't have been. I didn't know if Jolting Joe had gone on to play the drums, but when I was in the sixth grade my mother had donated my Kent drum kit to the Salvation Army because I refused to practice.

"All right," I said. "Give me a minute."

The drumbeats ceased immediately. I pulled on a pair of jeans and my Aspen State sweatshirt. I had left the *Aspen Times* on the foot of the bed, so I picked it up and folded it under a pillow. No one needed to see a picture of Dick Dupre circled in red in my possession. I opened the door and saw Byron the track star on the wooden deck outside my apartment. He was sitting on the railing, his long legs hooked around the pine rails and extending back and forth like he was doing sit-ups. He was wearing a fabulously expensive silk shirt printed with Picasso-like profiles, blousy white-linen pants, and teardrop Nike sunglasses. It was pitch black out and snowing like hell. I wondered if he was also wearing sunblock.

"What are you, deaf?" he said. "Been knocking on your door about two days."

"I thought it was Joe DiMaggio," I said.

"He dead," Byron said.

"But at least he got to bang Norma Jean," I said, faking a yawn and suddenly very nervous. "What time is it?"

"Don't matter," he said. "You on Ms. Laura's payroll. Lady wants to see you."

I looked behind Byron and saw, parked and running in the street, a long white Range Rover that had been customized into a stretch limo. Blue neon glowed around the borders of the rear windows. The mudflaps were chrome.

"Are you traveling with the Temptations?"

"Just put on some clothes that don't make you look like an asshole."

I went back into the apartment, pulled on some asshole-free clothes and scratched Winston behind his ears.

"If I don't come back, tell my mother I love her."

But Winston just licked his balls, so I don't know how much the moment really mattered to him. I headed down the stairs and slid into the rear of the Range Rover stretch. Blinking lights criss-crossed the headliner, and a Sony Trinitron paneled into the solid teak cabinetry was playing an exercise tape. On the tape, two men dressed in gym skivvies appeared to be using each other for bar-bells, or maybe Barbie dolls. I wasn't sure which.

Byron topped himself off a vodka rocks from a measure-pour nozzle like the ones used in airport bars, but he wasn't enough of a gentleman to offer me a drink—which was a very good thing, as I had moved rapidly from nervous to panicky while I was chang-ing my clothes. I was wearing my Keith Richards duster, a black turtleneck, and a pair of ostrich-skin cowboy boots I had pilfered from Mr. T when I was producing *The A-Team.*

"Nice boots," Byron said.

"I thought you'd like them," I said. "Where are we going?"

Apparently my rank didn't command an answer, and the all-terrain limo effortlessly drove off through the deep snow. Byron handed me *Aspen Daily News*. I could see that this copy also had the Dupre article circled in red.

"You see this?" he said.

"Mysteriously, someone was kind enough to deliver it to my bathroom," I said.

"How can you live in a shithole like that?" Byron said, solving the mystery.

"Less is more," I said.

Byron squirted himself another vodka rocks from the measure-pour nozzle.

"Less is bullshit," he said like a man who knew what he was talking about.

Chapter Twenty-Four

A valet in a red vest and white shirt opened the door for us as the Range Rover stretch stopped in front of the arcade on Hopkins Street. It was a short walk on a heated walkway to an oak door that closed off the Caribou Club to the Aspen masses. A second valet held an umbrella over Byron and me as we moved toward a large doorman who was really a bouncer to keep out the peasants and paparazzi.

"Mr. Byron and one," the valet said into the tiny microphone attached to his lapel.

The doorman opened the door, rogering the valet into the bug on his collar. They didn't really need the mini-mikes, but Aspen was a town where function followed form. We stepped downstairs into a large room warmed by a fireplace of flameproof logs and propane. The room was spectacular, clustered with leather couches and winged chairs, elk-horn chandeliers and original art.

Byron disappeared off to my left into a smaller room that I guessed was the bar, leaving me alone and conspicuous. I could hear a female singer singing an excellent rendition of Carly Simon's "You're So Vain." But I didn't think the song was about me. There were a number of homely old men fawning over a lesser number of beautiful young women. I figured that the song was about them.

In another room a great-looking middle-aged woman with a guitar was sitting on a stool and cooing beautifully from a small stage. There was a small dance floor, but nobody was dancing. The singer finished the ode to Mick Jagger (or Warren Beatty, as the debate goes) and then began to sing "Anticipation," another Simon cover, just as Ms. Laura tapped me on the shoulder. She was trying to smile her best smile, but I could see that Laura's dimples were twitching up and down as if she was suffering from an ongoing stroke.

"I've been looking for you," she said, or *"I've been losing a few."*

I couldn't tell which.

"What's the occasion?" I asked.

"My *birffh*-day."

"Not again?"

"Yeah, I'm thirty-nine. Can you believe it?"

"No," I said, honestly. "Thanks for inviting me, though."

Laura twisted the top of what looked like a silver tube of lipstick, put it to her nostril, and snorted loudly.

"Have you found my kid yet?"

"You'll be the first to know."

"Then why did you call me?"

"Dick Dupre told me Tinker was really twenty-one. Not seventeen."

"Big deal," she said. "I'm not thirty-nine."

Laura's fragment of honesty was pleasantly jolting, but I tried not to reward her.

"Why didn't you tell me the guy in the photos with Tinker was her teacher?"

"I'm not paying you two hundred a day so I can do all the work, Sherlock," Laura said, snatching a glass of Crystal off of a passing tray. "But just for your crib sheet, Tinker won't be eighteen until next March. Dupre's a child molester. What else is he going to tell you?"

I hate being put down by drunk women unless I'm naked and we've already had sex, but in spite of her *birffh*-day stupor, Laura might have been right. Maybe Dupre had told me Tinker was of legal age so he'd able to split town before I found out the truth. But I was clueless as to what question Jim Rockford might ask next.

"Did you know Tinker is into spelunking?" I asked, pretty sure Jim Rockford would never have asked it.

"Sounds perverted. What is it?" Laura lisped.

"Exploring caves and mineshafts."

"No," she said. "I didn't know."

"The kids she hung out with hung out in the Aspen mineshafts," I said.

"For *fun?*"

"Beats basketball practice, apparently."

"Yeah, well good golly and holy cow. But why don't you just find out why the little brat keeps running away?"

"Because I already know that."

"I'm all ears," she said.

"And nostrils."

Laura glared at me.

"Tinker wants to destroy your marriage to her father by making you look like a bad mother," I said, as if that would be hard to do. "And she's probably not crazy about you screwing Byron."

Laura laughed.

"Byron is my maid," she said. "And I don't screw him, sweetie. He borrows my panties."

Laura stepped onto the dance floor as if she had someone to dance with, snapping her fingers and listening to the singer, who had just begun another Carly Simon song.

"She's pretty good, isn't she?"

I nodded. "But doesn't this gal know anything besides Carly Simon songs?"

"That is Carly Simon," Laura said. "A present from my husband."

"Happy *Birffh*-day," I said.

Then I left Laura standing alone in the middle of the empty dance floor.

Chapter Twenty-Five

At eight the next morning I was scoping out a new pair of skis in Stapleton Sports while Winston lay flat on his back with all four of his feet straight up in the air. He looked like a glass coffee table without the glass. Stapleton Sports was the best ski shop in Aspen, owned by Dave Stapleton, a former member of the US Ski Team and a man of few words.

"I want to make a couple of turns," I said.

"Mountain's closed." Dave said.

"I'm going to drive up the backside."

"Don't get caught."

And that was all Dave said to me that morning. For just under twelve hundred dollars, I bought a pair of last year's Atomic 10 Ex powder skis, some discontinued Nordica ski boots, new Scott poles, a Patagonia powder suit, goggles, gloves and a hat.

I drove up the backside of Aspen Mountain on Midnight Mine Road, club-footing the clutch with my new ski boots as Winston shared his passenger seat with the ski gear. I was wearing the

Patagonia powder suit and the goggles, hat and gloves. In the fanny pack I had the Peacemaker along with a flashlight, dog biscuits, and a tofu energy bar.

I had not skied since 1980, but before that I'd logged at least one hundred days a year for nearly fifteen years. I looked forward to making some turns, but I also wanted to poke around my old abandoned mineshaft at the Zaugg Dump. Maybe that was where Tinker and her crew accessed the network of tunnels that criss-crossed under Aspen Mountain. I didn't know what I expected to find exactly, but it was a good excuse to ski the deep, and for the first time in years, my heart was beating against my chest with anticipation instead of anxiety. It felt good.

I parked next to a tall snowbank in front of a dilapidated miner's cabin. Anyone who thought Tim Lackey was still living off of drug money had never been up to his place. The cabin was circa 1880s and lacked plumbing and electricity. But the view of the surrounding mountain range was grand and peaceful. Winston jumped through the T-top and followed me to the door. I knocked and it opened immediately. A woman stared at me without smiling. It was Sarah Lackey, Tim's wife and best friend—a beautiful high-mountain gal with pale skin and coal black hair. Sarah Lackey was as pretty as it gets. She also hated my guts.

"Hello, Sarah," I said.

"Jake," she said, simply.

"Tim home?"

"Why?"

Sarah had never forgiven me for the pot bust, even though the original plan had been Tim's. She was a brilliant artist, but no one had ever heard of her because every time Sarah sold a painting, she used a different name. She knew the importance of anonymity firsthand.

"I wanted to get first tracks, and I thought maybe Tim could give me a lift to the summit."

"He's busy," she said, and started to close the door.

"C'mon, Sarah, it was all a long time ago."

"Not that long. You got rich and Timmy went to prison."

We always went through this when we saw each other again. It was why I didn't see Tim very much, even though at one time in my life I'd considered him my best friend. Sometimes I still did.

"Would it make you feel any better if I told you that maybe Timmy got the better end of the deal?"

"Just because you're a total fuck-up who couldn't handle success doesn't make the seventy-two months Timmy did doing your time any easier."

"Don't sugarcoat it for me, Sarah," I said.

"Holy smokes, look at you!"

It was Tim's voice, and he was coming around the cabin with a short stack of split logs in his arms. Tim had always chopped his own wood, grown his own vegetables, and played his own music on a homemade guitar.

"Yikes, what a surprise," he said.

"Hi, Tim," I said. "It's good to see you."

"Gosh almighty, it's even better to see you. When did you come back to paradise?"

Tim talked as if he lived in an Archie comic book. It was part of his charm and probably why he'd only been sentenced to seventy-two months.

"A couple of weeks ago, or so," I said.

"And you didn't come up and visit your best pal?"

Tim was golly-geeing all over me, and it made Sarah cringe. They were a match made in heaven, but Sarah thought I was the devil.

"I thought you'd be busy," I said.

"Too *busy* for a buddy, now what kind of a buddy would that be?"

For a genius, Tim was the simplest guy I knew.

"You have breakfast yet?" Tim asked. "How about some blueberry hot cakes? We grew the berries ourselves, right up here at the old homestead."

"I just came up to get some freshies," I said.

"Well then let me fire up the snowmobile and give you a lift to the top."

Tim was one of those increasingly rare people who offered to do you a favor before you could even ask for it. He loped off through the deep snow with Winston right on his tail, the dog wagging his like crazy. It looked like Winston already liked Tim better than he liked me. But I couldn't really blame him. So did I. Sarah touched my shoulder and I turned. She was standing very close to me.

"Don't start anything with Timmy, Jake," she said. "We have a nice life up here now."

She had the instincts of a vice cop.

"I won't," I said, hoping I wouldn't.

Chapter Twenty-Six

I had my arms tight around Tim's waist as he throttled a brand new Polaris snowmobile through about four feet of deep white toward the summit of Aspen Mountain. Miraculously, Winston was able to stay right behind us, his paws spreading into tiny snowshoes as he cantered through the drifts. He probably thought he was at a Club Med for Arctic dogs.

"Just like the good old days," I shouted.

"*These* are the good old days," Tim said.

"I've heard that. Last night, in fact," I said, thinking it must be Carly Simon week in Aspen.

Tim pulled onto the flats just northeast of the Sundeck and shut down his machine. There wasn't another person or an animal in sight, and the place looked like a golf course covered in high cotton.

"First tracks and a fine dog," Tim said. "You're a lucky man, Jake."

"It runs in streaks," I said.

The snow was at least chest deep, so I clicked into the 10 Ex's while still sitting on the buddy seat of the Polaris, I slipped my hands through the leather loops of the Scott poles, zipped my cuffs, adjusted my hat and flipped down my goggles. I did all this with the easy expertise of a retired ski instructor and was hoping that the rest of my muscle memory was still as memorable.

"Go for it!" Tim said.

"I haven't skied in a real long time."

"Like riding a bike."

"I better stretch."

"Good idea," he said, understanding immediately that I didn't want my old powder partner to see me ski for the first time in over twenty years.

He started up the Polaris and expertly looped it around in a tight circle.

"I'll get your car back to town," he said. "The keys in it?"

I nodded and then looked out across the Valley. I had forgotten how high nearly twelve thousand feet above sea level was, and the anticipation that was beating against my chest was now knocking on panic's door.

"I love you, man," Tim said. "And that's not the coke talking."

Tim slapped me a high-five and blasted off back toward his hideout. Winston looked up at me as if to ask if I was sure I knew what I was doing. I wasn't.

"Prepare to be amazed, Dogger," I said to the best friend a man can have.

I pushed off through the deep snow, poling myself up to speed and toward the pitch at the brink of Walsh's Gully. As the slope began to get steeper, I felt as if I was standing in the middle of a teeter-totter and trying to balance on it in an empty schoolyard on a snow day. The fat, parabolic skis were much more sensitive than I remembered my old-style boards to be, and every upper body motion I made was transmitted immediately to the skis. If I jerked for balance to the right, my skis turned left; if I jerked to the left they floated right. I was going faster than I wanted to go and wasn't sure if I liked it. Winston was right next to me, easily bounding through the snow. I thought I heard him laughing, but malamutes don't even bark so it had to have been me.

I made my first real ski turn in more than twenty years, and it wasn't bad. I easily linked into the next one, and the snow waved up over my face, filling my mouth and causing me to choke. I had forgotten that when skiing powder, skiers should only breathe between turns when the skis surface, not while still inside the pure white cocoon—but the face-shot felt magnificent. Skiing bottomless powder is the closest a human being can get to unencumbered flight, and I suddenly remembered that it was my favorite feeling in the world.

I began to make wider and faster turns, extending up and down as the Atomic 10 Ex's wrapped back and forth underneath me as though I were spreading frosting on a giant vanilla cake. The slope was getting considerably steeper, and I was going considerably faster. But the turns that made my rep as an Aspen Mountain powder pig were coming back to me like the lyrics to an old Beatles song, and I began to sing the title cut to their best album at the top of my lungs.

"It was twenty years ago today, Sergeant Pepper taught the band to play," I sang, with tears in my eyes.

As I cut deep S turns through a vertical glade of standing pines, I thought about why I had left Aspen. By comparison, Hollywood seemed like a lousy trade, and in the clear retrospect of the moment, a first-dollar back-end deal on a blockbuster or even an Academy Award seemed trite and unimportant. But regret is an emotion that is about as constructive as jealousy, and I concluded to keep my focus on the trees.

Unfortunately, I came to that conclusion a moment too late. My weight got a little too forward of center on the skis, and I submarined a tip, suddenly finding myself upside down in a tree well and fighting for breath as hundreds of pounds of snow piled in around me. It was pitch black, and I couldn't move. I frantically tried to maneuver my hands toward my mouth to push out an air pocket, but my entire body felt as if it were locked in a lead suit. It was a rookie's mistake and very possibly a fatal one. If I could have moved my feet, I would have kicked myself in the ass. But I couldn't even move my head. It was twisted around the base of a pine tree like a wheel boot on an illegally parked car. I could die here, I thought.

Tree wells result from the conical shape of pine trees. The diagonally vertical branches act as an umbrella that keeps the snow from filling in around the base of the tree. It is Mother Nature's way of protecting the roots from getting too much moisture when the snow melts. The hole I was in was about six feet deep, and given how much blood was pouring into my head I figured I was completely inverted. Every time I moved a muscle, loose snow would ramp down my back and continue to fill the well, reminding me that more powder skiers drown in tree wells than die in avalanches.

I stuck my tongue out as far as it would go, and I could feel a frozen pocket already forming an icy death mask around my face. It wasn't nice to fool with Mother Nature, I thought, for some reason remembering an old television commercial about margarine. Most people buried in snow don't suffocate. They die from carbon dioxide poisoning as they re-breathe their own air trapped in the ice pocket created by the moisture they exhale. My breath was heavy and wet—I was like a human humidifier in a meat locker.

I tried to stretch my legs out, but the effort exhausted me. I attempted to roll over but couldn't budge. Then a strange calm settled over me, and I was oddly content. I wondered if Annie Davenport would come to my funeral. The thought made me smile. I wondered if I would even have a funeral or if my body would ever be found. I stopped smiling. If my body were found, it wouldn't be until next summer after the spring runoff, and by then the mountain would be as empty as it is now. More likely, wild animals would eat my carcass. As that grim thought took shape, I was stricken with an attack of panic the level of which I had never experienced before—not from bad acid or the DTs or a network pitch meeting. I started to jerk and push with every ounce of strength I had left but could move nothing.

I was done for.

I began to imagine myself inside a huge silver toilet, circling toward the flush hole. Death wasn't as romantic as I had hoped, I thought. But it really wasn't very frightening either. It seemed a little silly, actually.

I felt someone tugging on the cuff of my right pant leg, and my brain recycled me out of the cosmic toilet and back to semiconsciousness. It had to be Tim Lackey, God bless him. But all I could do was go limp as my body was inched out of the snowpack; I couldn't even help save my own ass—Tim had to do it for me. It wasn't the first time.

Finally, my shoulders and head suction-cupped free of the tree well. The sunlight was blinding. I was gasping like a bellows.

"Thanks, Tim," I barely whispered. "Thank God, thank you."

All I could see was the yellow circle of the sun as I pushed myself up to a sitting position and tried to focus. I couldn't see Tim Lackey anywhere, but Winston was looking me in the face. He licked me on the lips, and I kissed him. It was my dog who had saved my life.

"I love you, man," I said, meaning every word of it.

Chapter Twenty-Seven

I had my skis angled through the loops of the Scott poles, and I was sitting against them as if sunning myself in a chaise longue. I tossed Winston the last of the dog biscuits and finished off the tofu bar. It tasted like a Milky Way made from topsoil.

"Coffee break's over folks, back on your knees," I said, mangling an old joke.

Winston jerked to his feet as I clicked into my Atomics and slipped on the Scott poles. My hat and gloves and goggles were at the bottom of the tree well, but I wasn't going to try to retrieve them; I knew that today I was the luckiest man since Ringo Starr, and only a fool on this hill would press that kind of providence.

I pushed off into the steeps and made a few quick turns to clear my head and get the rubber out of my legs. It felt like I was moving in slow motion, but I figured I was probably still a little in shock. Winston caught up to me while I navigated a narrow mountain artery clogged with white powder, fittingly called Elvis Presley Boulevard, finally taking the high traverse over to a secret chute

known as Bramble Bush. I pounded down the steep pine glade like
an old ski bum, then skidded to a stop and vomited into the fresh
snow.

My burial in a tree well was something I decided I'd never tell
anybody—which amazed me, given that I was a braggart and a
blowhard. It was how I'd stayed alive in Hollywood, a place where
blowhards and braggarts can still make a heck of living. But the
Monday night crowd at Morton's wouldn't believe me anyway,
and keeping a secret as impressive as this one might make me a
better man.

Zaugg Dump was steeper than I remembered, and the one-
hundred-yard climb up wasn't going to be an easy one. At the top
of the mine tailings, I could still make out the rock overhang where
the trapdoor-like opening to the abandoned mineshaft began, or
at least used to be. The snow on the abrupt slope was waist deep,
at least, and I started to sidestep up toward the hanging rocks.
My rate of climb was about ten feet a minute and I had to stop
and gag for oxygen every five. It was a laborious ascent, and even
though I had lived healthier during the last few weeks than I ever
had, I was still a fat flatlander at heart—a heart that was pounding
like a bowling ball bouncing down a flight of stairs as I toiled toward the Zaugg.

The opening to the abandoned mineshaft was buried somewhere
six feet underneath an area the size of a two-horse corral, and it
was going to take one very lucky horse's ass to find it. I clicked out
of my Atomics and stepped off into the soft white, instantly sink-
ing up to my chest. I started to panic, understandably hypersensi-
tive to being buried in snow. I tried to swim myself to my skis so
I could climb back on board, but when I reached for them I
knocked one free from its snow purchase. The ski surfed to the
base of the dump as if it was a kayak navigating a steep river.

"Fuck," I shouted.

The vulgarity echoed back at me, but I didn't need to be reminded just how screwed I was. I made a dramatic breaststroke
for my remaining ski, but suddenly the bottom fell out of the snow

pack and I plummeted straight down like Alice through the rabbit hole. I had found the abandoned mine.

Winston looked over the opening's rim and stared down at me. I had fallen about ten feet, but fortunately I was able to cushion most of the impact with my knees, my neck and the small of my back. The rest of it I'd absorbed with my teeth. I had bitten off a chunk of my tongue.

"Wince-thon" I said, as if he was Lassie and I was Laura Keller-Mellon at a *birffh*-day ball, "Goh geeth hellphh!"

But Winston may have had it with me, and he sauntered off. Who could blame him? I had been left for less. I took out my flashlight, flicking on a weak beam of light. I had been in this abandoned shaft many times before, and it didn't look as though it had changed much in the last twenty years. I could see the old cast iron silver gurneys and rusted mining gear that Tim Lackey and I used to pilfer for souvenirs. There was still the old wooden table where we used to chop up our coke, and I smiled at the decrepit nineteenth-century tool chest we had used to store our valuable weed. It was padlocked with a fancy new lock. I kicked at the lock, easily busting it out of the rusted lock loops, and swung open the door. A large twenty-first-century Igloo cooler had been fitted wall-to-wall into the chest. I opened the cooler.

Countless sandwich-sized Ziploc plastic bags were filled with little green pills emblazoned with tiny aspen leaves. I guessed that what I was looking at was at least a million hits of sexstasy, a mother lode of grin-making pelvis motivators. I closed the cooler and shut the tool chest's wooden door. It was suddenly very difficult to breathe, and I could smell a rancid mixture of mildew and sweat. I felt nauseous and fought back a dry heave. I swung the flashlight around the mineshaft and could see two brand new Black & Decker utility tables and large commercial-sized cartons of Ziploc bags. There were three pharmaceutical scales and a Vegas-style money counter.

Richard Dupre was sitting quietly in an old wooden rocking chair, and I sucked in what little breath I had left. He was wearing white sweatpants, Reebok runners, a vintage Aspen State Teachers College sweatshirt, and a beret. His eyes were wide open and there was a slight smile on his lips. There was also a silver dollar-sized hole in the center of his forehead. Sprayed on the rock wall behind him was a Rorschach of blood, hair, and gray bone in the shape of a reclining cow. Or at least that's what it looked like to me. I backed away, praying that the vintage State Teachers sweatshirt wasn't mine, and stepped into the bright shaft of sunlight beaming down through the mine's opening.

"Beam me up, Scotty," I whispered, to no one.

I could see that a rope ladder had been rolled up and attached at the underside of the shaft's trapdoor. If I'd had a long stick or a rake, I could have unhooked it. But like an idiot, I had forgotten to bring a rake. Then my blood chilled as I heard the sound of someone moving toward me from deeper inside the mine. The footsteps were light and quick. I looked up at the shaft's opening and tried to make like Michael Jordan, but I missed by two feet. The steps were getting louder and coming toward me at a much quicker pace. I fumbled the Peacemaker out of my fanny pack and extended it in front of me with both hands, the barrel sweeping like a metronome. I took a breath, determined to shoot whatever was coming toward me through the mine tunnel. The footsteps were very close now. I laid both index fingers on the Peacemaker's hair trigger. I was ready.

It was Winston.

Chapter Twenty-Eight

Malamutes can sniff out mice in a snowfield the size of Manhattan, so rooting out my sweating sponge of humanity probably wasn't a very big deal for Winston. Who knows how many abandoned mine accesses there are under Aspen Mountain, but Winston must have found a connecting one and tracked me down through the maze of tunnels. Then he led me out through a narrow gap in the rocks not a hundred feet from where I'd fallen into the shaft. I got to my other ski and made it down the mountain without killing myself, my perfect powder day somewhat less than perfect.

The Corvette was parked in the City Market parking lot, and Ernie Grubbs had his Saab angled behind it to prevent any chance of escape. He was writing me a ticket.

"You can only park here if you're shopping at the market," he said.

The parking lot was completely empty except for my car; it wasn't like I was taking up anyone else's space.

"I know better. Sorry," I said, for once not wanting to bait him and trying to hide my newly acquired lisp.

"What happened to your face?"

I bent down to the side view mirror of his Saab and could see that my face was brush-burned and scabbed. My ride into the pine tree had left me looking as though I had shaved with a sharp stone, Indian style.

"Oh, that," I said. "I'm having laser treatments to get rid of all those broken blood vessels I got from drinking."

"You look like shit."

"But it's worth it."

Once I actually had gotten laser treatments from a famous Beverly Hills dermatologist who had been made rich from injecting Botox and bleaching buttholes, and the broken blood vessels caused by my heavy drinking were exactly why I did it.

"You're still not drinking?"

"So far."

"I'm happy for you," Ernie said.

"Thanks," I said.

I put my Atomics into the Corvette, and Winston jumped through the T-top.

"You look pretty shaken up," Ernie said.

I looked around the parking lot.

"I need to talk to you," I said.

"Talk."

"Seriously."

"Okay."

"But no one else can know about what I tell you."

"Any friend of Bill W. is a friend of mine," Ernie said.

"He's only an acquaintance," I said.

But I did need some help.

"Are you in the program?" I asked Ernie, hoping to God he wasn't.

He shook his head.

"But my dad was," Ernie said, maybe explaining some of his ass-busting attitude toward me.

A few minutes later we were sitting at the counter in Marshman's Munchies, a spectacular sandwich joint popular with the board bums and the construction guys. There were four stools anchored by pipe to decoratively painted steel wheel rims. We sat on two of them; the remaining two were empty. I was having a small bowl of free soup, the Marshman's idea of loss-leader marketing. Ernie chomped on a Philly cheese steak, the lucky glutton. I told him how I'd found Richard Dupre dead as a boot and about the cooler full of ecstasy. But I left out the parts about the tree well and how I had almost shot my dog.

"Have you had much experience with murder, Mr. Wheeler?" he said, all business.

"Weekly," I said, literarily, not literally. "But my victims always came back to life in syndication. So I was only charged with humiliating actors."

I was trying to be funny, but it didn't look like funny was on the menu.

"Did you kill Richard Dupre?"

The way he asked the question, I could tell Ernie was pretty certain he already knew the answer. But I wanted to be respectful and answer the question directly.

"Are you out of your fucking head?"

He looked at me for what seemed like about a whole minute.

"So that's a no?"

"Duh," I said.

Ernie sucked up the rest of his Coke.

"Do you have a gun?"

Ernie knew I had a gun from when I was busted with the open bottle of Scotch in my car.

"Well, an old gun, yeah," I said. "I do."

"Do you have it on you?" he asked.

I nodded. Ernie's right hand slipped toward his holster.

"Give it to me," he said, quietly.

"Why?"

"I want to send it down to our department's forensic lab, check the ballistics. See if we can get a match."

It seemed to me that when Ernie tried to talk like a cop, it came off clumsy, as though he was pretending to say cop stuff for the first time—as though he was imitating a flathead rookie. I could feel sweat pooling in the small of my back. I reached into my fanny pack and grabbed the Peacemaker. I held it by the barrel and handed it to Ernie, butt-first. If he didn't know what he was doing, he could have put a .45-caliber slug into my chest. But it looked like he knew.

"It hasn't been fired since the Civil War," I said, lying.

Ernie didn't need to know that I almost blew a hole through my knee and that the Colt nearly winged a state trooper on a bad bounce. He slipped my gun into his vest.

"Were you going to tell the chief this?" Ernie asked.

It was a good question.

"I haven't decided," I said.

"He's your buddy, isn't he?"

"Sorta," I said. "But I think the chief is under a lot of stress."

"From what?"

Better question.

"His kid left for college," I said. "That empty nest syndrome thing."

"You think Rick's a fairy?"

"I haven't thought about it," I said, lying again.

"Dresses like one," Ernie said.

"Clothes don't make the man."

Ernie broke off a piece of crust and popped it into his mouth, following it with a handful of potato chips. He took another bite of the Philly Cheese and then crunched off the end of a dill pickle. While I was waiting for him to swallow, I remembered a kid at camp who choked to death after inserting the top half of a jar of peanut butter into his mouth. Ernie finally swallowed and reached for the stick of complimentary celery I was saving for desert.

"You lost weight," he said.

"Working on it."

"Getting old sucks, doesn't it?"

"Depends."

"If you got to use them," Ernie said, humoring himself with the oldest joke at the rest home.

He chewed on the celery.

"I break with procedure and the chief could ream my ass."

"Once a philosopher," I said, "twice a pervert."

Ernie sort of smiled, but I couldn't imagine that he understood what I meant.

"I'm not going tell the chief about this. Not yet, anyway," Ernie said. "I'm going to have to trust you."

"I'm honored."

"Don't be."

Ernie got up to leave.

"Hey, Ernie," I said. "The Aspen PD doesn't have a forensic lab."

"*Duh,*" he said, and stuck me with the check.

Chapter Twenty-Nine

It had been two days since I had survived my dip in the tree well and happened upon the most recent member of the Hole in the Head Gang. My face was healing up, but the scabs still made me look like I'd lost a sandblasting contest. Winston and I had just returned from a run. Most of the snow in town had melted, and I was impressed that I'd covered the three-mile loop without stopping, peeing, or puking. According to my new plastic watch, I was clocking eight-minute miles at eight thousand feet above sea level.

I stripped down to take a shower and noticed that today's edition of the *Aspen Daily News* had been once again delivered to the back of my toilet. I was either getting braver or dumber, because I just sat down on the can and read the headlines without spiking my blood pressure. In death, Richard Dupre was now newsworthy of an above-the-fold mention. There was a photograph of him teaching his French class. Tinker Mellon was still in the front row and swooning over the late teacher, but in this picture Dupre was gesturing with his hands as if he was trying to levitate his class to a higher standard of education—or maybe curl an invisible elephant.

I generally don't like to think ill of the dead, but I still couldn't stand the guy. He was a pompous ass—a dead pompous ass, maybe, but I wasn't going to give him any bonus points for getting whacked. Though Dupre's obit certainly did. His mother must have written the piece, and I just about got diabetes reading it. After restating a dozen times that the whole town continued to be in mourning, the obit mentioned how stunned and saddened everyone was that such a fine teacher would have taken his own life.

Chief Rankin was quoted as saying, "A tragedy of epic proportions has befallen the City of Aspen." My not winning an Emmy was an epic tragedy. Dupre was a chicken hawk who got off on sticking high school students. The suicide thing was also a giant crock. There was no way that this guy croaked himself. It's pretty hard to shoot a hole in your forehead and then get rid of the gun. It was something I had thought about, so I knew. The piece also spun that Dupre's body had been found in the rear seat of his Renault up in the ghost town of Ashcroft. It went on to say that the ghost town was a "special place . . . a *warren* where Richard enjoyed meditating on life and contemplating the future." The article didn't mention anything about consummating predatory relationships with young girls.

But I had underestimated Ernie Grubbs. Apparently he'd been able to retrieve Dupre's body, get it out of a mineshaft, down the mountain through six feet of snow, into the back of the Renault and up to a ghost town ten miles from Aspen to make an obvious murder look like a suicide. I started to think that maybe he'd had some help.

The memorial service was to be held at the Prince of Peace Chapel at the edge of town. I had about an hour. I slipped on a fresh pair of Loose Fit Gap jeans that were surprisingly loose, a denim work shirt, my brand new Lowa hiking boots and a hounds-tooth blazer. I'd purchased the blazer years ago when I was still under the misconception that television writers could pass them-selves off as intellectuals. I put a quart of dry dog meal into an empty half-gallon milk carton I had torn in half for a dog bowl. I lifted up the toilet seat so Winston would have something to drink, turned on CNBC so he would have something to watch, grabbed a banana, and walked out the door.

Winter was coming; there was no doubt about it, as I almost broke my neck on a patch of ice at the bottom of the stairs from my apartment. The new Lowa hikers were touted to be state-of-the-art trekkers, but the titanium-reinforced hard rubber soles gripped the ice about as well as a hockey puck. I probably should have gotten the solid chrome clamp-on crampon ice climbing op-tion when I bought them. The boots' inflexible soles might be ef-fective for scurrying over scree fields and climbing up narrow rock chimneys, but I looked like Herman Munster with every step I took.

On the chapel's lawn a lectern had been set up in a position that made it nearly impossible to look at the speaker without gaz-ing skyward to Maroon Peak, the lead ringer of the Bells. But when I arrived, Chief Rankin was just wrapping up his tribute, so it was pretty easy for me to concentrate. I didn't know they were such good friends. Big Ricky was retelling some quaint tale about the time when he and the French pedophile had been lost on a mountain trek and Richard had led him out of the wilderness. It was supposed to be a metaphor, I guess. Then he said something about meeting his good pal *Froggy* farther on down the cosmic highway, bowed his head, and waited for some applause. The clapping was mercifully short and sweet, and the police chief re-luctantly left the limelight.

The next speaker took the lectern, and I settled into the back of the crowd. There were maybe three hundred people there, most of them students. I also saw a number of trustafarians from my old days in Aspen. But their faces weren't older and fatter like mine. They were chemically peeled and excessively tailored: the tribe of the chronically astonished. I flipped up my houndstooth collar and self-consciously tried to hide my brush burns and the Gucci bags under my eyes. The speaker was a girl, maybe eighteen years old, with blonde dreadlocks and silver bangles at the ends of the braids. She was wearing knee-high red leather boots and a tight black wool dress that scarcely reached the top of her deliciously butterscotch thighs. Her ample cleavage was apparent and barely respectful, and she wore a white rose above each ear. She was trying to weep and doing a lousy job of it.

"Mr. Dupre was my best friend," she said, sounding like she was auditioning for dinner theater. "And I let him down."

The girl went on to say something in French that I couldn't understand, and her first-rate accent didn't hide the second-rate performance. I was pretty good with actors and thought that this young lady needed to take a cold reading class. Then my legs jellied when I realized that the speaker was Tinker Mellon. But before I could freak out completely, Laura Keller-Mellon leaned in next to me.

"Looks like you're out of a job," she said.

She pronounced job "jobe" but I didn't think she was trying to be biblical. I could smell vodka on her breath, and she left a hand on my shoulder to keep steady.

"Looks like it," I said. "When did Tinker come home?"

"This is the first time I'm seeing her," Laura said. "The little bitch must be out of money."

I was hoping that Laura wasn't going to ask me for a refund, because I was also out of money, having blown her cash advances on skis and hiking boots.

"Let me know if you need someone to paint your house," I said.

"What house?" Laura laughed, and then faltered off as if she was trying to qualify for the finals at a Twister competition.

I walked back to the Corvette, which was parked within an armada of SUVs and pricey mountain bikes. Rick Rankin was sitting on the hood. I still had the banana in my pocket, but I wasn't happy to see him.

"What a bitch," he said.

"Laura?"

I was thinking Tinker but didn't want to bring it up.

"Life," he said. "Got a smoke?"

"I quit."

Rick drummed on the fiberglass hood and looked a little spooked.

"Froggy wasn't that bad a guy, you know," he said. "He shouldn't have killed himself."

"I didn't know him," I said solemnly.

Rick looked at me hard and tried to hold my gaze, but I turned my head.

"Then what are you doing here?"

"I read about it," I said. "And all the bars are closed in honor of the occasion."

I could see he was trying to get a better look at the scabs on my face.

"What happened, are you drinking again?"

"Just a little," I said, planting a seed I might need to water later.

"Well, try'n stay on your feet next time."

Rick got off the hood and stood a little too close, making the point even clearer that he was at least half a foot taller than I was.

"I'm taking the car back," he said. "My kid wants to cruise for pussy at college."

"My favorite major," I said.

Big Rick and I watched Tinker walk through the parking lot and climb into a brand new yellow Jeep. It looked like her tears had already dried.

"What was the point of all this?" I said. "This Tinker missing gig."

"Her stepmom thought she was," Rick shrugged. "Guess she wasn't."

"That's it?"

"Hey, you made a couple of bucks," he said, shrugging for the second time.

I handed Chief Rankin the Corvette's keys, and he drove it off, leaving me stranded in the church parking lot.

Chapter Thirty

I took the residential walking tour back to my apartment, passing the Jerome family mansion that had been turned into the Aspen Historical Society museum. I smiled at the irony that the mansion probably couldn't be built today due to the protests of the Aspen Historical Society. But it was a half smile. I felt awful. There was an ugly thought rebounding against the inside of my forehead like a ping-pong ball. But at least my forehead didn't have a ping-pong ball–sized entry wound in the middle of it. I was pretty stick-to-my-stomach, sure that if I had not confronted Richard Dupre in the school parking lot, he would probably be alive today. Some of his blood had splattered onto my hands. It was that simple.

I can generally make myself culpable for just about any terrible deed that may have taken place within my immediate reach and even beyond. I am the kind of guy who can hold himself personally responsible for the Vietnam War or the death of a waitress I banged once but who died two years later on her honeymoon. But I didn't have to reach too far to take at least some responsibility for Dupre's death. He was dead. If I hadn't moved back to Aspen, my guess is he probably wouldn't be.

When I got to my street corner, I could see that the door to my apartment was open. I called out for Winston, but he didn't come out, and my pulse began to pound.

"Winston?" I said again, and started to jog.

I could hear CNBC still broadcasting from my television.

"Winston? Hey, boy, I'm home."

I looked up and down the street. No dog. Then I heard a weak moan—the kind a coyote might make when caught in a clamp trap and about to chew off its own leg. I bounded up the stairs. I didn't have my Peacemaker handy, thanks to the officious Officer Ernie, but I bolted through the door, unarmed and unafraid. Winston was prostrate on the bed. His legs were bent at odd angles, and I could see a bit of foam drooling from his muzzle. His eyes were half closed, and there was a peculiar look on his face.

There was also a beautiful young woman lounging next to him and stroking his belly. Winston was in heaven, and he continued to moan probably just to rub it in. The woman had an auburn page-boy do and tasteful pearl dot earrings. She wore a pink North Face windbreaker, khaki Patagonia hiking shorts, wool knee socks and Salomon *après ski* clogs. The woman was maybe twenty, if barely.

"I missed my dog," she said.

And I not so instantly realized it was Laser. But this was not the Laser I knew. There was no nut and bolt through her lip, no shower curtain ring gracing her brow, no ten-penny nails penetrating her ears—though I could still see the rim of her chainlink tattoo peeking above the brim of a white turtleneck.

"Laser?" I said.

"It's Lynda now," she said, like a flight attendant.

"Christ, you scared the shit out of me," I said. "I thought Winston was hurt."

"If this is hurt, I wish someone would hurt me."

Lynda smiled a smile that I thought was a little too seductive and laid back on the pillow. I tried to look out the window but couldn't make my neck turn. Lynda grimaced at my face.

"What'd you do, make out with a belt sander?"

"A pine tree," I said. "I hiked up and skied the glades."

I took off my houndstooth jacket and hooked it on the back of the door.

"Aren't you supposed to be up in Seattle cutting an album?"

"I quit the music business," she said.

"Already?"

"It's full of assholes," she said. "Why bother."

"How far did you get?"

"Vail. I met this pathetic old guy driving one of those please-look-at-me Beemers who said he'd give me a ride back here if I gave him a hand job."

"Jesus, Laser."

"Don't have a fit. I hitched," she said.

"Good choice."

"I got nothing against hand jobs but the guy looked like a perv."

"And he was in a Beemer," I said, remembering I had leased at least two of them.

"Can I stay here for a while?"

"Why not stay with your parents?"

"My dad's on the ski patrol up in Jackson Hole, and my mom runs a ceramic workshop in Carmel," she said.

"Since when?"

"Since I was fourteen," she said. "I'm an emancipated minor."

I knew some minors in show business who had emancipated themselves so they could keep their parents from emancipating off with their dough. But I had a feeling this was different.

"As soon as I got tits, my mom put me on the pill and adiosed."

Lynda sat up on the bed, guru style, and I went to the fridge to get something to drink. But a recently purchased quart of orange juice had been recently emptied. I shot Laser a look and then threw out the carton.

"Was that yours?"

"No. It came with the apartment," I said.

I filled a coffee cup from the tap and chugged it.

"Can I stay here?"

"No."

"I'm almost eighteen, so it's not really a felony," she said, doing a pretty felonious Lolita. "And anyway, the other pedophile in town suicided himself."

"The *other* pedophile?"

"If you're going to be so fucking touchy, I won't live here."

"You're not living here, Laser."

"Lynda," she said, a little miffed. "Why the fuck not?"

"Because you're only seventeen."

"Until next January. And I'm emancipated, like I told you."

"So was John Brown, and his body lies a-moldering in the grave," I said, punting one way over her head.

She grabbed Winston with a headlock and blew into his ear. He seemed to like it.

"Look, it'll be so *sick*. I was conceived here, *c'mon*," she said.

I was hoping that she meant "sick" like in "cool" and not sick like I used it, as in uncool and perverted.

"How old are you?" Lynda asked.

"Older than you."

"How much older?"

"What difference does it make? *Older.*"

"It could make a shitload of difference," she said. "How fucking much older are you?"

Lynda talked like a trucker who hauled manure. But she was pretty as hell.

"I'm fifty-three," I said evenly.

"The Muslims say the perfect age for a man's wife is half his age plus seven years."

I am not a big fan of Islam, but there are no atheists in foxholes, so I quickly did the arithmetic. I came up fifteen years too short. I did it again, this time using the new math I was taught in junior high but was still light by nine years. Lynda apparently came to an equivalent number by using her fingers.

"Holy shit," she said. "I would have to be like almost thirty."

"Thirty-three and a half," I said, a little more disappointed than I wanted to be.

Lynda got up from the bed, stripping off her windbreaker as she walked into the bathroom.

"Think about it," she said.

"A couple of days, maybe," I said. "But that's it."

"Thanks."

She turned the shower on, pulled the turtleneck over her head, dropped her shorts and kicked out of her clogs. Lynda wasn't wearing underwear. She closed the toilet, sat down on the lid, and began to unroll her knee socks. I moved to close the bathroom door and could see a rendition of the Morton's Salt girl with the raincoat and the umbrella perfectly tattooed on Lynda's back. I was suddenly quite sad.

"You don't have to close that, you know," Lynda said.

Her eyes had the look of an abandoned puppy.

"I know," I said, closing the door.

Chapter Thirty-One

Winston and Lynda slept together on the Murphy bed, and they both snored, something I rediscovered every time my sleep apnea choked me back to consciousness as if I was trying to snorkel a golf ball through a garden hose from the bottom of an ocean. The two of them looked as if they had been dropped onto the bed from a great height, landing all akimbo. Nobody sleeps better than teenagers do, and I had to resist an urge to bend down and kiss them on their foreheads. But it really wasn't that hard to resist, because my back was killing me. I had bunked out on the floor, using a bedroll of dirty clothes with my knapsack for a pillow. I could only stretch out if I angled my legs into the bathroom and jackknifed at the waist. I dreamed I was a sand wedge.

I didn't bother to shower and grabbed a quick bowl of Mueslix, then slipped into my Patagonia powder suit and pulled on my Lowa neck breakers. They were the only hiking boots I had, so I had no choice but to try to break them in. Winston woke up and stretched, but Lynda was sleeping like a woman with a clear conscience. I was glad she had decided to pass on the Beemer-man's offer. My generation had left hers in the sexual wasteland without a compass, and I hoped she would find her way out—but not by following our lead. I patted Lynda on the cheek and was glad when she didn't wake up, because I was staring at her a little too hard and long. Lynda was a beautiful young woman, and at that moment I longed for Annie Davenport like a sailor lost at sea. But this wasn't my port no matter how fierce a storm I might be in. Winston licked my hand. He was good to go and we did.

It was just before first light, and what was left of the night sky was so clear and close it looked like you could hit your head on the moon. We had hiked about two miles up the Smuggler Mine trail, planning to loop through Four Corners and back into town. Smuggler was one of the more popular hikes in Aspen, but it was off season, and Winston and I hadn't seen a soul—though we had heard one, and it was probably a living person. Winston was staying tight to me, ears laid back, stopping every hundred yards or so to sniff the air. Every once in a while we heard the distinct tumble of a trail rock or the crack of a branch. When we did, Winston froze and growled.

"Easy, boy," I said. "Just an elk."

But I think Winston knew I was lying. My shins had been splinting from all the running miles I had been pounding out, so a long slow hike at dawn seemed like a good idea. When Byron walked out into a clearing in front of us, I immediately realized it hadn't been. He stopped and stared at us. He was about a hundred feet away but didn't say a word. He didn't have to. The three of us knew what the deal was. Byron had come to kill us. Or at least he had come to kill me. Winston growled, bending low on his haunches, tail down and ready to charge. I grabbed a handful of fur behind his collar.

"Don't hurt my dog," I said.

It was a plea, not a threat.

"Mutt, don't get in the way," Byron nodded.

He pulled a small pistol from the pocket of his silk workout pants and began to walk toward us. For some reason, I noted that he was also wearing a chartreuse cashmere sweater and a matching open-collar shirt of a slightly lighter shade. I let go of Winston, and he charged at Byron as I started to run away. The Lowa boots were clumsy and the rock trail was slick, so I couldn't really get up to speed. But the last thing a man like me wants to do is turn and fight. It was treason, I knew it, and a coward's bile boiled into my throat. I have never been big on heroism, except, of course, on paper. In the event of an emergency, I'm the one who should go get help. But inexplicably, a wave of fearlessness swept over me. I stopped my gutless retreat, turned, yelled my loudest rebel yell, and charged back to save the dog that had saved my life.

The first thing I discovered about heroism is that it's scary as hell, and the scene that was unfolding in front of me appeared as if I was looking at it through a pair of binoculars turned backwards—tiny and far away. Byron was ferociously wrestling Winston to get a grip on the dog's collar, to steady him and then shoot him. As I got closer, Byron turned the gun on me, and my legs suddenly felt like they were without bones. I buckled, covered my head, wet my pants, and waited to die. But when I heard the three quick caps from Byron's trim .22 and then Winston's painful howl, the Schwarzenegger in me returned and I got back to my feet.

I could see that Winston had taken at least one slug, and his right hindquarter was collapsing. But somehow he had managed to gain a bite on Byron's gun hand. The dog was fearless, grappling with the bigger man with what little strength he had left. There was blood spurting from a through-hole in Winston's ear, and I could see that one of his eyes was shut. Still the malamute wouldn't let go of Byron's gun hand no matter how many times the brutal track star kicked him in the ribs. I jumped onto Byron's back, but he shook me off as if I was an ugly scarf. Then he switched the .22 to his free hand and shot Winston one last time in the chest. My dog squealed and went limp.

"You son of a bitch!" I screamed.

I picked up a jagged stone and hurled it at Byron's head. But the pitch was high and outside. Byron smiled. Then he leveled the revolver at my heart. Winston whimpered, and Byron kicked him again.

"It's going to be fun killing you," he said.

I didn't doubt it.

Byron squeezed the trigger, and all I could do was I shut my eyes. I had already wet my pants. The gun clicked. I opened my eyes and the .22 clicked again. Byron was out of bullets.

I ran.

Byron threw the gun and it caught me square in the back of my head. I stumbled but stayed on my feet, scrambling over a scree field, the Lowa boots finally performing as intended. I figured I had to be putting good distance between Byron and me, but when I slowed to look at how far behind he was, he grabbed me by the ankles and wheelbarrowed me backwards across the rocks, tearing my Patagonia and a chunk of meat out of my chin. I rolled over on my back and looked up at him. He grabbed a basketball-sized boulder and hoisted it over his head.

"Goodbye, asshole."

Byron hefted the rock, and I prepared myself to be pummeled like an Iranian adulteress. But then Byron staggered just as the left side of his head caved in. I could hear what sounded like someone opening a six-pack of beer bottles with a church key. It was a sound I knew well, and with every pop and piffle, Byron jerked as if he was a marionette whose strings were being cut one by one. Maybe it was a twelve-pack. Byron did his best to stay on his feet, but it's hard to balance with a perforated head, and he finally fell on top of me in a bloody pile. The NBA boulder missed me by less than an inch. I pushed him off and nearly puked.

"That was close," Ernie said.

I peeked over Byron's bloody hulk and saw Ernie reloading a sleek 9mm pistol with a wire rifle stock and an attached silencer. It wasn't beer bottles; it was bullets. He reloaded a twelve-shot clip, flipped out a cell phone and punched the recall button.

"Cell phones don't work up here," I said, still a local know-it-all even when slipping into shock.

"Satellite," Ernie said, and then whispered at the phone. "Lariat, this is Sofa-One. Byron's sanctioned, bring the bag."

"He killed my dog," I said, as if it was one word.

But I don't think Ernie could hear me, because of the sound of an approaching helicopter. I tried to stand but I couldn't.

Chapter Thirty-Two

A black Special Ops helicopter that had flown off minutes before with Winston onboard circled again over an aspen grove and then spiked its second landing on a small clearing next to the scree field. The chopper's twin blades had only inches to spare, but whoever was at the stick knew what he was doing. The landings were impressive and quick. Two men in blue FBI jumpsuits bailed out of the big Chinook's cargo door, unrolled a body bag, and sprinted to Byron's corpse, which was still splayed across the rocks as if he was suntanning in hell. I hoped that he was. The men wore thin rubber gloves and surgical masks, and I wondered if maybe the track star had something contagious I should ask about. There was about a quart of his blood still drying on my face and chest. It had tasted like salty salad dressing, and I spit again.

The two agents dragged Byron's body bag toward the helicopter like it was a rug on its way to a flea market. I could see where Byron's head was in the bag, and it bounced across the serrated rocks with sickening thuds and squishes. The guy hadn't looked that good when they'd zipped him in there, but by the time they got him back to wherever he was going, he was going to be a human smoothie.

The agents strapped Byron to the chopper's landing skids, and a lady FBI agent motioned to me from inside the cargo door. She was maybe fifty but still looked as if she could clean and jerk a small car. I walked over to her.

"You okay?" she said.

"I'm not worried about me," I said, to my surprise.

I was really trying not to start bawling. Every time I pictured Winston, I had to bend down, like the weight of it was making me smaller. It was grief, I think.

"Your dog's gonna be okay."

At first I didn't understand what she'd said, even though her sentence was simple and well within my grasp of the language.

"What?"

I looked behind the woman and could see Winston bandaged and strapped to a small stretcher. His one good eye was open, and he was awake, though sedated.

"Winston, Jesus," I said. "He's not dead?"

"Must be part cat," the woman said. "I stitched up the hole in his ear and one in his front paw. But he's still got a slug in his ass and one in his ribs, so I'll let the vet go after those. I'm just a paramedic."

More like a saint, I thought. I grabbed her hand and kissed it.

"Go easy, cowboy, I'm married," she said.

"I'm too old for you anyway," I said.

"No shit."

We could have gone to the prom together, but I let it slide.

"I love you, Winston," I said, reaching to him and rubbing his head.

I didn't want to leave my dog, but I could hear the Chinook spooling up again.

"Hey, Winston, this is the guy who shot your paw," I said, like I was in a corny western. Then I kicked the body bag as hard as I could, a little mortified.

"You write TV shows, right?"

"Used to," I said, really mortified.

"I liked that one with the judge and that kid who stole cars," she said like a fan.

"Thanks."

I stepped back as the Special Ops helicopter rose into the sky, continuing to wave until it disappeared over a mountain ridge. Ernie walked up to me, clicking off his satellite phone and holstering it next to the high-tech 9mm. He had already broken down the stock, but I could see that the silencer was still clipped to the barrel.

"Looks like you could use some cleaning up," he said.

I noticed that Ernie had mysteriously lost his Texas twang and his IQ was climbing by the minute.

"I'd rather have an explanation," I said, but politely.

"That's fair," he said. "But let's get the heck out of here first."

Ernie signaled to a flat black Hummer that I had not seen but which must have been supplying cover just beyond the clearing. It had every off-road option imaginable and easily clambered over the scree field as if it was paved road. This was not a low-dollar operation.

"Where's your Saab?" I asked.

"I just use that for my day job," Ernie said. "Makes me look like a Democrat."

He smiled and slapped me on the back.

"This has been some morning, huh, Pops?"

"Indeed it has, *Son,*" I said.

We climbed into the Humvee, and it headed up toward Independence Pass.

Chapter Thirty-Three

The road to Independence Pass was prematurely closed because of all the early snow, but the Hummer didn't even pause. We were motoring over the Lost Man Trail like we were in a golf cart, and the agent behind the wheel was trying not to let Ernie know just how much fun he was having. He was at least ten years older than Ernie, but it was clear who pulled rank in this vehicle. The agent blasted the Humvee through a deep drift, and a wave of snow briefly covered the windshield.

"Keep a grip on her, Larry," Ernie said. "We have important cargo here."

"Yes, sir," the agent nodded.

Ernie and I were dropped off at a squatter's cabin left over from the silver bust. The cabin was hidden behind a thick row of trees and couldn't be seen from the road or the sky, but I had been here before. It was where I had proposed to Annie Davenport the night before I'd left for my double decade binge in LA. She'd said no and left the next day for Minneapolis. I hadn't seen or heard from her since. But I often wondered if she ever saw my name on television.

"Cool place, huh?" Ernie said.

But I just nodded, and tried to remember Annie's smell. The inside of the cabin had been turned into an FBI field headquarters. There were three computers, two printers, a fax machine, a water purifier and a microwave oven. Ernie handed me some disposable medical wipes, and I cleaned myself off as best I could, stripping off my Patagonia one-piece, down to my long johns. It felt good to get the blood off my hands. Ernie removed two Healthy Choice frozen dinners from the microwave and placed them neatly on a portable camping table. He unrolled some flatware from two cloth napkins and filled a couple of white wine glasses with chilled water.

"Nice place you have here."

"The western front," he said quietly.

I wondered what had happened to the bunk where I'd held Annie in my arms for the last time.

"Sit down, I'm starving," Ernie said.

I sat down but didn't feel like eating, so I just watched Ernie. I don't know where he had gotten his manners since we had last broken bread together. But he now ate with the protocol of a Miss Manners poster child, elegantly switching his knife to his fork hand and slowly swallowing small bites. It was very clear that the Ernie Grubbs I'd known was an act.

"Virginia," he said, apropos of nothing.

"Pardon me?" I said, Ernie's good manners apparently rubbing off.

"Quantico's in Virginia," he said. "You said FBI headquarters was in Maryland."

I remembered my meeting with Ernie on the Hyman Avenue Mall and was a little embarrassed.

"I get the facts mixed up," I said.

"I know," he said. "I've watched your TV stuff."

But he wasn't being mean about it and just smiled.

"We think Aspen is part of an international drug ring," Ernie said, swirling the water in his glass as if it were wine, "mostly for ecstasy, but some cocaine, and a little OxyContin. We don't know all the players yet. But we're getting together a list."

"What does that have to do with me?"

"Bad luck on your part," he said. "Most of my field agents were shipped overseas to search for the WMDs."

"And when they get back I got some swampland to sell them in Florida."

I sort of laughed, but Ernie sort of didn't.

"Saddam Hussein was a weapon of mass destruction himself," Ernie said, like he had changed his hick-from-the-sticks facade but not his political perspective.

"Some weapon. Guy was hiding in a hole with a bag of hot-dogs and a Mars Bar. And spare me the twirl about how the CIA spooks flushed him. Mr. WMD was ratted out to the Kurds by the father of a girl who was raped by one of Saddam's twin turds, Cutesy or Utesy. It was a blood feud. Our glorious fight for free-dom had nothing to do with it."

He waited to make sure I was finished. I was.

"We're not digging up tulip bulbs over there. We're digging up bodies."

"I'm sorry," I said, caught slightly off guard by his reasonable conservatism not to mention embarrassed by the size and speed of my gag-reflexing liberalism. "I might still be in some shock."

Ernie nodded and swallowed slowly.

"That'll pass," he said. "I'm going to need you."

"You are?" I said, swallowing slower.

"The way you went after Byron showed me you've got eggs."

"Robin's eggs," I said.

"Doesn't matter. Since Agent Dupre was murdered, I need an-other man inside."

"*Agent* Dupre?"

"His real name was Bill Carter. He had a wife and two kids."

The room started to spin a little, and I held on to the table.

"I have some photographs of him with Tinker Mellon," I said. "They're not nice."

"We know all about that," he said. "We put Bill in deep as a high school teacher because he had a degree in education and was fluent in French. We usually alert the local authorities that there is an agent in their jurisdiction, but the way money and drugs spiderweb through this community we decided not to. Part of Bill's job was playing the creep, and apparently he had to decide between Miss Mellon blowing him—or his cover."

"It's tough work but someone has to do it."

"An FBI agent is dead."

I was immediately sorry I'd said what I'd just said.

"Tinker doesn't want to be an Olympian?"

"Not in basketball," Ernie said. "When Rankin had Tinker's stepmom hire you to find her, it was a complication. But we thought we'd live with it and see how it turned out. The chief probably figured you were still a boozer and wouldn't locate the kid and it would keep Laura out of the way. But then it turns out she wasn't even missing."

"So Laura's not involved in this?"

"We don't think so."

"But that's how I got here?"

"Bingo, Charlie," he said, as if I had written the line. "Rankin figures in somewhere, but we think maybe he is just a peripheral. Big Ricky probably got sucked in because he's a guy who likes money more than the law."

"And drugs, I think," I said, like Judas.

"And maybe boys," Ernie said. "We put Carter in as Rankin's liaison to some mob muscle out of Phoenix who wanted to handle the ecstasy's distribution in the southwest."

"Actually, it's sextasy, sir," I said, suddenly an expert. "Finally supposed to be like that Spanish fly I kept hearing about when I was a horny kid in high school."

"An aphrodisiac property wouldn't change the name of the drug, Jake. Ecstasy is a drug *type*, not a specific, and the bureau doesn't use nicknames in order to avoid confusion."

"Of course."

I was a little embarrassed, but Ernie just smiled at me again.

"We're pretty sure Big Ricky is going to offer you Agent Carter's old spot on the team," he said. "It's why we need to keep you inside."

"How do you know I'm getting the offer?" I asked.

"Someone's been running your package at Quantico," he said. "We think it's been Rankin, making sure you're still approachable."

"I have a package at Quantico?"

"Everybody does," Ernie said. "That's how I knew about that pot bust with your buddy, Tim Lackey."

I took a bite of the Healthy Choice. It wasn't bad.

"As chief of police he still needs to keep a distance between himself and the Arizona dealers. We think Rankin wants you to be his new liaison. And we need you to do it."

"Can I just say no?"

"You can."

Ernie reached into his pocket, took out a small photograph and handed it to me. My heart stopped when I recognized the beautiful woman in the picture as Annie Davenport. She was holding the hand of a young boy. I felt even dizzier than before, but I couldn't stop staring at the photograph.

"She looks good, doesn't she?" Ernie said.

Annie's hair was still long and red, and she was on a vintage mountain bike. Mud was splattered all over her wonderful body, and I remembered just how hard-core Annie was. The little kid was also on a bike, and he had red hair like his mom.

"If you think Annie is involved in this, you're wrong," I said. "I won't help you if this is some kind of blackmail."

Then I looked at Ernie with as much tough guy as I had.

"And if you hurt her, I'll kill you," I said.

Ernie laughed.

"I will," I said.

"Man, you are a piece of work."

"I'm not kidding."

"Go easy, killer," he said. "I just thought you might want to see the picture."

I took some deep breaths.

"Who's the kid?"

"Me," Ernie said. "Annie Davenport is my mom. I'm Agent Davenport."

"Ernie Davenport?"

"Jensen Davenport. I came up with Ernie because I needed a redneck name."

"Davenport. As in *Sofa-One?*" I said, a little slow on the uptake.

"Bingo, Charlie," he said.

"Nice to meet you, Jensen."

Jensen was my middle name but for some reason it didn't register—maybe because I was about to slip into a coma.

"Likewise," he smiled.

"I didn't know Annie was married," I said, my heart breaking a little.

"A single mom," Ernie said, nodding to the photograph. "You can keep that."

I shook my head.

"Looking at it all the time would be too hard on me."

"Every dad should have a picture of his kid."

I pretended not to hear and focused on Annie's photograph. Jensen tapped me on the shoulder, but I still didn't look at him.

"You're my dad, Jake," he said.

I finally looked up at Jensen.

"Who is?"

"You are."

He had Annie's red hair and slate gray eyes.

"I am?"

"Afraid so," he said.

Chapter Thirty-Four

The flat black Hummer had dropped us off at the Saab, which was parked behind a snowbank at the end of the plowed portion of Highway 82. We were driving back toward town, and Jensen was dictating some notes into a tiny voice-activated digital recorder. I was still pretty much in a trance. But every once in a while I would steal a look at Jensen and compare his nose to mine. It looked like we had about the same profile, and sometimes the way he phrased a sentence sounded exactly like how I would have phrased it.

Jensen's sense of recall was outstanding, and he detailed every moment of what had happened from when he'd first arrived on the scene, as well as everything that was said inside the cabin, verbatim. What he hadn't observed personally, he speculated upon. His scenarios were concise and well thought out, and I was suddenly very proud of him. Maybe he had inherited my flair for storytelling but dodged my weakness for bullshit, a gene that has been contaminating the Wheeler bloodline for generations.

"Pretty amazing, huh?" Jensen said.

But I just sort of smiled.

"Did you ever even want kids?"

Jensen understood what a hard question that was, so I only nodded.

"They're great," Jensen said.

He flipped down the Saab's sun visor, although it wasn't sunny out.

"You have two grandsons."

He pointed to a picture of two identical baby boys in a photograph rubber banded to the visor. They were dressed up for Halloween. One was wearing a Hershey's Kiss costume, and the other one looked like he was supposed to be a bean pod.

"Jensen Junior and Jacob Junior," he said. "Jensen is two minutes older than Jacob, so he lucked out with your middle name. Like I did."

I tasted salt from the tears that were streaming down my face.

"How old are they?" I said in a voice that sounded like it was coming from outside the car.

"Three. That's an old picture."

"They look just like their grandmother," I said, lying.

My two grandsons looked exactly like I had when I was their age. But for Halloween, the only costume my folks could afford was an old white sheet with a black magic marker face, so I always looked like Casper on his way to a meeting of the Klan.

"Are you sure I'm your father, Jake?" I said.

The word "father" felt as if it weighed ten thousand pounds and I could hardly lift it out of my mouth.

"You're *Jake*," he said, "*I'm* Jensen."

"Sorry," I said.

"Don't be."

I shifted in my seat and moved to roll the window down for more air, but it was already wide open. I was sweating.

"It's just that I haven't seen your mom in a very long time . . ."

I was on some very new ground here and couldn't find the

words I needed to say what I thought I needed to say. Jensen looked at me.

"What, you think I'm after all your *money* and that I'm not really your kid?"

He smiled. It was my smile—or at least the one I used to have.

"How old are you?" I asked, grasping at the last straw.

"Do the math."

I computed forty weeks from the night of April 15, 1976.

"Your birthday around the end of December?" I asked.

"Twenty-seventh," he said.

"Twenty-six years old?"

"In December. Mom said I was conceived in that cabin."

It must have also been Celebrate Where You Were Conceived Week in Aspen. I didn't want to say the wrong thing so I started to count to ten. But I only made it to five.

"I think I really need to call your mom."

Suddenly I missed Annie Davenport as much as I had ever missed her. As if the gauze I had packed around my heart all those years ago had finally started to soak through.

"If Mom wanted to hear from you I think she would have let you know by now."

Jensen said it as nicely as he could but it still wasn't nice to hear. He turned off the heater and buzzed up my window.

"I just put in for this gig because I knew you guys used to live here. I wanted to find out about Aspen. I had no idea you had moved back to town."

"So this is all just a coincidence," I said.

It wasn't a question.

"Yup," he said.

We drove for a while in silence, and I kept looking over at Jensen, regarding his size and shape, the way he held his hands on the steering wheel and how he perfectly shifted the Saab. He seemed deliberate and focused—things he must have inherited from his mother's side of the family. I was thankful.

"Who is Byron?" I asked.

"I think that's a who *was* Byron," he said. "And we're not sure."

Jensen downshifted perfectly and turned the Saab into the City Market lot.

"At first we thought he was just some goon Rick put in place to keep Laura from screwing up the deal," he said. "But after Agent Carter was murdered and Byron tried to pop you, I think he is much farther up the food chain."

"*Was,*" I said.

Jensen smiled.

"Laura told me Byron was her drug dealer."

"But we don't think this is just about drugs," he said. "Too much money."

"There's big money in drugs," I said, with the wisdom of a father and former pot dealer.

"Been about five million dollars floating around Aspen," Jensen said. "Even figuring two bucks a hit wholesale for a million hits, that still leaves us way short."

Jensen's satellite phone buzzed. He answered it, listened for a few seconds and then hung up.

"Byron field-tested positive for HIV," he said.

"That's not good," I said.

"No, it isn't. How much of his blood did you come into contact with?"

I remembered I had tasted some of Byron's blood, and there was also the exposed gash on my chin. The realization freaked me out more than a little, but I wanted to look in control for my kid, so I just shrugged.

"Not much," I said, not true.

"I want you to get tested for the next month or so," he said. "If you have sex, wear a condom."

This was the kind of advice I should have been giving him ten years earlier.

"Thanks," I said. "But it probably won't come up."

"Bummer," he said.

We both laughed.

"I've been a pretty lousy dad, huh?"

"But you weren't a dad," he said, "because you didn't know. There's a difference."

Jensen reached for my hand. I let him hold it.

"Look, if you knew I was your kid and you split on me, I probably would have hated you. But Mom told me you asked her to marry you and she said no."

"But Annie didn't know she was pregnant."

"But she wanted to be," he said.

Chief Rankin exited the liquor store next door to the market and looked straight at us. I pulled my hand from Jensen's, but it was too late. Rankin had seen us. He wasn't happy about it— not because his officer was holding hands in public with another man but because he was carrying a gallon of tequila in a brown bag.

"You still harassing my buddy here, Ernie?" Rankin said, his eyes spinning like a juggler's plates on the Ed Sullivan show.

"The idiot lost his dog," Jensen said. "I'm just trying to help him find it."

Jensen again sounded just like a redneck cop with a room-temperature IQ, and I marveled at his undercover skills.

"The malamute?" Rick asked. "I didn't know Jake had a dog."

Then how did he know Winston was a malamute, I thought.

"Yeah, and you got to be some kind of a shithead not to know we got a leash law here in town."

Rankin shifted the brown bag to the hand behind his back.

"I hope you find him," Rick said.

The chief walked off. I looked at Jensen.

"That any way to talk about your father?" I said.

"Sorry, Dad," my son said.

I got out of the Saab and took a long walk through town before heading back toward the Snow Eagle. I thought about my new son, my wounded dog, and my old life.

Even Hollywood hadn't prepared me for this.

Chapter Thirty-Five

My apartment door was mysteriously open again, but thankfully this time all I could hear was Bob Marley wailing that he was "comin' in from da cold." It sounded like a good idea, so I did. There was a boom box set up on a small antique table, both of which I had never seen before. I had also never seen the large poster of a rock star of undetermined gender hanging over my bed. It may have been Marilyn Manson, but when it came to androgyny I was still a David Bowie fan, so I wasn't sure.

The television had been moved from the floor in the corner and placed on a cinder-brick-and-beaverboard bookshelf that was crammed with CDs and self-help books. A withered rattan loveseat short a cushion and a pink chair in the shape of a high-heeled shoe filled up what had formerly been the apartment's only open space. My once-humble studio digs now had the radical chic of a community college dorm room, with the architectural flow of a storage bin.

Lynda was on her hands and knees in the bathroom scrubbing

out the shower with a putty knife and a sponge. She was wearing my Aspen State sweatshirt and a pair of painter's pants rolled up to mid-calf. I was relieved to see my old sweatshirt.

"Take off your shoes," Lynda said. "I just vacuumed."

"What's a vacuum?" I said, untying my Lowa boots.

"How can you live like this?"

"You get used to it."

I was never a spick-and-span freak but after having daily maids in LA, I had slid into condemnable now that I was in charge of my own cleaning again.

"This scum is from the turn of the century."

"Turn of the century was only a few years ago," I said. "Is this all your stuff?"

Lynda backed out of the bathroom and climbed to her bare feet. I could now see that she had cut the midriff off my classic sweatshirt. The little vixen had also ripped the collar off into a deep V. It was a bit too clear that she wasn't wearing a bra, and a brass ring was piercing her navel. But Jimmy didn't reach for it. I was a father now, and even though he knew parenthood was something we had to keep secret, we could both use it for an excuse—should one fail to arise.

"Gracie's was throwing it out," she said. "Can you believe it?"

Gracie's was an Aspen thrift shop where ski bums would pawn whatever they hadn't broken or burned on their way out of town when the snow melted.

"I'm astonished," I said.

Lynda looked at me as I stripped off my bloodstained Patagonia.

"What the hell happened to you?" she said.

"Winston's okay. Don't go nuts."

"What *happened* to him?" she said, going nuts.

"He's fine," I said. "He's going to be fine, I mean."

"Oh, Jesus," she said. "If you let something happen to my dog . . ."

"He's going to be okay," I said. "He just got hit by a car."

"*Just* hit by a car?" she said. "Oh, my God, where is he?"

"At the vet's."

Lynda grabbed her coat and slipped into her clogs.

"I have to go see him."

"In Denver."

Lynda put her face in her hands. She was really upset.

"How the fuck did he get to Denver?"

"By helicopter."

"Helicopter?"

"He's a very important dog," I said. "I thought it'd be worth it."

"Tell me how it happened."

"I was walking him, and he took off after a deer and, then he was hit, I guess."

For some reason my bullshit gene was malfunctioning.

"Did you have him on a leash?"

"No."

"What kind of a person walks a dog without a leash?"

"A shithead, I've heard," I said. "But he's going to be okay, Lynda. I promise."

"I only gave him to you because I thought you would take care of him."

"I know."

I wasn't feeling good about it.

"But at least you got him the right kind of care," Lynda said, taking my hand.

And I immediately decided she could live with me as long as she felt like it.

"I wanted to do the right thing," I said. "Winston saved my life."

"He did? How?"

Whoops.

"I was dying of loneliness," I said.

The Murphy had a new bedspread that was fashioned out of an old parachute.

"The place looks great," I said. "Ever thought of going into interior design?"

"But you said I can't stay here," she said. "I just needed something to do while you were out trying to kill my dog."

"Okay, you can stay here," I said.

Lynda smiled at me.

"Really?"

Lynda put her arms around my neck and kissed me on the cheek. It was a tender kiss—the kind one might give their grandfather on his deathbed. But I *was* a grandfather now, and even though I wasn't dying, I had almost died today. The kiss felt very nice.

"Thank you," she said.

"What for?" I said. "I put our dog in the hospital."

"For not poking me last night."

It wasn't the most romantic thing I'd ever heard. But I understood her point.

"It would've been a mistake, and then I would've had to move out," Lynda said.

"Who knows, we may have liked it," I said.

"I doubt it. And anyway, I think I have chlamydia."

"It's very common," I said, like a veteran who'd been awarded a Purple Heart or two during the sexual revolution.

"But I'm still pretty, right?"

"Gorgeous," I said.

Chapter Thirty-Six

It had been nearly a month since I'd had the misfortune of becoming blood brothers with the late Byron. I took my first HIV test at the Aspen STD Clinic and failed it. But it was the kind of test I wanted to fail. The results were negative. The lady who took my blood was appropriately discreet and didn't make me feel more conspicuous than I already did as I thumbed through an issue of the *Advocate* and sat on a steel stool. I had asked her for a copy of *Sports Illustrated*, but she just gently patted my arm.

"It's okay," she said, and winked. "My son's in ladies' shoes."

"He must have small feet," I said, winking back.

I had gotten a job tending bar at the Rude Goose on off nights for eight dollars an hour plus tips and all the beer I could drink. I still wasn't drinking, so I sold my freebies to understanding locals and pocketed the cash. Lynda had begged back her old job at the animal shelter, and it seemed that about every other day we had another furry freeloader for a temporary houseguest. She had turned out to be a great roommate and an even better cook.

I generally never ate anything unless it came with a free toy, but the teenage temptress's no-meat-no-wheat-no-treat diet was actually quelling my Quarter Pounder with Cheese compulsions. As a result, I was getting into the best shape of my life. Every morning Lynda and I got up at first light and double-looped the three miles to Slaughterhouse Bridge and back.

I had faked strep throat and a scrip to an old familiar dupe at Carl's Pharmacy and brought Lynda home a bottle of Cipro to clear up her little social bug. The only way I could get her to take it was to tell her that Aspen was on the alert for an anthrax attack. I also embarrassed her by bringing her home a box of condoms. She told me that using a condom was like taking a shower with a raincoat on and gave them back to me.

Lynda kept asking me when Winston was coming home. I told her it would be a while because I had sent him away to dog discipline school, and then he still had to be castrated and de-clawed. She called me a *pet*-ophile and fascist and didn't speak to me for a week. Jensen took a chunk of his vacation time to go surfing down in Mexico, but he was probably refreshing his night-fighting skills at Quantico. Before my secret son left he had slipped me some new photographs of my grandkids to cheer me up. The twins were growing like weeds, reminding me that all the clichés are true.

I showed up for my late shift at the Goose around seven-thirty and was just tying on my apron when I noticed Laura Keller-Mellon at the bar. She was nursing what looked like a tall vodka rocks and cranberry juice—although for Laura, nursing a cocktail was not using a straw, so I had no idea what condition she was in. She blew me a kiss and wrinkled her nose, and I moved down to her end of the bar. I had seen her look better, but it was probably time for her plastic surgeon to pull up on the skin at the top of her head and snip off a few inches. It would yank the creases out of her face, but at the rate Laura was getting lifted, sooner or later she was going to end up with a goatee.

"I tried to buy this and put it in my game room," she said, stroking the hand-carved bar. "But the assholes wouldn't sell it to me."

"It's an Aspen point of interest," I said. "Some very famous cowboys got very famously shitfaced while leaning against it."

And I wondered what Doc Holliday might think about the Keller-Mellon gang chopping up coke on his bar.

"What can I get you?" I asked.

"Vodka cranberry," she said. "When did you start working here?"

"When I started to feel dizzy from a lack of protein," I said.

"Isn't it embarrassing? I mean, you were a *writer*."

"I was a word merchant at a garage sale," I said. "Let's not get carried away."

But I could see I was confusing Laura, so I just slid her over the vodka C-berry.

"Tinker home?"

"Who cares?" Laura said. "I moved into a condo."

"Really?" I said.

"I'm getting a divorce."

"I'm sorry," I said, and actually meant it. "But this town is hell on marriage."

"Tinker got what she wanted," she said, "but it doesn't matter. Her old man was the worse hump I ever had."

"Well, they say when a marriage is working, sex is ten percent," I declared, like Master Johnson, "and when it's not, it's ninety percent."

"Charles was a hundred percent lousy in the sack and an asshole a hundred and fifty percent of the time."

"He must work for Enron."

Laura crunched some ice and shrugged *whatever*.

"Could you talk to Javier for me?" Laura asked.

Javier was a Salvadorian dishwasher who made up for his minimum wage by dealing cocaine out the kitchen's back door.

"About what?"

Laura knew that I knew what she wanted me to talk to Javier about, but business was slow and I wanted to entertain myself for a while.

"Don't be an asshole," Laura said, un-entertained.

"What happened to Byron?" I asked.

"He's down under," Laura said.

It was an interesting choice of words.

"*Where?*" I said.

"Australia," she said. "I just got an e-mail from him."

"What's he doing there?"

"Raising daisies, apparently," she said. "I didn't even know he liked flowers."

I smiled. Maybe the FBI had a hell of a sense of humor after all.

"Let me see if I can do something for you," I said.

I headed back toward the kitchen. Scoring a little blow for Laura would be a fine way for me to establish myself with the drug-dealing evildoers of Aspen. I was getting the hang of this under-cover thing. Jensen would have been proud of me.

"*Hola, mi amigos,*" I said, entering the kitchen.

There were two Latino cooks and another Hispanic guy barely four feet tall working the dishwasher. The kitchen was hotter than a Mexican Julio but these guys didn't seem to notice. The cooks were wearing Dallas Stars jackets, and the miniature plate scraper was wearing a hooded Calgary Flames sweatshirt—Mexican hockey fans, apparently.

"Javier?"

The little man peeked out from his hood.

"*Si,*" he said with blank eyes.

"Anything happening?" I said.

"What do you mean, *amigo*?"

"What do *you* mean, what do *I* mean?" I said, like a guy trying to buy drugs. "Anything *hap-pen-ing*?"

"I don't know you, man," he said, but not nervously.

"I'm the bartender."

Javier asked one of the cooks in Spanish if I was indeed the bartender. The cook nodded.

"I got a customer who needs to be helped out."

Javier pushed past me, climbed a potato box, stuck his head out the kitchen's ready counter and looked toward the bar.

"I got *mucho* help enough for that *puta, señor.*"

Javier thrust his hips at the rim of a garbage can, and his buddies just about killed themselves cracking up.

"Smaller packages come good in things, no?"

I didn't know if he was trying to be funny or he just mangled the language because he had only been in the country for about ten minutes. But Javier finally fronted me the coke, and I returned to the Rude Goose's bartending sector.

I slipped the bindles underneath Laura's cocktail napkin. Laura reached into her purse and then tried to slide two one hundred dollar bills across the bar. I didn't let her.

"On the house," I said. "I owe you."

"For what?" she said.

"I got to meet interesting people and make new friends," I said.

Laura sucked down the rest of her drink as if she was siphoning gas.

"Be careful," she said, like she really meant it.

Laura slipped into a mink ski parka and left the bar. I wondered how long it would take for Chief Rankin to find out I was dealing drugs from behind the bar in the Rude Goose. Not long was my guess.

Chapter Thirty-Seven

"How's the modeling agency?" Herman said with a head as loose as a circus wheel. "You meeting any chicks?"

It was about closing time, and Herman was the only guy sitting at the bar.

"It was a bad idea," I said. "All the good-looking *chicks* are in New York."

"I hate New York," he said. "All the people care about there is how good the rye bread is."

I didn't want to get Herman started so I just nodded and kept washing glasses.

"That Tinker girl is back in town," he said. "You see her?"

I shook my head. "Have you?"

"Once," he said. "I wanted to buy some dope, but she said she didn't have any.

"Tinker sells dope?" I said.

"Supposed to," Herman said. "But now she's just stuck-up like every other chick in this town."

I think "chick" was the first English word Herman had ever learned, and he had never bothered to update his language file.

"The chicks in this town all suck," he said.

"That's why there's so little air."

"Give me two for the road," he said. "I'm out of here."

I poured Herman a shot of tequila and backed him up with an O'Doul's draft, but he pointed to his other empty shot glass on the bar.

"Both of them," he said.

"Are you driving?" I said.

"Pour," he said, more belligerently than usual.

I poured. I wasn't in the mood to get my ass kicked by a Swiss ski bum. I considered Herman a friend, but it was clear he had been drinking all day and only occasionally appeared to recognize who I was. Twice he had called me Bob.

"So, does Tinker sell that new X stuff," I said. "What is it, sextasy?"

Even though I hadn't received any specific undercover orders yet, I thought I would continue to chum the pond.

"Who are you, *a cop?*" he said, trying to keep his eyes from crossing.

"You know who I am, Hermy."

"Don't call me Hermy. I hate that."

"Sorry," I said. "I was just trying to connect."

But Herman just glared at me.

"I'm Jake."

Chief Rankin entered the bar. Herman turned to him, wavered and then focused.

"Thanks a lot, Bob," he said. "Why'd you call the cops?"

"Wasn't me," I said, trying to keep Herman from igniting.

"All I was having was just a couple of drinks."

Herman got up from his stool and squared off with Rankin.

"I never saw Bob before in my life," Herman said, pointing to me.

Herman careened out the door as Rick sat down at the bar.

"Remind me to kill that guy someday," he said.

"It'd be redundant."

"Are you closed?"

"Just about," I said, stacking some glasses.

"Anybody else here?"

"Just me. What's up?"

"Lock the door."

Rick looked as sober as I had seen him in a while. He was wearing a wool tweed skeet-shooting jacket with leather shoulder guards, a white oxford shirt, a red ascot, Basswood English Walkers and pleated gray slacks.

"How was the fox hunt?" I said.

"Just lock the door, smartass," he said, a little too seriously.

I locked the door and dimmed the outside lights.

"Want a drink?" I asked.

"No."

I sat down on the stool next to Rick. He lit a cigarette.

"When did you start smoking?"

He made the cigarette look like it tasted good but didn't answer me.

"How do you like working for a living?" he said.

"Not bad."

"It sucks."

Rick pulled a long a swig from Herman's O'Doul's, but I think he probably thought it was mine. "A guy could starve to death busting his ass in this town."

"But the weather's great," I said. "Very little humidity."

Rick glared at me. He wasn't in the mood for my witty repartee.

"I need a favor," he said.

"Okay."

"My kid's up for getting killed."

"That's a big favor," I said. "Let me check my calendar."

"Don't fuck with me, Mogul."

Rick sipped the faux beer.

"Last year I busted two meatheads from Arizona with about a million hits of ecstasy," he said, lying through his teeth. "Maybe you read about it?"

"I was still in LA," I said. "It didn't make the trades."

"Their lawyer got them a change of venue to Denver, and they walked. I think maybe they greased the judge. These guys are pretty big players—Vegas connections."

"What does that have to do with Little Ricky?"

"Nothing," he said. "But they told me they're going to kill my kid unless I give them the ecstasy back."

"Can you go to the FBI or somewhere?" I said, without a net. "The state police, maybe?"

"And look like I can't do my job here?" he said. "I'm the chief of police for fuck sake."

"It was just a thought."

"I need someone to get the X back to them."

"You still have it?"

I didn't want to remind Rick that the evidence would have followed the case in a change of venue. I had written a few episodes of *LA Law* and picked up a little legal knowledge before drinking my way off the show. What Rick was telling me lacked verisimilitude, as the network execs liked to say. But thanks to my kid, I knew where this plotline was going. Jensen was way ahead of Rankin. I hoped he stayed there.

"Yeah, in a cooler in the evidence room," he said.

The cooler had to be the same one from the Zaugg Dump shaft. So it must have been the late Byron who had removed Agent Carter's body from the mineshaft—not Jensen, who I had thought was Ernie at the time.

"I need someone to get it to Las Vegas," he said.

"How much?" I said.

"I told you," Rick said. "A million hits."

"How much do I *get*?" I said.

"This is just a favor, Jake," he said. "You owe me."

"Forget it," I said. "I was in the drug-dealing business, remember? It's an industry that isn't big on favors."

I thought I'd better hold back a little to protect my cover.

"I could still open your case," Rick said. "It never came to trial."

"Lackey's a buddy. He still won't testify."

"Maybe I could change his mind," Rick said. "Ask him what he's been living off of all these years."

"The guy lives like a sharecropper," I said. "Tim doesn't have any money."

He finished off Herman's beer.

"They're going to kill my kid, Jake," Rick said, like he was auditioning for a soap. "You're not a father. You don't know what that's like."

"Maybe not like you do," I said, riding no-handed, "but I still have to protect my back end."

I had Rankin by his back end. He didn't like it.

"How much do you want?" he said.

"At a few dollars a hit wholesale, that's at least two million dollars," I said. "So my delivery fee's got to be at least the standard ten percent."

"Two *hundred* thousand dollars?" he said.

"In *advance*."

Rankin looked at me for a long time, as if he was trying to make up his mind to either hire me or kill me—or eventually both.

"That's an awful lot of money," he said.

"I'm an experienced professional."

"Then you better start looking like one."

Chief Rankin walked out. I thought I got the job.

Chapter Thirty-Eight

I had slept like a rock and was showered and shaved before six, but Lynda was already at the hot plate, scrambling a half a dozen egg whites with basil, fresh tomatoes, and mushrooms. She was wearing a favorite T-shirt of mine that barely covered her ridiculously round ass. I had asked her to not wear the shirt. But like a good roommate, I didn't harp on it. I could smell what must have been some new kind of exotic coffee brewing. Lynda was always field-testing the latest in hip caffeine, and she ground the beans by hand in my old Gearing Grinder, the one I'd once used to grind coke so I could grind my teeth.

"What the hell is this?" I said, sipping my cup.

"Postum," she said. "I want to eliminate caffeine from our lives."

"I'm not ready to do that."

"It's a drug, Jake."

"But on the low end of the speed spectrum," I said. "And it's legal."

"So are cigarettes," she said, "and war."

I loved how Lynda looked at the world and wondered if I had ever seen things in such clear and simple terms. But lately I had begun to enjoy the fact that I was fifty-three. Lynda handed me a plate of the scrambled whites and fresh veggies.

"I didn't have any cheese, sorry," she said.

"I'm off dairy."

"Since when?"

"Since it's mostly fat."

"A little fat is good for you."

"How would you know?"

"Cause I know," she said. "I used to be bulimic."

"So was my wife," I said. "Binge, purge, nag." I took a bite of the scramble. It was delicious. "And did you know that if Karen Carpenter and Mama Cass had shared that sandwich they would both be alive today?"

"And if Ted Kennedy drove a Volkswagen, he'd be president," she said, surprising the hell out of me. "My dad used to tell me all those old jokes. They're not funny."

"You had to be there," I said.

I gobbled the rest of my breakfast and then watched Lynda eat for a while. She took very small bites and separated the mushrooms and the tomatoes from the egg whites, swallowing each ingredient individually. I wondered why she bothered to cook them all together, but she probably knew that was the way I liked it— my roomie was a hell of a kid.

"Are we going on a run?" I asked.

We always went on a run. I just wanted to say something to break the silence. It looked like there was something on Lynda's mind.

"Well, I'm going to go on a run," she said. "But I was wondering if you'd mind if I ran with somebody else."

"Depends where to," I said, a little hurt.

"I met someone."

"With a penis?"

"Duh," she said. "That was just a stage."

There was no reason in the world for me to be jealous. But I think I was.

"Congratulations."

"But he's older."

"How older?" I said, remembering the Muslim math.

"Twenty-four."

"Yikes," I said. "Don't run him into the ground. Can I meet him?"

Lynda nibbled a tiny flake of egg white and then nodded.

"But I want to sleep with him first," she said. "I don't know if it's going to last."

Lynda kissed me on the cheek and put away her plate.

"He's a Cancer."

"That doesn't even sound good," I said. "And what if it's hereditary in Canadian mice?"

"What?" she said.

"An old Johnny Carson joke."

"Who's Johnny Carson?"

"The only guy who ever got out of Hollywood alive," I said.

In about two minutes Lynda was in her running gear. She took a quick look at herself in the bathroom mirror and nodded her approval. I was happy that she liked what she saw.

"Don't pull any muscles," I said.

"Well, maybe just one," she smiled.

And ran out the door.

Chapter Thirty-Nine

I had cut my solo run in half, doing only a single loop of our usual Slaughterhouse dash. I felt sluggish, but maybe it was because I wasn't chasing Lynda, at least not consciously. When I got back to my apartment, there was a note fixed to the door:

FRYING PAN HEADWATERS.

That was it. Three words. No signature.

The headwaters of the Frying Pan River were six miles northwest and three miles below the summit of Independence Pass, at the base of Mount Massive, at the corner of Backwoods and Boondocks. It was a perfect locale for the next cycle of *Survivor* or to pop somebody and hide the body. But maybe Big Rick simply wanted to give me my delivery fee in advance and didn't want an audience. I called Jensen, but all I got was his office answering machine. I should have left a message, but I didn't want anybody to get hip to the fact that we were father and son instead of Cain and Abel. I decided to go into the wilderness alone.

It was late October but still pretty warm. I put on a pair of tan hiking shorts, a gray cotton turtleneck and a blue fleece pullover. I wished that Winston was coming with me and realized that I missed him almost as much as I used to miss Annie. But I didn't miss that both of them probably didn't miss me.

I grabbed two bottles of water, put them in my fanny pack, and headed out the door. My mouth was dryer than usual, and I wished I still had the Peacemaker. The old Colt would have helped quench my thirst.

Independence Pass had been reopened since our first big snow was defeated in overtime by an Indian summer, so I decided to grab one of Aspen's historic Mellow Yellow Cabs with the built-in bongs and the free bar, though I decided not to partake while riding toward the summit. I had the taxi drop me off at the Lost Man trailhead. Not the best trail name I've ever heard.

Most of the snow had melted, and the steep trail was slick and muddy. But my Lowas lumbered along reasonably well, and I calculated that I could make the Frying Pan headwaters in about an hour and a half. The hike was uneventful. I saw two mule deer, one elk, three otters, and an occasional pile of bear scat chock full of chokecherries. I made as much noise as I could make, singing all four sides of The Who's *Tommy* at the top of my lungs. I was in mountain lion country and hoped that the big cats weren't rock opera buffs. I can't remember a single thing I learned in high school, but I had total recall of every record album I'd listened to while stoned on pot in Joey Noonan's basement during the summer after twelfth grade.

When I finished with Peter Townshend's elegy to the "Pinball Wizard," I started howling on Cream's *Disraeli Gears*. But I didn't get past the first chorus of "White Room" before I heard the distinct sound of a wild animal busting through the underbrush. I froze. Maybe mountain lions were Eric Clapton fans. I couldn't tell which direction the sound was coming from, so I just rotated in slow, defensive circles and double-timed the pace of my hike.

The trail had gotten steeper and slicker, and I frightened myself with the thought that maybe the Lost Man wasn't lost. Maybe he had been eaten. I tumbled backwards into a clearing and sat down hard on my tailbone. It hurt like hell. I tried to get up, but something grabbed hold of my fleece sleeve and yanked. I screamed.

Winston was wearing a patch over his left eye and wagging his tail. He looked like the Hathaway shirt dog. But Winston was as glad to see me as I was to see him. I put him in a headlock and hugged.

"Winston! Jesus Christ," I said, "You want to give me a heart attack?"

Winston let go of my sleeve and licked my face. He looked good. The fur on his hindquarter that had been shaved for surgery was growing back in, and he didn't appear to be limping, though when I squeezed him too hard, he yelped. I looked farther into the clearing and could see a slow-moving spring creek, apparently the headwaters of the Frying Pan River. The Frying Pan flows into the Roaring Fork, a river that runs into the Colorado, which supplies drinking water to LA. I thought about sending my old agent a message, but I didn't have to take a leak.

A man was knee-deep in the creek. He was fly-fishing, gracefully laying out maybe fifty feet of light line with a long bamboo rod. At the end of the line was a tiny Royal Wulff, a hand-tied speck of elk fur and peacock herl that somehow rode on the end of the filament as if it was surfing a silent Doppler wave. The Royal Wulff touched down without a ripple at the top of a riffle and floated downstream below a large rock. The presentation was a perfect imitation of a caddis fly about to take flight for the first time, and within seconds a large cutthroat trout took the bait. The man moved slowly upstream and gently drew the trout toward shore, winding his reel as if it were a delicate pocket watch. He quickly released the trout from a minute barbless hook without touching the fish or taking it out of the water. The trophy swam off, unharmed.

The man, of course, was my son, Jensen, and I watched him repeat his elegant skills as he pulled a half dozen more cutthroats to shore, freeing each of them with the tenderness of a pediatrician. Jensen was aware that I was watching him, but neither of us felt the need to speak. Winston sat down next to me, and the three of us savored the moment. I could see an eagle circling high over Jensen, patiently waiting for one false move from my expert son so the bird of prey could gobble an easy lunch. There was no such chance; Jensen never even bobbled. I finally got up and walked toward him.

"You're a heck of a fisherman," I said.

"Thanks," he said. "I had to work at it."

Fishing, like baseball, was the kind of American pastime a boy learned from his father, and I suddenly felt the hollow knock of guilt in my gut. Jensen must have sensed it.

"My mom taught me," he said.

"She's a heck of a fisherman, too."

"I know," Jensen said. "You taught her."

"I just put her in the river," I said. "Annie always taught herself whatever she wanted to learn."

Jensen made another cast and hooked another fish.

"What do you say I build a fire and we have trout for lunch?" I said.

"I'm a catch-and-release man," Jensen said.

"Me, too, but I only apply that regulation to women."

Jensen looked away from me and shook his head, and I was immediately sorry I'd made the smart-ass quip. My son clearly wasn't impressed with my wordplay. I couldn't blame him. But I had only been a father for a little while and still had a lot to learn.

"Sorry," I said. "Sometimes I use humor like a helmet."

And Jensen let me off the hook with a grin.

"You want to try for a cutty?" he said.

"*Try?*" I said.

Jensen handed me the fly rod and sat down on a streamside rock. He sipped a can of Budweiser and watched me as I stripped out some line. I hadn't been in a river in years, but the rod felt right and natural in my hands. I waved the tall, thin bamboo and immediately caught a bush on my backcast. Jensen untangled the fly.

"Keep your wrist stiff," he said.

"I know how to do it," I said. "Give me a chance."

My next cast was dead solid perfect, and a mid-sized cutthroat hit the Wulff as if the fish hadn't eaten in a month. I mended my line, turned the trout upstream and eased it to shore. I released the fish and looked at Jensen.

"Your old man isn't a complete screw-up," I said.

Jensen sipped his Bud and then handed it toward me.

"I only bought one of these," he said. "There's a gulp left."

"You can buy beers *one at a time?*" I said, and laughed.

Jensen laughed with me, not at me, and I was proud that a son whose dad had a tiny substance abuse problem—with maybe a dash of denial—could maintain such restraint.

"How does it feel not drinking?" Jensen said.

"It feels good," I said.

And made another cast.

Chapter Forty

Jensen and I were sprawled out under a royal blue sky full of fat white clouds.

"What about that one," I said, pointing to a pure white pillow about the size of a baseball stadium.

"Another rocking horse," Jensen said.

"They can't all look like rocking horses, Jensen. Get creative."

Jensen squinted up at the clouds. My one-eyed dog was squinting at beavers by the stream.

"Okay," he said. "A rocking chair with a horse on it."

"You're no fun," I said. "It looks just like the state of California. Exactly. But with feet."

"I never had any reason to go to California."

"Ouch."

But Jensen threw a small stone at my head to show me how much he loved me.

"You didn't miss much," I said.

"But *you* did."

Ouch again.

Jensen sat up and handed me the last half of the turkey sandwiches he had made. He had a weakness for mayonnaise that I didn't share, but the sourdough was perfect, and the onions were fresh and firm and perfectly sliced.

"Great sandwiches," I said. "The bread's perfect."

"I baked it."

"No kidding?"

"I've spent a lot of time on stakeouts. Eating well passed the time."

I swallowed the last bite of the turkey sandwich and licked a drop of mayonnaise off my thumb.

"Rankin wants me to deliver a million hits of ecstasy to Las Vegas," I said.

"I know."

"I told him I would do it."

"For two hundred grand."

I was impressed.

"Wire taps?" I asked.

"Waste of time," he shrugged. "You guys aren't talking on the phone."

Jensen sort of raised an eyebrow and then came as close to smirking as he probably ever does.

"The day after you got the job at the Goose, we bugged the whole place."

"What, you don't trust your old man?"

"I trust you," he said simply. "Everything you said made me proud."

"And that's legal? Bugging the Goose?"

"The Patriot Act is a beautiful thing."

"In Peking, maybe" I said. "But I forgot, you're a right-wing Christian and a George Bush fan."

Jensen tilted his head slightly and looked me in the eyes.

"Actually, I'm a God-fearing conservative," he said, like he meant it. "And I think George Bush is a good man."

"Who grew up signing Daddy's name at the country club while the family caddy kicked in his short putts."

My son looked genuinely disappointed by what I had just said, or maybe by how I had said it. I didn't like the way that made me feel.

"Dad, if you can't respect the man, at least respect the office," he said. "When you're around me, anyway."

"I'm sorry."

"I think our president is doing the best he can do in a very dangerous world. When I don't think that anymore, I won't vote for him."

I remembered back to the days when my only occasionally ashore Merchant Marine father and I nearly got into fistfights over Nixon and the Vietnam War, but Jensen sounded so logical and sincere, I found myself almost nodding my head in agreement.

"But you don't really believe all that stuff about the Clintons, do you?" I said.

"No, that's just my Ernie act," Jensen said. "But I have to admit, it's fun tormenting you lefties."

"Are you sure you're my son?"

"No doubt," he said and smiled.

I picked up a stick and pretended it was a sword.

"When am I going to Vegas?"

"Soon."

"I'm going to need my gun back."

"That's not a gun," Jensen said. "It's a collector's item."

"I know," I said. "Big Nose Kate got it for a wedding present."

Jensen removed two weapons from his tackle bag. One of the weapons was a small pistol that looked like it was made of Teflon. It was tucked inside a holster about the size of a change purse. I recognized the other gun as a Mac Ten machine gun pistol, the preferred choice of gang-bangers everywhere. Jensen hefted both pistols and then slammed a full clip into the Mac Ten.

"This is a Mac Ten," he said, "but you probably already know about these because this is what you guys always give the punks on TV."

"It looks familiar."

"It's for big game."

I nodded.

"But unlike television, you can't bring down a bad guy from a moving car hanging out the window with one hand on the steering wheel."

"What are you, a critic?"

"I'm still alive, Dad," he said. "I'd like to keep you that way, too."

Jensen stood up, spread his feet and held the Mac Ten straight out in front of him.

"This is a machine gun, so don't try and aim it. Just sweep it toward your target in short strokes, like you're painting some trim, but with both hands."

It was a peculiar analogy, but I knew exactly what he meant.

"And don't hold the trigger down. Use short squeezes. That way, you won't run out of bullets with the bad guys still on their feet."

"We never run out of bullets on TV," I said.

Jensen fired a burst of the Mac Ten and cut down a small aspen tree like a neo-con environmentalist. Then he handed me the paint-sprayer-sized weapon.

"I know you're a fly-fisherman," he said. "Now show me if you're a marksman."

I stood up, took a grip on the Mac Ten, jerked back the trigger and swept it toward a small stand of Douglas fir, cutting one of the little buggers in half.

"Is that the tree you were trying to cut down?"

"I think so."

"*Think so* won't kill the guy who's trying to kill you," Jensen said, and then pointed. "Try that one."

I leveled the Mac toward a six-foot pinion pine about thirty feet away. I squeezed the trigger and pruned the tree to just about shoulder height.

"Nice work," Jensen said. "You took off his head."

I handed Jensen back the Mac Ten.

"What's the Derringer for?" I asked. "Card games?"

Jensen unclipped the small-caliber pistol from its holster and tossed it to me. It was light and felt like a toy gun.

"When an agent working undercover gets caught by the bad guys, they like to make an example out of him."

"I would imagine."

Jensen looked at me. It was a no-bullshit look.

"If you get caught they might torture you, Dad. They could fill your head with LSD and light you on fire or cut your arms and legs off while keeping you conscious with crystal meth. Depends on how angry they are or what kind of drugs they're on. But that little gun could maybe save you from those miseries."

"*Wait.* You want me to *kill* myself?"

"I want you to have the choice if you get caught," Jensen said.

"You guys don't actually do that?"

"Agent Carter was killed with his own service revolver. According to the lab report, he pulled the trigger."

Jensen drove me in the Hummer to just short of the Lost Man trailhead. I didn't have a lot to say on the ride back and mostly just sat there, petting Winston and fingering the small-caliber suicide revolver. For the first time in my life, I was certain I didn't want to kill myself.

"You don't have to do this," Jensen said.

"I want to help you out."

I had to help him out, actually; he was my son. Jensen tossed me his satellite phone.

"This is a secured Bureau sat-phone. I'm in the index at number one," he said. "It's also a GPS, so I can know where you are every minute."

"I don't know if I like that."

"Give it a chance."

I powered up the satellite phone and put it in my pocket. Jensen looked as though he may have been having second thoughts. He tapped the steering wheel.

"You're in their movie now, Dad," he said. "Do whatever you have to do to make it look real."

"If you say so," I said.

Chapter Forty-One

Lynda was naked on the bed in my apartment and making like the beast with two backs with a man I didn't recognize. I guess I should have knocked, but it was too late for that, so I simply coughed. Lynda froze mid-thrust. She was on top. If the man beneath her was twenty-four years old, I was fifteen. He had the complexion of a walnut, and if he'd shaved this morning, his five o'clock shadow was already approaching midnight blue. I could see that he was in extraordinary condition, although short and wiry, like his hair.

"Doo yoose minded, pleeze?" he said, I think.

And yes, I did *minded pleeze,* and I had to throttle back the urge to twist the little bastard's head off. Lynda wrapped herself in a sheet and covered the Walnut's nuts with a pillow.

"*Busted,*" Lynda said. "I didn't know you'd be coming home."

"Who iz thiz man?" the Walnut said.

"My roommate," Lynda told him. "Jake, this is Youssef."

"*Yourself,*" I said. "If he's me, who's he?"

I was trying to stay cute in lieu of turning into a homicidal maniac.

"*Sef,*" he said.

"The guy I told you about this morning," Lynda said.

"The runner?" I said.

"Youssef is here with the summer music school. He's a violinist."

"The summer's over," I said.

"But I found a reason to stay," Youssef said with a smile that had been selling rugs since the time of Christ.

"Put some pants on," I said. "I stopped talking to naked men back in gym class."

I took off my fleece pullover.

"Where you from, You-*sef?*"

"Persia."

"I didn't know there still was a Persia," I said, steady.

"It's Iran now," he said, steadier.

"But aren't you guys merging with Iraq so you can call the whole place Irate?"

It was a cheap shot, but it was better than throwing one at his head.

"That's funny," he said finally.

Youssef put on his pants and a shirt, slipping into an expensive pair of black loafers. I watched him, and he watched me, and Lynda watched us both.

"How old are you, Youssef?"

"I'm half his age plus seven years," Lynda said, suddenly an actuary.

"So that's what? Twenty-one?"

"Twenty-four," Youssef stated, a little too clearly.

But he knew that I knew he wasn't even close; thirty-four *maybe*.

"Praise Allah," I said.

He didn't think that was funny.

"God is the law," he said.

"So is statutory rape."

"Don't be ridiculous, Jake. I've been emancipated since I was fourteen."

But neither of us was listening to her.

"It's midnight at the oasis, Sinbad," I said. "Hit the road."

Youssef glared at me for a few seconds to show me how tough he was, but I towered over the guy by about eight inches and broke his stare. I also had a Mac Ten in my satchel, and it made me feel tough. He kissed Lynda on the lips.

"See you later, lover," he said, and walked out the door.

It was now Lynda's turn to glare at me.

"I fucking *hate you* for doing that."

"This is my home, I make the rules," I said, exactly the way my dad used to say it.

"So I can't date some guy?"

"He's not *some guy*. He's a man."

"You're just jealous and that is *so* sick."

"I'm not jealous," I said, convincing nobody.

Lynda put on some clothes and didn't seem to care if I watched her. So I did.

"Where did you meet this character?"

"His *name* is Youssef," she said. "And he's a genius."

"Look, I come home, and you're in my bed screwing some guy that looks like he should be on the cover of *Newsweek*," I said. "It's hard to tell if he's a genius."

"I met him at the Wheeler," she said. "At *Prisoners of the Mountain*."

"What's that?"

"A film about the atrocities of the Afghan war," she said.

"They're only atrocities if you're on the side that's losing."

"So now you're a racist, too?"

"No," I said. "It's just that maybe this isn't the best time to be humping Bedouins."

"I bet you don't say that when the Prince and his posse of Arab ass-grabbers are in town."

"Bandar has diplomatic immunity. They can grab any ass they want so long as it isn't Condoleezza Rice's."

"This is so disappointing," she said. "I like the guy, big deal."

"But you don't even know him."

"His father's a surgeon, he went to Yale, he's a dedicated violinist and he likes me," Lynda said. "How well did you know that airhead actress you married?"

She was right. I didn't even know my wife couldn't read until after our divorce.

"I'm sorry," I said. "Do you want to move out?"

"Move *where?*" she said. "I'm stuck here."

Lynda walked out the door. I felt like a shit-heel.

"Winston!" Lynda said from outside the apartment.

I could hear her laughing, but then the laughter stopped. Lynda came back into the apartment. She had Winston by the collar.

"What *happened* to his eye?" she said.

"It was put out for looking at another man's wife," I said, like a mullah.

"You're such an asshole."

Lynda left again, but this time she slammed the door. Winston sniffed the bed.

"I know," I said to Winston. "Something stinks."

Chapter Forty-Two

I must have been trying to stake out some kind of primal territory, because I had slept in Lynda's bed without changing the sheets. She hadn't come home. I got up and took a shower but passed on my morning run. Running just wasn't the same alone. I kept telling myself it wasn't because I was jealous—which was the truth, actually. I was happy for Lynda. I just wished the guy were more age appropriate. I had overreacted to the young Persian. I didn't feel good about it.

I put on jeans and a turtleneck and an old motorcycle jacket Lynda had bought for me at Gracie's, and then I opened the door to face the day. I had no idea where I was going, but my trip was a short one. I tumbled face first over a cooler that had been placed, apparently sometime during the night, in front of my door. It was the Zaugg Dump cooler—the one filled with a million hits of the sexy ecstasy.

The cooler tipped over but didn't open, though I did knock off a gift box of Johnnie Walker Red that had been placed on top of it. I opened the box to see if I had broken the bottle, and was slightly disappointed to discover that instead of Scotch, the box was filled with twenty bundles of hundred-dollar bills a thousand bills thick. There was a room key from the Moroccan Bay Hotel in Las Vegas taped to the bottom of the box. There was also a note from the concierge. "See you Friday night," it said. It was Wednesday. I had two days.

Las Vegas was a couple of short hops out of Aspen on America West, connecting in Phoenix. But there was no way I could carry on two million dollars worth of love drugs unless I was a college prankster and disguised them as plastique. The whiz kids from Homeland Security were still body-searching our nooks and crannies in case they contained anything Tom Ridge deemed deadly. That's probably why I'd heard about some poor bastard being arrested for carrying tweezers. But maybe he was planning to pluck the pilot's nose hairs unless he was flown to Algiers. I decided it would be best to drive.

I looked at Winston and then at the two hundred grand.

"Let's go shopping," I said.

Winston and I got off the bus in front of the Hummer dealership next to Big O Tires down in Basalt. I walked in and purchased a top-of-the-line Hummer II right off the showroom floor for the full sticker price of $82,969, not including the break I got with the global-warming-gas-guzzler tax credit. But I wanted to drive a hard bargain, so I didn't spring for the extended warranty or the after-market floor mats. The Hummer was fire-engine red with carbon fiber wheels, huge off-road tires, a front bumper winch and an electric sunroof with broad spectrum UVA/UVB-blocking tinted glass. Two jerry cans were strapped on the roof rack for extra water or fuel. Apparently this was a vehicle designed for soccer moms who wanted to make sure their kids would still get to practice in the event of a nuclear attack.

The Hummer had a CD player but we didn't have any CDs, so we stopped by Great Divide Music and spent several hundred dollars on the history of rock 'n' roll. We also swung by Ute Mountaineering, where I bought a pair of Maui Jim sunglasses that were so expensive they should have been called Maui James. I also spent a thousand dollars for five silk Hawaiian shirts. I was having fun, but maybe it was a way to keep from feeling scared.

I drove through Aspen hoping somebody would see us, but apparently nobody was looking for Winston and me behind the wheel of a new Hummer II. I did see Tinker Mellon chatting up Youssef at the corner of Cooper and Galena. They were sharing what appeared to be a fat-free yogurt from the Paradise Bakery. I honked at them and nudged close as they crossed the crosswalk, but the Persian just flipped me off like a lifetime local without giving me a look.

I could see that they were arguing about something. Maybe Mohammed was ringing the bell for Tinker in favor of Lynda. I had mixed emotions about that, though it was fun to imagine that maybe the goes-around-comes-around karma was going to come around and kick Tinker in her precious little pooper.

I went by the apartment and loaded up the cooler of sextasy, my shaving kit, the Mac Ten and the tiny pistol. I left the refrigerator full of food but grabbed what few possessions Lynda had brought with her. I vacated the apartment in about two minutes, no doubt a Spread Eagle record.

Chapter Forty-Three

"Want to go for a ride in my new Hummer II?" I said.

I was leaning against the chainlink fence at the halfway house for mutts, but Lynda, pretending to be busy, wouldn't look in my direction. Two dogs came over to the fence, and I fed them a couple of Winston's biscuits through the links. I had left him in the Hummer listening to the CDs.

"Don't feed the dogs, please, sir," Lynda said, as if I was a stranger.

"Look, I'm really sorry," I said. "A guy with my record in busted relationships has no right to give advice."

"You embarrassed the shit out of me."

"I know."

"I don't hardly even like the guy," she said. "I was just horny."

If there was one word I hated, it was *horny,* especially the way Lynda had just used it.

"And he puts olive oil on everything," she said.

"Experiencing different cultures can be a wonderful thing."

"Not when he puts it on me."

We both laughed, even though Lynda thought it was funnier than I did.

"C'mon, let me take you for a ride."

Lynda looked at the Hummer II and then at me.

"What are you, the fire chief now?"

"If you love summer drive a Hummer."

"You look like every other middle-aged idiot in this town."

"I'm trying to fit in."

We walked over to the Hummer and climbed in. Winston licked Lynda's face.

"He didn't buy this, did he?" she said to Winston.

"He did," I said.

"With what?"

"My good looks."

"I thought they were expensive," Lynda said, and slugged me in the arm.

After my shopping binge earlier in the day, I had stopped in at Fat City Realty. Since the Iraqi war games and the global economic bust, Aspen real estate had plummeted for the first time in decades, and I had been able to rent a freestanding townhouse that overlooked Aspen Mountain for a meager twenty thousand dollars a month plus first and last and security. The move-in cost was fifty grand, but I was a man who had been used to devouring large wads of cash, and my appetite was coming back. I had not previewed the place, but I was told it was the kind of pad Elvis Presley would have liked if he had lived and had taste, which meant little to me except that the toilets might be equipped with defibrillators.

I turned into the underground parking lot and pulled into one of two slots that were already designated with my name on brass plates.

"What are we doing here?" Lynda said. "And how come they got your name on the parking spots?"

"You ask too many questions," I said.

We went up a flight of mosaic-tile stairs and down a long hall with a parquet floor. I punched in a four-digit code on an electric pad, two large teak doors opened automatically, and Lynda and I stepped into what can only be described as a shrine to excess and conspicuous consumption. Winston sniffed and followed us in.

"Holy shit," Lynda said.

The great room had twenty-foot ceilings, with open beams and whale tusk chandeliers. There were wood-burning fireplaces at either end of the forty-foot-long room, each presently burning wood. Four suede couches filled the conversation pit, and a full bar was sunken below a big-screen television the size of a baseball backstop. There were also a high-speed internet terminal niche, a library, a game room, a gym, four bathrooms and two complete master and mistress bedroom suites with matching waist-deep Jacuzzi tubs and wet steam showers.

"It's so *huge*," Lynda said.

"I thought you might want your own room," I said. "Follow me."

We entered the mistress suite. There was a king-sized canopy bed draped in pink silk fit for a queen.

"I always wanted a canopy bed," Lynda said, like any little girl would.

In the suite's master bath, there was a group-sized shower with tile benches and dozens of spigots and steamers looking like it was intended to treat burn victims. There were also two toilets, side-by-side, for crapping contests, apparently. I didn't see a defibrillator, but a gold-plated bidet separated the commodes, maybe for the referee.

"Oh, my God," Lynda said, looking at the bidet. "A wheelchair drinking fountain."

"It's a bidet," I said.

"What's it for?"

"Mistakes."

I poured us each a Diet Pepsi at the bar and unwrapped a complimentary wheel of Brie. Lynda was already lounging in the great room on one of the suede couches. Winston was next to her and curiously watching the big screen as she channeled through the satellite reception. I sat down across from them on a wicker chair with a hooded back.

"I have to leave town," I said, biting a wedge of Brie.

"We just moved in."

"I won't be long," I said. "But I want you to be extra careful and to take care of Winston."

I handed Lynda a thousand dollars in cash. She was suspiciously speechless.

"And buy yourself some nice clothes," I said.

Lynda looked at the money for a moment, and then finally took it.

"You're not getting involved in drugs, are you?"

The great room suddenly didn't seem so great.

"Don't be silly," I said.

"Then where'd you get all this money?"

"They're re-running one of my series in late night," I said. "I get royalties."

Lynda didn't know much about show business, but I think she knew I was lying.

"If that's the line you want to feed me, fine," she said. "When'll you get back?"

"Couple days."

"Good luck," she said.

Chapter Forty-Four

I left for Las Vegas at six the next morning, when it was still only about ten degrees outside. But the Hummer II's heater was on and I had a hot CD spinning in the player: *The Very Best of the Rascals*. The Mac Ten was locked away in the wheel well storage bin. I wore the little Teflon terminator at the small of my back.

"I ain't gonna eat out my heart anymore," I sang, instantly hungry.

I rounded Philips curve on Highway 82, six miles west of town, and slowed. There were a half a dozen fire trucks and police cars flashing their emergency lights in the middle of the road, and a tow truck was dragging a Mercedes SUV away from the trunk of a giant ponderosa pine. It was a terrible wreck—a fireman was hosing gasoline off the asphalt—and I could see the impression of the pine tree horseshoed three feet into the Mercedes' driver-side door.

An Aspen cop waved a flare and I rolled to a stop. It was

Jensen. There were two other cops standing maybe twenty feet from him, waving flares and directing the busier up-valley traffic. I buzzed down the Hummer II's window, resisting the urge to get out and give my son a hug. Jensen was still Ernie to these guys. I couldn't even brag to him about my new ride.

"What happened, Officer?" I said.

"Laura Keller just got herself killed," Jensen said.

I instantly felt like I was going to vomit and gripped the wheel with both hands.

"Oh, Jesus," I said. "Was she loaded?"

"That's a good bet," Jensen said.

I quickly counted back how many days it had been since I had procured cocaine for Laura and decided in my favor that two grams wouldn't have lasted a user like her this long.

"But it doesn't matter," Jensen said. "She had a bullet hole through her temple."

He whispered the last part.

"Be careful, Dad," he said, between his teeth. "They're raising the stakes."

I was going to say something clever about Las Vegas and stakes being raised, but Jensen waved me on. As I idled off, I thought I could read his lips say "I love you," but I couldn't be sure. And to be honest, I think he might've just actually mouthed *I'll call you.*

I stopped in Green River, Utah, and grabbed a heart-clogging cheeseburger at a fabulous little joint called Ray's Tavern. I filled the jerry cans with gas to impress a legit off-road enthusiast driving a less pretentious four-wheeler, refueled the Hummer and merged back into the truck traffic on Interstate 70. Las Vegas was a ten-hour drive from Aspen, but you got back one hour once you crossed into Pacific Time from the Rocky Mountain zone, so everybody thought it only took nine hours. It was ten in the morning and I had about seven hours to go. I would be in Vegas before sundown.

I put Jackson Browne's *Saturate Before Using* CD into the

player and thought back to when Annie and I wore out our vinyl version of the same album on our Zenith Hi-Fi. We loved to make love while listening to the A-side, and by the end of the winter, the grooves were worn smooth and Jackson Browne was rendered speechless. So was I.

I let the Hummer glide down the last long grade into Vegas. The fuel light had been on for the last twenty miles, but I was one of these guys who thought stopping for gas before the motor conked was a sign of weakness. I exited Interstate 15 at Tropicana Boulevard and drove down the strip toward the Moroccan Bay Hotel. I passed the MGM Mirage, former home of Siegfried and Roy, the illusional animal act that was closed down after the younger of the significant others had finally gotten a tiger to act like a real tiger. A block down on my left was the Paris Casino. A quarter-scale Eiffel Tower straddled over it like a giant stick figure attempting to crap on the roof. On my right was the New York, New York Hotel & Casino, built in an exact replica of the Manhattan skyline. Formerly exact, actually.

I pulled into the Moroccan Bay Hotel, and a valet in a silk fez handed me a claim ticket with my name on it. A bellman snatched up my duffle bag but didn't let on that my new duds made me look like a Parrot Head searching for his lost shaker of salt.

"Welcome, Mr. Wheeler," he said.

I took the cooler out of the Hummer's rear seat.

"I'll have someone get that for you, sir."

"I'll carry it," I said. "It's medical."

The bellman looked at me as if I was trying to beat him out of a bigger tip.

"I'm on the list for a liver transplant," I said. "This is a portable dialysis machine."

"*Liver* dialysis?"

"The latest thing," I said, "but I'm still touch and go."

"I'm sorry to hear that, sir."

They probably go through a ton of livers in this town, so it didn't look like he was going to break into tears. I handed him a twenty and headed toward the front desk. A small man in a red sport coat and a wig that made him look like a chimp doing a Moe Howard impersonation greeted me with an enduring smile. I put down the cooler but stood close to it.

"Mr. Wheeler, we've been waiting for you. Safe trip?"

"For me," I said.

I reached for my wallet.

"It's taken care of, sir," he said. "Suite 32-101. Can one of our bellpersons show you the way?"

"Thank you," I said. "But I think I can find it."

"Excellent," he said. "We have you down for dinner for three at nine at Aureole?"

"Oreo?"

"*Aureole.*"

"The cookie or the nipple?" I asked.

But he didn't answer me. I picked up the cooler by both handles.

"You have a courtesy bar in your suite, Mr. Wheeler," the little man said, sniffing at my cooler.

"Special diet," I said. "I'm a diabetic."

He nodded understandingly. At the rate I was lying about my health, the sports book in this place would probably put the over-under for my death at about 55 years.

It was only five o'clock, but the casino was jammed, and every single gambler appeared to have a cigarette in one hand and a drink in the other. These were my people, and I breathed in as much of the smoke-heavy oxygen as I could. The nicotine tasted great, and whoever came up with the concept that gamblers could drink for free should be honored by the Las Vegas city fathers with a statue in the center of the Bellagio Fountain. The free drinks were why I had doubled down with tens nearly thirty years ago. I could feel that the casino's air conditioning was on full blast; the temperature was about forty degrees. I was wearing one of my new Hawaiian shirts, Bermuda shorts, and sandals, and I was shaking like everyone else. But, just like them, my shakes weren't because of the cold. Lost Wages lured out the worst in me.

Another bellman came out of nowhere and tried to relieve me of the cooler. It must have been embarrassing the management.

"Sir, please," he said, reaching for the cooler. "Let me help."

"It's my lucky cooler," I said. "No one else can touch it."

The bellman understood immediately and backed off.

"I have a lucky hat," he said.

But not that lucky, I thought. He was still a bellman.

We shot up a high-speed elevator and walked down a super-long hall. The bellman opened the door to suite 32-101 with the obsequiousness of a caddy and I was relieved he didn't ask me if he could wash my balls. I tipped him a twenty and told him I could play in from here on my own.

"It's no problem, sir," he said.

"I know," I said, "but I spent my honeymoon in this room, and I want to cherish the memory alone."

The bellman smiled.

"Las Vegas marriages are the best," he said.

"Because they're the shortest," I said.

He left and I entered suite 32-101. If the townhouse in Aspen was a shrine to excess, this suite was a tribute to minimalism. Aside from a small swimming pool in the middle of the main room, the digs were Spartan by Vegas standards. There was a queen-sized Japanese-style bed on the floor of the bedroom nook, one courtesy bar, a small TV and a stainless steel desk. That was it. The management probably didn't want to encourage guests to spend too much time away from the tables, and the pool was most likely only there to sober them up. The floor was large black and white marble squares, and there wasn't even a plastic plant in the place. The room looked like in a pinch it could be swabbed out with a garden hose and made ready for its next victim in five minutes.

I put the cooler in the closet and slid under the bed's rice-paper comforter. I turned on the Golf Channel, shivered, and instantly fell asleep. I dreamed that I was meeting Annie Davenport in the Oreo Room at nine o'clock for milk and cookies. But even in my dream I knew I wouldn't have such luck. This was Vegas and luck was rare—except for bad luck, which lumbered along like plagued cattle instead of stampeding in streaks.

Chapter Forty-Five

I woke up two hours later to the sound of four muffled buzzes. I took a pee and heard the four buzzes again. I checked the TV. It wasn't buzzing. I opened the courtesy bar. There was no buzz in there, although it had the potential for a big one. Top-shelf miniatures were lined up like little soldiers ready to battle the night, and a bottle of Crystal stood available for the victory celebration. I licked my lips and closed the door. The origin of the buzzing was still a mystery to me, but maybe it was some kind of Pavlovian wake-up call rousting me out to the tables. It was Friday night, and downstairs the games had more than likely already begun.

I took a shower that tested the limits of Las Vegas's hot water supply and then put on another of my new Hawaiian shirts. This one was emblazoned with a collage of surfboards and, for some mysterious reason, Egyptian sphinxes. I pulled on a pair of white cotton pants, socks monogrammed with seahorses, and brand-new tennis shoes. I probably looked like I sold used cars in Honolulu, but I was working undercover in Las Vegas and wanted to fit in.

I heard the four muffled buzzes again and finally deduced that it was coming from the Bermuda shorts that I had kicked off at the foot of the bed. I picked them up. In the pocket of the shorts was Jensen's satellite phone. It was blinking and continued to buzz. It was a pretty complicated phone, and I fiddled with it, an analog man doomed in a digital world. I finally figured out how to answer it by pushing the green "answer" button.

"Hey, Jensen," I said, smiling. "I arrived alive."

"Who?" the voice said.

It was a man's voice but it didn't sound like my son's.

"Who is this?" I said, a little tight.

"Who is this?" the voice said.

It was familiar but I couldn't place it.

"Jake," I said.

"You big dummy. It's Tim."

"Hey, Tim."

My throat got even tighter when I wondered how my old pot partner had gotten the number to Jensen's secret FBI phone.

"Where are you?"

"Los Angeles," I said, lying quickly.

"Don't tell me you're going to do something stupid and get back into show business."

"Nah," I said. "Just doing my taxes."

"Good deal."

"Say, Tim?" I said. "How did you get my number?"

"From Ernie."

"Who?"

"You know, that darn cop that keeps giving everybody a hard time?"

"Oh, him."

"You want to talk to the guy?" Tim said. "He's right here. I'm using his phone."

"Sure."

There was a pause, and I could hear the sound of Jensen's voice in the background. Tim came back on the line.

"He said he doesn't want to talk to you," Tim said.

"That's Ernie," I said.

"He's okay, just a grouch," Tim said. "Hey, when you get back, Sarah and I want you to come over for dinner."

"Great."

"And bring back a big appetite because Sarah wants to make up for being so mean."

"She hasn't been mean."

"Oh, c'mon, every once in a while she gets a bee in her bonnet about the old days."

"I don't blame her," I said.

"Me neither," Tim said. "Talk to you soon, buddy-boy."

He clicked off.

Tim Lackey was my best friend, but in the thirty years I had known him, that was probably only the second time I had talked to him by phone. The first time was when he was on his way to federal prison. It gave me an uneasy feeling. I put the phone in my pocket, checked the plastic pistol at the small of my back, left the suite, and walked down the hallway that was about as long as a runway at Heathrow. I finally arrived at the elevators and pushed the "down" button. The phone buzzed again. I flipped it open.

"You actually were in the pot business with that guy?"

It was Jensen. I was relieved.

"Tim's a good man," I said.

"He's lucky he's not doing life for impersonating Wally Cleaver," my son said.

"I just about shit when it wasn't you."

"Tim said he hadn't seen you since he took you skiing and was getting nervous," Jensen said. "Came into the station and wanted to file a missing persons report."

"Tim's like that," I said. "And he doesn't have a phone."

"Is that cornpone routine real?"

"Terminally," I said. "But thanks for putting him through."

"We get a deal on long distance," he said. "You okay?"

"So far."

"Good," he said. "But remember, you're a lowlife drug dealer, so act like one."

"I'll do my best," I said.

"Be careful, Dad," Jensen said.

He hung up and the elevator doors opened. I got in and pushed the button marked with a "C" for casino—not coincidence. I won two hundred and sixty bucks at the dollar slots and then lost twice that at the craps tables. It was almost nine o'clock.

I headed over toward the Aureole Room.

Chapter Forty-Six

I was sitting in a private booth at the outer rim of Aureole and couldn't ignore the fact that the restaurant was about as understated and tasteful as my Hawaiian shirt. It was a sunken dungeon filled with hard chrome and sharp edges. What looked like a discarded elevator shaft was crammed with bottles full of precious wine in the center of the restaurant. The wine tower was a little over the top, even by Vegas's lack of standards, and looked about as natural as a church steeple on a freeway medium. My table had a centerpiece of fresh-cut flowers; two bottles of Dom and a chilled bottle of Stoli Crystal were neatly arranged on a Lazy Susan. There was also a room-temperature carafe of burgundy port.

It had been over an hour since I had sat down, but I entertained myself watching the scantly clad sommelier hoist herself up the three-story wine rack in a climbing belay, snatch a bottle of wine and rappel down. It looked like some kind of game show for rich alcoholics. I was working my way through another Diet Pepsi and was impressed that I no longer had to fortify it with a spoonful of sugar. The placebo went down easily now without it. A waiter came over and popped open a bottle of the champagne, not wasting a bubble. He filled two crystal glasses. I covered the top of a third with my linen napkin.

"No, thank you," I said.

He nodded and left.

During the twenty years I spent in Hollywood, I had been exposed, sometimes intimately, to beautiful women of all shapes, sizes, and pedigrees, but I was absolutely unprepared for the two extraordinary creatures that joined me at my table. One appeared to be an extravagant mixture of every race that has ever populated our planet. She was maybe six feet tall and wrapped in a Prada sheath that was apparently made out of tissue paper. I could easily see this woman's entire inventory, and to say the least, her store was well stocked. Her hair was the color of rusting charcoal, and her skin had the complexion of lightly toasted dough. I don't think I have ever seen a woman as beautiful. The other woman was barely a woman at all. She was a girl of maybe twenty-one with the butterscotch buoyancy of a cheerleader. Her hair was blonde and pigtailed. She wore skintight jeans and a pink denim shirt that was unbuttoned to her navel. Her breasts were small but confident, and I could see a diamond engagement ring pierced through each nipple. She probably took them like scalps from previous lovers, or maybe clients. The cheerleader was as white as the other woman wasn't, and each of them smiled with teeth that appeared to be battery powered. They took a seat on each side of me. I spilled my drink.

"Hi," the taller woman said. "Sorry we're late."

"Not a problem," I stammered.

The cheerleader emptied her entire glass of champagne in one long slow sip. The tissue-paper gal poured herself a glass of the Crystal vodka and chugged it.

"I'm Enova," she said, like a character on *Star Trek*. "This is Cynthia."

"Cindy," the blonde said, outlining the silk sphinxes on my

Hawaiian shirt with a finger. The nail was long and purple and looked as if it could be used as a tiny spoon.

"Are you from Hawaii, Jake?"

"Egypt," I said, palming the spilt ice back into my glass. "How did you know I was Jake?"

I was feeling slightly vulnerable and uncovered.

"Because you used to write for the TV, you goose," Cindy golly-geed. "That is *so* amazingly neat."

I wondered for a minute if Tim Lackey had a little sister who hooked in Vegas.

"It's just that I was expecting to be meeting somebody else," I said.

"Who?" Enova said.

"Who knows?" I smiled.

"Would you like us to leave?" she said.

It wasn't suspicious, exactly. But there was an edge on it.

"Are you kidding, I want you to move in," I said, half-serious.

"Fabulous," Cindy said.

The waiter put down a platter of duck pate, imported cheese, and tiny oval slices of fancy bread. But I suddenly wasn't hungry. Cindy made herself a cheese sandwich and swallowed it.

"How's Big Ricky?" Cindy said. "That guy is such a blast."

"For a cop," Enova said.

"He's a cop like we're models," Cindy laughed. "This is Vegas."

"Are you a cop?" Enova asked.

"What?"

"Sorry," she said, "but I have to ask."

"I'm not," I said and nodded to Cindy. "I used to write for the TV."

"And that is so neat," Cindy said again, sipping some more Dom.

"Then you won't mind if we entertain you?" Enova asked.

"This is Vegas," I said. "It's why Bugsy Siegel built the place, isn't it?"

"Good," she said.

"Is anybody even hungry?" Cindy said. "I'm not."

"I had a burger in Green River," I said, patting my stomach. "Still stuffed."

Enova was watching me closely. I could tell she was the leader of this dynamic duo.

"Then let's just have dessert," she said.

Enova poured herself another drink and then produced a small silver compact. I had no idea where she had been keeping it, although I could venture a guess. She popped opened the compact, and I could see six of the little green aspen leaf tabs and maybe an eight ball of cocaine. There were two silver straws, a razorblade, and a mirror all neatly fitted into the compact. Cindy flipped two of the tabs on her tongue, made a face, and smiled.

"Blasting off, Captain," she said.

Enova held the compact out to me.

"Maybe later," I said.

"This is your brand," she said.

It was obviously a test.

"I know," I said. "But I'm the designated driver."

"We're not going anywhere until tomorrow."

"Absolutely," Cindy giggled.

"And we wouldn't want Little Ricky to get into any more trouble than he already is," Enova said.

"*Little* Ricky?" Cindy asked, obviously confused.

Batman shot Robin a look.

"Cindy," Enova said. "Will you shut. The fuck. Up. Please?"

"Oops, I did it again," Cindy said. "No wonder I love that song."

Jensen was right. I was in their movie now, and it would be wise to give them the performance of a lifetime, or I might not have a lifetime left to give. Anyway, this was Las Vegas, and it is generally unwise to bet against the house. I picked up a tab of ecstasy, placed it on my tongue as if it were a communion host and then washed it down with what was left of my Diet Pepsi.

"Take two," Enova said.

"*Two?*" I said, like a guy who had flipped out at Woodstock.

"There's two of us, darling," Enova said.

I tried to look casual.

"Is this stuff any good?"

"It's so good you'll wish it wasn't so good," Cindy said.

Oh, great.

I took the second tab and waited for the room to start melting. I wondered what the X would feel like and how long it would last. My guess was not good and too long.

"Cheers," Enova said.

She snorted a line of coke and took a tab.

"Hey," Cindy said. "Let's go swimming."

"Where?" I said.

"Your room, Dumbo," Cindy said.

I faked a smile. The three of us got up from the table and headed toward my room. Three months of sobriety down the drain.

But I was only following orders.

Chapter Forty-Seven

I was sitting on the steel desk chair in my stainless steel suite and sipping a ginger ale that I had made up with a swizzle stick and a lime to look like a real cocktail. Cindy was trying to find VH1 as Enova paced in front of the huge windows that framed the lights of Las Vegas below. I felt grim but still grounded. Enova looked like a boa ready to constrict a gerbil.

"When does this stuff come on?" I said.

Enova pulled the drapes and dimmed the lights.

"You don't know?"

It was clear the woman didn't like me and was still suspicious. But maybe cocaine made her paranoid.

"I'm generally a boozer," I said. "But I am looking forward to the flight."

"Buckle up," she said.

Cindy found some music and began to dance. She pulled off her blouse and slipped out of her jeans. She wasn't wearing any underwear, but I couldn't tell if she was a natural blonde or not, because the evidence had been recently removed. Cindy eased into the little swimming pool. The girl was absolutely stunning. I suddenly began to feel my face flush and my entire body tingle. *Tingle* may not be a strong enough word, but *pleasantly epileptic* or *delightfully seizurelike* seem oxymoronic. I wondered if one of these girls had shoved a cattle prod into my rectum when I wasn't looking. It was a crazy thought, I knew. But it made some sense to me at the moment. My whole body began to quiver as if I was being electrocuted—but in a nice way.

"What is this stuff supposed to feel like?"

"What do you mean, Jelly-head?" Cindy said.

She started to laugh uncontrollably. I didn't know what was so funny but began to laugh along with her anyway. The cattle prod felt good, and for some reason, I kicked off my shoes and unbuttoned my shirt.

"This water feels like rainbows," she said. "C'mon in you guys."

Enova dropped her tissue paper sheath to the floor, stepped out of her heels and poured herself another drink from the courtesy bar. She came over and stood directly in front of me, parting her legs slightly. Her pubic hair had been shaved into a three-inch diamond-shaped patch. It looked like the infield at Yankee Stadium miniaturized in Velcro.

"Nice work," I said. "I used to play shortstop."

Enova bent down and kissed me gently on the lips and then began darting her tongue in and out of my mouth as if my mouth was a vagina and her tongue was a penis. I'm sure there was another way to describe it, but this was what came into my head. I almost had an orgasm, which surprised me because Jimmy was still faking a coma, and I wondered who was sending in the plays. It wasn't me. I was losing control and a little bit of my mind. I looked at Enova. She looked Chinese.

"Am I the Mandarin Candidate?" I said.

And I instantly had an idea for a new hit TV series about a guy who was a CIA operative but also delivered Chinese takeout in New York City—on a scooter. The idea came to me in a nanosecond, completely whole. But then it disappeared. I heard someone laughing hard and loud. I think it was me. Enova joined Cindy in the pool. She sat on the very edge of the tile and began slowly frog-kicking while the cheerleader licked up and down her thighs. I suddenly felt like I was levitating. I had never levitated before, but I was convinced that this was how it would feel. I was watching Cindy and Enova from the ceiling directly over the pool, although I was certain I had not moved. But Jimmy did, and I began to experience the fiercest erection I have had since the ninth grade. I shifted on the ceiling, still in my seat. No wonder this stuff was illegal. I felt wonderful. I dropped my shorts, pulled off my shirt, and unhooked the little holstered pistol from the small of my back, placing it in the courtesy bar. No matter how tough the going was going to get, I decided that under no circumstances would I kill myself. Not tonight, anyway. I had a job to do. I dove into the pool.

"It does feel like rainbows," I said, understanding exactly what Cindy meant, but clueless as to why.

Cindy pushed away from Enova and floated over to me, anchoring herself with both hands on my erection.

"I love you," she said.

"I love you, too." I said. "But what about your fiancés?"

I had a hand on each of Cindy's breasts, engaging her engagement rings, as it were.

"I'm going to marry them both," she laughed.

"Are you a Mormon?"

"I'm a whore, silly," she said, laughing harder.

I laughed too, but wondered how funny all this really was. Cindy's eyes were blue and shiny, but empty. Enova wore the soul-free expression of an eel. What little Catholicism I had left was trying to swim to the surface, but I didn't throw it a rope.

Enova kissed me hard with an open mouth. Then Cindy kissed Enova and then kissed me. I kissed Enova and then kissed Cindy. Enova kissed me again and then kissed Cindy. My tongue was getting some very pleasant—though strenuous—exercise, but no doubt my diction would improve. Cindy pulled Enova out of the pool and led her to the bed that was on the floor in the suite's other room. I was no dummy and followed them, but stopped to hang a linen napkin from the courtesy bar on my erection. I thought it was the funniest thing I had ever done. Enova began to pleasure Cindy, and Cindy began to pleasure me. I had an orgasm and almost fainted, but Jimmy bravely remained at attention. I climbed onto the bed and entered Enova from behind, riding her as if I was trying to win the Kentucky Derby.

To say I had never had sex like this in my life would be an obvious understatement. There were moments when I actually felt I was truly in heaven. But I knew that God would punish me. I was a New Age Adam eating the bad apple with a couple of Eves. Then again, who has time to make a novena at a time like this? I finished with Enova and climbed on top of Cindy. She welcomed me with her knees in the air and then tilted her head back to mow the Yankee infield. I pulled a hard line drive to left-center and rounded third, heading for home.

Chapter Forty-Eight

Someone was kicking the bed. It woke me up, but it was hard to open my eyes because they were crusted shut. I was lying on my back on top of the covers, stark naked. I still had an erection, and globs and drops of the previous night trickled out from the holes in my head like gasoline from a leaky tank. I hoped it wouldn't ignite. I tried to focus.

"Cindy?" I said.

"The girls left," a man said.

I opened one eye and could see two men in the room. The cooler was out of the closet and open, and one of the men was counting the Ziploc bags of sextasy. He looked Italian and wore black Banlon pants, a polyester turtleneck, fake patent leather loafers and an antiquated Members Only jacket. There was a cheap plastic suitcase next to him. He was smoking—bravely. The other man was Asian and, by contrast, fastidiously dressed in a midnight blue Armani suit. His hair transplants looked like corn stalks on a hockey rink, but I didn't think I should mention it, because he was standing at the foot of the bed with a gun pointed at my erection. Apparently I had woken up in an episode of *The Sopranos.*

"You call that a cock?" The Asian guy said.

"Afraid so," I said.

"Too bad," he said, with a lot of nerve for an Asian guy.

Jimmy realized that a gun was pointed at him, but he was a brave little bugger and only wilted a little. This hybrid ecstasy could probably keep a guy stiff during a root canal. I covered myself with the rice-paper comforter.

"Who are you guys?" I said, politely as I could.

"Wake-up call," the Italian guy said.

"What time is it?"

"Around three."

"In the morning?"

"In Singapore, maybe."

He pulled open the heavy drapes, and a late-afternoon sun burned into the room.

"You have fun last night?" the Asian guy said.

"I can't remember," I said.

"You did," the Italian guy said. "Went through about five grand worth of pussy."

"Put it on my expense account," I said.

The Asian guy laughed and put his gun away.

"I didn't want you to wake up and go nuts 'cause we was in your room," he said.

"Yo, thanks," I said like a made guy.

He tossed me my Teflon revolver.

"Why the hell you keep that in the ice box?" he said.

"I'm a cold killer," I said.

And these two jamooks went off like I was Bob Hope.

"How come your TV stuff isn't this funny?"

But before I could make up an answer, the telephone rang. The Italian guy picked it up, grunted and handed it to the Asian. The Asian grunted and handed it to me.

"Hello," I said.

"Hey, Mogul, how'd it go?"

It was Chief Rankin.

"Not bad."

"You like the twins?"

"Yeah," I said. "I could hardly tell them apart."

"That's because they were upside down," the Asian guy said, causing his goombah buddy to almost have a stroke.

"Perks of the job," Rick said.

"I'm glad it's over," I said.

"It's not."

"Yeah, it is. These guys are counting it out right now," I said. "Right guys?"

But neither of them grunted.

"I just told you that was the job to get you in," Rick said.

"In what?"

"Deep shit," he said. "Last night was like initiation night."

"To what?"

"Like a fraternity," he said. "Pretend you're pledging."

"Look, Rick," I said. "I was glad to help you out but I'm a little over my head here."

"Just wait," he said.

I didn't like the sound of that, and my hands started to jitter. But maybe it was because I was finally coming down.

"They were never going to kill my kid," he said. "That was just a joke."

"That isn't a very funny joke," I said.

"These guys are going to give you a suitcase of money. I want you to take it to Idaho."

"I don't want to do that, Rick."

"Let me talk to one of the other guys."

I handed the phone to the Asian. He listened to Rick for a minute and then nodded to his Italian partner. The Italian walked toward me, sneezed, and blew his nose into his hand.

"I hate this fucking air conditioning," he said to no one.

Then he put a 9mm Beretta into my mouth. I could barely get my mouth around the barrel, and I gagged—he pushed the gun deeper down my throat.

"That better?" he said.

It wasn't. My tongue was killing me and I remembered why. If this was the last thing on my mind before I entered the Great Perhaps, Saint Peter would be very pissed.

"Here's the gig," the Asian guy said, hanging up the phone. "We're going to give you a suitcase of cash. Exactly two mil except for what you spent on the trim. You hav'ta pay that part back yourself."

I gagged and nodded.

"He's getting the hang of this, I think," the Italian said.

"We got an address of a bar in Idaho and a phone number," the Asian said. "You go there, make a call, they come get you, you deliver the dough, you're done."

"Badda bing," the Italian guy said, like a blurb for HBO.

"Cool?" the Asian said.

I shook my head no.

"Okay, I was wrong," the Italian said.

"Kill him," the Asian said.

I could see the Italian's finger tighten on the Beretta's trigger.

"*Ol ooh id,*" I said, my diction unimproved in spite of the recent tongue exercises.

"What?" the Italian guy said.

"*Owl ooooh idd.*"

"Owl is Ed?" the Asian guy said.

"Who the fuck is Ed?" the Italian said.

"Are you speaking in code?" the Asian said. "We don't use any fucking codes, okay?"

Okay, I nodded.

But he was fucking with me, and they both laughed. The Italian took his gun out of my mouth.

"I'll *do* it," I said.

"Now was that hard?"

He threw me my shorts and my Hawaiian shirt. I rubbed my mouth.

"You know where Idaho is?" the Italian said.

"I can find it," I said.

Chapter Forty-Nine

I drove northeast just about all night on I-15 toward the Canadian border heading to the other side of Coeur d'Alene, Idaho. I was very depressed. Bad flashes and snatches of me performing various acts of depravation were ricocheting back at me as if attached to a Catholic tether. And even though I'd been under the influence of drugs the previous evening, in the harsh darkness of Big Sky country, I could see that my behavior was despicable and loathsome. I had taken advantage of the cheerful Cindy and her Amazon sidekick. They hadn't taken advantage of me. I had exploited their dysfunction for my own pleasure. Prostitution was a crime against women, and last night I'd been a criminal—not to mention that my back was killing me and I had bruises on both knees.

The greaseball brothers had given me the address of a tavern in Moose Head, Idaho, called the Volunteers Gunnery & Grill. Northern Idaho was a popular neighborhood for right-wing extremists and bush vets who were delaying their stress and living off the fat of the land while they planned the overthrow of the United States government. The Volunteers G & G sounded like one of their clubhouses. I was keeping the Hummer well under the speed limit, even though it's generally cool with the Potato State cops for drivers to have a loaded gun and an open beer in the car. But I wondered what they might say about a plastic suitcase stuffed with two million dollars in cash.

I had called Jensen four times during my journey into the wild, but each time I got an automated message. It made me nervous that I hadn't heard from him. Maybe he had already found out about my tag team escapade in Vegas. I knew that the late Agent Carter may have been in a similar predicament with Tinker, and he seemed to get a break on it from the Bureau—although the FBI may have just wanted to clean up Carter's reputation because he was a family man. I really hoped my son didn't know the details of my latest bacchanal. They would not have made him proud of his old man.

The satellite phone rang. It was Jensen.

"Jesus Christ, am I glad to hear from you," I said.

"How'd it go?"

"Awful," I said. "It was a setup."

"There was a high probability that would be the case."

"Thanks for telling me."

"We're all on a need-to-know basis," he said. "Sorry. That's how it works."

"Then you *need to know* that I'm on my way to the Volunteers Gunnery & Grill in Moose Head, Idaho."

"You are?"

"Two guys asked me not so nicely to deliver two million dollars in cash."

"Dad, this isn't smart."

"You're probably right, but one of them put a gun down my throat," I said.

I could hear Jensen tapping a pencil.

"We have a lot of customers up there," he said, finally. "The radical Christian right."

"Yeah, and so few lions," I said. "I think I just passed the Timothy McVeigh Bible Camp and Trade Show."

"That's the cost of living in a free country, Dad. People get the freedom to be lunatics."

"You don't need two million dollars to buy a truckload of fertilizer," I said.

Jensen paused.

"What do you say about turning around and coming home?"

"What do you say you give me a chance not to be a punch-line?"

"I don't think that."

But he probably did, and I tried to imagine the expression on my son's face as our voices connected via satellite somewhere in outer space.

"You stay sober in Vegas?" Jensen asked.

"I didn't drink, if that's what you mean," I said, splitting pubic hairs.

"It's what I meant."

"Let me just go up to Moose Head and play dumb," I said. "I'm great at it."

"I don't like this."

"It doesn't matter—I'm your father," I said, and shut off the cell phone.

I pulled into the Volunteers Gunnery & Grill parking lot at about eight in the morning. It was a Lincoln Logs prefab next to an A-frame fly-fishing shop, cleverly named Master Bait & Tackle—but maybe these guys knew the Vegas tag-team. The Gunnery had a Confederate flag and a Vietnam-era howitzer on a grassy knoll in the center of the parking lot surrounded by two chopped Harleys and a broken down pickup truck. On the door was a life-sized target of Bill Clinton crisscrossed with bullet holes and insults:

NO FAGS
NO LEZBIANS
NO JEWS
NO NIGGERS
NO LIBERALS
NO SHIT

The bar was still open. I entered.

Chapter Fifty

Two pensioners from the Hell's Angels were playing pool on a coin-operated table that had the quarter slot duct-taped shut. Another man in camouflage pants whispered at a pay phone. There was sawdust on the floor, but not for ambiance. It looked like the kind of dive where Rush Limbaugh might try and score some hillbilly heroin.

The bartender was six foot six and bald. He wore a sidearm, and an extra bandoleer of ammo was slung around a chest the size of a snow tire. His pecs stretched the limits of a T-shirt that, in turn, pushed the boundaries of far-right-wing humor. ASSASSINATING BUSH WOULD BE REDUNDANT, the T-shirt stated. The bartender was apparently even to the right of Ann Coulter—the bleached bag of neocon bones who mixed WMDs with PMS for the electronic media—but with firmer boobs.

Sitting at the bar were two barking beauties in their fifties. They wore cowboy boots and had blonde helmet-hairdos and looked like they could've made the finals of an *I'd Rather Be a*

Dolly Parton with My Husband's Face on a Milk Carton contest.
Jerry Jeff Walker sang "Desperados Waiting for a Train" on an
old Wurlitzer.

"Closed," the bald man said.

"Lights are still on."

"We're waiting up for freedom to come home."

Oh, brother.

"How can I help you?" he said.

Probably by not having children, I thought, but instead said,
"I think I'm supposed to make a phone call from here."

But the bald man was apparently selectively deaf. It was probably time to use a small piece of my politically inappropriate person-
ality and show these guys that sometimes I was still one of them.

"Know what they call a hundred lesbians with M-16s?" I said,
inappropriately.

Nobody looked at me.

"*Militia* Etheridge," I said.

The two Partons laughed but the bartender didn't. I could see
he had "Onward Christian Soldiers" tattooed on his arm. The tattoo was sloppy, the kind done in prison with a carpet needle and
India ink. One of the Dollies moved over two stools and sat next
to me with a smile while the other Dolly winked and waved.
Maybe they were the clones.

"Lost?" she said.

"The journey is the destination," I said.

"Don't talk to him, Darlene," the bartender said.

"It's a free country," I said.

But apparently that was the wrong thing to say, and he stuck
his sidearm against my lips. I knew exactly what to do and
opened my mouth.

"Make your call, and then go wait outside," the bald man said.

He took back his gun and wiped my phlegm off the barrel with
a bar rag.

"He just gets jealous, is all," Darlene said.

"Petey, off the phone," the bartender said, motioning to the
man in the camouflage pants.

I moved to the phone. There was a faded decal advertising a regional taxidermist. There was also what I thought to be some appropriate graffiti about where the bartender could stuff his head. Local calls were still only a dime. I dialed a four-digit number, heard someone answer and then hang up.

"Thanks," I said, and left.

Chapter Fifty-One

I sat in the Hummer outside the Gunnery & Grill for about an hour. A man on a bicycle rode into the parking lot and began to open up the fishing shop. I didn't want to masturbate or tackle anyone, having been masturbated and tackled plenty in Vegas, so when he waved, I didn't wave back. Anyway, it was a good time for a review of what I knew.

Three months ago I had defected from Hollywood and the loosening grip of a semi-illiterate writing career. I'd been flat broke but was saved from painting houses with the insane Swiss refugee, Herman Thayer, when I was hired by Aspen's insane police chief, Rick Rankin, to find a possibly insane runaway teenager named Tinker Mellon. Tinker was the stepdaughter of the certifiably insane, but now tragically deceased and murdered, Laura Keller-Mellon. It had become clear to me that Big Ricky only hired me to find Tinker because he believed I couldn't or wouldn't. He'd figured correctly that a washed-up Hollywood drunk was all it would take to appease a washed-up Aspen drunk when it came to searching for her missing stepkid.

But Tinker hadn't really been missing and was apparently only a part of a much larger picture—one that included the nationwide distribution of ecstasy, which was really sextasy on account of it was laced with Viagra. Rick's kid was somehow involved, and so was the deceased Byron, who had probably killed Agent Carter and tried to kill me, possibly twice. Also, Big Ricky and Byron may have been an item.

I had acquired a promiscuous teenage roommate and a great Arctic dog. I missed them both. I'd also discovered I had a son and two grandkids, both boys, all three of whom I was learning to miss. I'd learned that the long-lost love of my life, Annie Davenport, my son's mother, still hadn't married, and the discovery made my heart beat with relief. I had never stopped missing her. My son, Jensen, was a hotshot undercover agent for the FBI but was working with limited resources and personnel because of the continuing war on terrorism. This was almost certainly the only reason he'd pressed his old man into service. I knew that in peacetime I wouldn't be allowed to help. Our blood wasn't thicker than the water that had run under the bridge—not yet.

The two meatheads in Vegas were more than likely just regional distributors who paid cash up front for quantities of the sextasy, then broke down the Ziplocs for their junior partners, who worked the dance-mix concerts and the high-school proms. It was big business but conceivably separate from, or only a small part of, a bigger one—at least as far as my genius son was concerned. But I was now sitting in the gravel parking lot of a right-wing dive in Idaho, so the family genius was probably right.

A nearly middle-aged Iranian named Youssef had been banging my underage roommate, unfortunately once right in front of my eyes. But the US was lousy with Muslims, and his piece, if it was a piece, had nowhere to fit—though Youssef somehow knew Tinker, who'd stolen Little Ricky away from Lynda back when Lynda's name had been Laser.

Jensen was passing himself off as a dim Aspen cop named Ernie, who let my old drug-dealing partner and best pal, Tim Lackey, call me in Las Vegas on an FBI satellite phone.

This was easily the most convoluted scenario I had ever found myself trying to figure out. I was usually pretty good at creating clever dramatic turns and hiding the obvious from the eight o'clock audience. But then I realized I had missed the most obvious of the many ham-handed beats in this typically cruel reality show. After I delivered the two million dollars, I would no longer be needed by Chief Rankin. The smart move on his part would be to make me disappear.

Now would be a good time to get the Mac Ten out of the wheel well, I thought. I was opening the door to climb behind the rear seat when a guy in a vintage Willy's Jeep pulled up alongside me. He was dressed in full battle fatigues. Next to him was a kid maybe sixteen years old, similarly dressed but distinguished by a crewcut and an Uzi that he cradled in his arms.

"Follow us," the young man said.

He flicked the safety off on his Uzi. I followed him.

Chapter Fifty-Two

I followed the Willy's over a logging road bordered on each side by tall Douglas firs and thick ferns. After about thirty minutes we entered a small clearing. We crossed a fast-moving creek which powered a waterwheel rigged to an electric generator and then idled up to a large steel gate with two gun turrets set upon elevated elk blinds, the kind intended for trees. Standing at each perch was a man in military dress with an M16.

The gate was connected to ten-foot-tall steel corrugated walls, which formed a large rectangle that appeared from my vantage point to be about the size of a soccer field. The gate opened, and we entered what could pass for the type of terrorist camp described regularly on *Nightline*. There were maybe fifty ragtag soldiers, a couple of small kids playing with empty coffee cans and yarn, and a handful of painfully thin women with bundled hair, long dresses, and vacuous expressions. The men were armed with M4 carbines, a shortened version of the standard US Army Issue M16, and M9 Beretta sidearms. I knew this because the prop

man on my last television series had been a gun nut and a merce-
nary wannabe.

We stopped our vehicles and the two men in the Jeep climbed
out. The young kid waved his Uzi at me while the driver went to
the Hummer and took out the suitcase of cash.

"I always wanted one of these," the kid said, like any teen cov-
eting a cool ride.

"It's yours," I said.

"I know," he said, nudging me with his gun. "Get out."

A man the two guys saluted and called "general" walked up to
me. He was maybe seventy years old and looked as if he was chis-
eled out of baked mud. The driver of the Willy's counted the cash
from the suitcases.

"It all there?" the general said.

"Doesn't look like it, sir," the driver said, holding a broken-
open bundle of hundred-dollar bills.

The general punched me straight in the face and almost
knocked me out.

"Whoremonger," he said.

"Fornicator!" the crewcut screamed.

Word travels fast up here.

"I know you been waiting for this, Joshua," the general said to
the young kid.

The kid smiled as if someone had given him a new bike.

"But not here," he continued. "Not in front of the women and
children."

"Not *what* in front of the women and children?" I asked, but
only in a very general way to the general.

"He's a POW, sir," the Jeep driver said. "He deserves a fair
judging."

"He's got a judging coming from the fairest judge," the mud-
made man said.

"You guys are new at this, aren't you?" I said, squeaking
through a tight smile. "I mean, nobody ever kills the delivery guy.
That's not how it's done."

The general glared at me.

"How about I help you set up some protocols and procedures here?" I said. "It'd be fun and I'd be glad to do it."

But the kid just spun me around and cuffed my hands behind my back with a short length of chain and two small padlocks. He pushed me into the Hummer's passenger seat, jumped behind the wheel, and burned dirt out the front gate.

"This has a CD player," I said. "Anything you'd like to hear?"

"Music is the devil's work."

"Some heavy metal, maybe," I said. "But some of that other stuff can be spiritually uplifting."

"Don't worry," he said. "I'll let you get right with the Lord Jesus Christ our Savior."

"I'm not ready to be saved."

"You're not a Jew, are you?"

"Only if it'll make a difference."

But apparently it wouldn't. The kid drove about a mile into the bush and then stopped at a clearing. We got out of the Hummer II. I could see that a pit had been dug. Already in it were the smoldering remains of last night's dinner: two mule deer carcasses, about a dozen milk cartons, and maybe fifty charred and empty tuna fish cans.

"I don't want to do this much," the kid said. "But it's God's law."

"A lot of that's been going around," I said.

"You ask for His tender mercies, I'll wait."

"Can I get down on my knees?"

"Of course."

I got down on my knees and slipped the chain handcuffs under my feet so I could get both my hands in front of me. I had already taken the tiny Teflon pistol out if its holster at the small of my back. I started to recite as much of the Lord's Prayer as I could remember, and the young kid bowed his head. Then I stood up and leveled the revolver at the top of that head, firing four shots directly into the boy's brain. He glanced up at me for a split second and then collapsed straight to the ground. The boy was the first person I had ever killed. But I had saved my own ass, and at that moment it felt very good.

Chapter Fifty-Three

I had about ten inches of chrome chainlink attached to each of my wrists, but I could still hold the dead kid's Uzi with my left hand while steering the Hummer with my right. I hit a chuckhole, and the armor-piercing ammo ripped a ten-inch gash through the headliner, cutting clean through the steel and a corner of the tinted sunroof before I could coordinate my finger off the Uzi's trigger.

I entered a meadow that was relatively treeless and flat. I set the cruise control to ten miles per hour, angled the Uzi under my chin, twisted my right hand to its trigger, stretched my left hand out to the end of the barrel and pinched a piece of the chain-link over the machine gun's muzzle. I hit another chuckhole and blew off the ring finger of my left hand just above the big knuckle. What was left of my wedding ring finger felt red hot and about the size of a sweet potato. I stuck the stub into my mouth and bit down hard.

I had also blown the chainlink apart, freeing my hands. I flat-footed the Hummer back into the firs, bending trees and bouncing off boulders, the Soccer Mom Classic kicking classic off-road ass.

But there was no reason for me to be driving like a wanted man. No one was chasing me—which was good, because the Hummer II ran out of gas.

I removed an Adventure Medical Kit that was stored under the passenger seat, opened it and bandaged up the remains of my ring finger with white adhesive tape and gauze. My finger hurt like hell, especially the part that wasn't there. I climbed on top of the Hummer, unhooked a jerry can using my one good hand and both feet, and somehow emptied it into the gas tank without gassing myself.

I kept hearing the four gunshots in my head and the sound of the laundry bag crumple as the kid collapsed to the ground, as if it was on a loop—as if it was something I was going to be hearing over and over for a long time. The good feeling about saving my own ass wasn't lasting.

For no other reason than that it was easier to turn left than right, I chose the left fork in the logging road and immediately found the main highway. I turned left again and called Jensen.

"I delivered the money," I said, "to some kind of militia camp in the boonies."

"Could you find it again if you had to?"

"Probably not," I said. "But we can get it off the GPS."

"Not if you don't leave the phone on, Dad," Jensen said, a bit tweaked. "How are we going to find this place in the middle of the Idaho wilderness?"

"I'm sorry."

My lips began to tremble.

"I killed a kid," I said.

I waited for Jensen to say something that would make me feel okay—some cool FBI lingo about death and the line of duty, but all I could hear him do was breathe.

"It's okay to kill somebody if they're going to kill you, right?"

"Usually," Jensen said, finally.

It started to rain, and water began to trickle through the bullet holes in the roof.

"And I shot off my finger," I said.

"I told you to come home," he said.

The usually scenic ride back to Pitkin County turned into a nineteen hour pukeathon. I tried to force down a box of saltines but the uncomplicated Keeblers kept rebounding into the plastic grocery sack I had strung from my ears like a feedbag. Apparently killing kids made me carsick. It was good to know.

Chapter Fifty-Four

On my way into town I stopped by the emergency room at Aspen Valley Hospital and had a young intern stitch up what was left of the ring finger on my left hand. The baby doc told me if I had saved an inch or two he probably could have reattached it, but I told him it was in a garbage disposal. He gave me a scrip for Percocet along with a handful of free samples. I took three of them.

I pulled into underground parking at the townhouse. The yellow Corvette was parked in the spot next to mine. But I was in too much pain and too tired to try and make sense of it, so I just climbed up the Spanish-tiled stairway, walked down the parquet hallway, took out my tiny pistol, and kicked open the two teak doors.

Lynda was sitting on one of the suede couches holding Little Ricky's hand. The young man was crying and looked a lot more vulnerable than he had in the photos with Tinker. Ricky was clearly the runt of the Rankin litter. He was almost pretty, but in a painfully hip, Winona Ryder sort of way. Or maybe it was the handcuffs.

My son was in the kitchen, elaborately tossing an omelet and wearing an apron over his police uniform. Winston was making like the glass-free coffee table on a fur rug, sound asleep. Two FBI agents were standing stoically at each end of the suede couch.

"Honey, I'm home," I said.

"Well, now, isn't this a wonderful surprise," Lynda said, like Katharine Hepburn in a Christmas movie.

Jensen shook his head at my roommate's attitude.

"I can make you one of these," he said. "But we just ran out of pimentos."

"In that case, forget it," I said.

Jensen flipped the omelet onto a plate and then put it down in front of Little Ricky. The kid whimpered. Lynda stroked his hair.

"It's going to be okay," she said.

"But *when?*" Little Ricky whined.

I put my gun away and Jensen came over to me.

"You okay?"

"I'm surviving," I said.

The smell of the omelet nearly made me swoon.

"What's going on?" I said.

Jensen looked at Lynda and then at Ricky.

"You want to tell him or should I?" Jensen said.

Lynda took a bite of Little Ricky's omelet.

"Ricky got busted in Boulder for dealing," she said matter-of-factly and with her mouth full. "What happened to your finger?"

"I lost it in a card game."

"Bummer."

"My dad will get me out of this," Ricky said.

"We can't find your dad," Jensen said.

Lynda tried to feed Little Ricky a bite of the omelet.

"Eat something," she said.

"The eggs are too runny," he said.

"But they're not too runny in prison," Jensen said. "In the big house they use fake ones made out of powder."

"I'm not going to *the big house,*" Ricky said. "My dad won't let that happen."

"We can't find your dad."

"Where's Dad?" I said.

"He checked himself into rehab," Jensen said, "at an undisclosed location."

"Anonymity is a very important part of the treatment," I said.

"Haven't you ever known anyone with a drug problem?" Little Ricky said.

"Only personally," I said.

"I'm going into rehab, too," he said.

"No. You're going to jail," Jensen said.

"Am not."

"Are too," Jensen said. "But you'll like prison. You get free cigarettes for letting the real big guys teach you how to do the bump."

"They still do the bump?" I said, like Paula Abdul.

"Only in prison."

This time it was Jensen who took a bite of Ricky's omelet. At this rate the kid was going to starve to death.

"Where is your dad?" Jensen asked Ricky again.

"I told you. In *ree-haab,*" he said.

"Where's rehab?"

"That's private."

"Did your dad supply you with the ecstasy?"

Little Ricky didn't answer.

"Did you know Laura Keller was murdered?" Jensen said.

"That was just a car crash," Little Ricky said.

"Laura had a bullet in her head."

"Maybe she shot herself," Ricky said. "She was a loon, anyway."

"And an FBI agent was murdered. Do you know that?"

"Big deal," Ricky said.

Jensen took out his service revolver.

"Murder one, two counts," he said. "You're involved, you get the death penalty."

Jensen took the safety off his gun. Little Ricky stared at it.

"But I can save the taxpayers money and take care of that right here," he said.

And Little Ricky began to click and blink as if he was coming down with a case of Tourette's.

"I don't know where my dad is," he said. "I don't. Honest."

Jensen put his service revolver in Little Ricky's ear and twisted it in a way that looked like it would hurt like hell. This was a side of my son I had not seen.

"What about Tinker Mellon?" Jensen asked.

Little Ricky shook his head.

"You can tell him about that bitch," Lynda said and pinched her ex-boyfriend.

Little Ricky squealed.

"She wasn't really a very good dealer, just mostly a user," Ricky said between snivels.

"And a blowjob," Lynda said, but Jensen ignored her and continued.

"Where is she?" Jensen asked.

"I don't know."

"What about the Arab?"

"The who?" Little Ricky said.

"The guy Lynda here has been doing while you were dealing drugs in Boulder."

"An *Arab?*" Ricky said.

"He's a violinist, actually," Lynda said.

Little Ricky looked at Lynda as if he actually had a heart that could be broken.

"A couple of times. Big deal," she said.

Jensen nodded to the two FBI agents. They hoisted Little Ricky to his feet and bitch-slapped him out the door. Jensen moved to a chair across from Lynda and sat down.

"Young lady," he said. "I have to ask you to keep what you saw here today confidential or the FBI will pursue charges against you as an accessory after the fact to felony drug dealing and murder."

"Who is *this*, Buzz Lightyear?" Lynda said, looking at me. "And tell him if he wants me to shut up, he has to ask nice."

Jensen looked at me.

"I must have been a very bad guy in a previous life," I said.

"But you're doing a little better in this one," Jensen said.

I didn't hear him, because the painkillers had kicked in and I passed out.

Chapter Fifty-Five

Jensen ran a check through most of the high-end rehab ranches in the country, but none them came back with a possible on Rick Rankin—which wasn't surprising. The secrecy thing was a big deal with the rich and famously inebriated when trying to get sober, so getting an ID on anyone taking the cure was almost impossible. I told Jensen we'd probably have to wait until Big Ricky went on Letterman to find out where he'd been drying out. But my son never believed Rick was in rehab to begin with.

A team of FBI agents had combed the wilds in a fifty-mile square surrounding the Volunteers Gunnery & Grill. They'd found the militia camp abandoned, and a bundle of human remains in a pit full of deer carcasses and empty tuna cans. I still felt bad about killing the kid.

The city council had taken over Rankin's duties as Aspen chief of police and the elected members took turns running the day-to-day of the Aspen PD as if it were a celebrity pro-am. Lynda and

I were still squatting at Presley Memorial Digs, at least until the rental deposits dwindled to zilch and we had to move. In the meantime my roomie was either logging onto gawker.com to find out who the Hilton sisters were hoteling up with or rabidly pursuing an Australian massage therapist who avoided dairy products but seemed to daily drink his weight in Foster's. My finger had healed into a handsome stub but ached like hell whenever the temperature dropped below freezing. Little Ricky had copped a plea and was on a school-release program, attending college classes. The FBI was hoping that Big Ricky might show up to see his kid, but so far he was still a deadbeat dad. Tinker had resurfaced and was waiting tables part-time at the Ajax Tavern where Youssef was tending bar. Tinker had also re-enrolled in the twelfth grade and was going to basketball practice.

FBI headquarters wanted Jensen to wrap up his investigation and head back to Quantico to wait for his next assignment. The Bureau figured that until Chief Rankin resurfaced, Jensen was chasing a cold case. But Jensen didn't agree and stalled. I was glad because we had been meeting three mornings a week at my place for breakfast. Jensen cooked and I drank coffee.

"Tell me about your wife," I said.

I had mentioned this once or twice before, but Jensen had always changed the subject. We were cleaning up after breakfast. I was washing and he was drying. The place had a dishwasher but I liked the ritual. It was the kind of thing we both had missed.

"You keep asking me that," Jensen said.

"I'm your dad. I want to know about your wife."

"Don't have one."

"Never married?"

"*Was* married," he said. "How else you think you got two grandkids?"

"I never married your mom."

"I didn't want to put that on the boys."

Touché.

"Do you get to see them much?"

"I have full custody."

"I'm impressed."

"Don't be."

Jensen snapped a dishtowel.

"My wife fell in love with a professional golfer and left us."

"That's tough."

"Very."

"Did she play?" I asked, then immediately regretted it.

"She caddied," he said, "for the LPGA."

"No kidding?"

And then it sunk in all at once.

"Oh," I said.

Jensen wiped his face with the dish towel. Apparently he healed slowly, too.

"She wasn't a lesbian when I met her, Dad," he said.

"Yes, she was," I said.

"That life goes against what I believe in. I'm a *Republican* conservative."

"You're a *compassionate* conservative, a GOP subspecies rarer than the ivory-billed woodpecker. And you're also a very good guy, Jensen. That probably helped your wife come out."

"The guys down at the Bureau thought it was hysterical."

"Yeah, well tell'em if your old man had any Hollywood clout left he'd get Rosie O'Donnell to star in *The J. Edgar Hoover Story*."

Jensen almost laughed and shook his head.

"The boys need their mom, Dad."

"You tell her that, son," I said, like it was an order.

Jensen ran some water in the sink and washed his hands.

"Annie takes care of the boys when you're gone?" I said.

"Isn't that just like her?"

"It is."

Lynda's new Aussie squeeze stumbled out of her bedroom and grabbed a giant can of Foster's out of the fridge.

"G'day," he said, as if he was in a beer commercial.

"*G'mornin'*," Jensen said pointedly.

But the Aussie just shrugged and headed back down under into Lynda's room.

"Whatever happened to marriage?" Jensen said.

I didn't have an answer.

Chapter Fifty-Six

Aspen Mountain had opened early for the season, and it was an epic day. I was at the bottom of a run named Aztec trying to catch my breath. The slope was narrow and steep, and today it was as smooth as a custard pie standing on its side. A skier careened down the fall line in a series of tight, high speed turns, bashing moguls and catching air in a display of freestyle skiing that I had not seen in years—not since I had skied with Tim Lackey. He was unmistakable. Tim stopped at the bottom of a lower run called Spring Pitch.

"What's the matter, old man," Tim shouted. "You run out of legs?"

"Serotonin," I called back.

I took off after Tim, nicely slicing through the steep powder and then covering him in a cloak of snow when I stopped.

"Not bad," he said.

"It's all gravity," I said. "I just hang on for the ride."

We nonstopped it to the bottom and grabbed the gondola for

another lap. I was sweating like a Budweiser clydesdale, but Tim looked as if he had just finished taking a nap. The mountain below us was empty. We were alone in the gondola.

"You haven't lost much," he said.

"What I lost doesn't show."

Tim pulled out a joint and lit it. I was shocked, but maybe he had glaucoma. He offered it to me.

"I'm sober," I said.

"Since when does pot count?"

"Since I started counting."

We rode up the mountain in silence. I looked to my right and could see the Dumps covered in a deep, quiet white. Tim saw that I was staring over at the Zaugg.

"I went into Zaugg's," he said, simply.

"Oh, yeah, when?" I said, flashing on the hole in Agent Carter's head.

"A while ago."

"How the hell did you find it?"

"Wasn't hard," he said. "Just have to know where to look."

Tim aimed a finger at where the mine's opening would be. Then he pointed his finger at me. I kept my gloves on so he wouldn't see that I was missing one of mine.

"I wanted to find that money of ours," Tim said.

I didn't like the look in his eyes, but after all, he had just sparked a fatty.

"But it wasn't there," Tim said.

He wetted the joint and put the roach in his pocket.

"Any idea what happened to it?" he asked.

I really didn't like this.

"Actually, yes," I said.

"Tell me, buddy."

I took a deep breath.

"I blew it on a coke binge in Vegas when you were on your way to prison."

Tim looked at me and then started to laugh.

"Well, thank goodness," he said. "I thought somebody got in there and filched it on us."

"*I* filched it," I said, using the word for the first time.

Tim's eyes went flat black and he stared at me hard. I was suddenly quite chilled.

"I'm sorry I blew your money, Tim," I said. "I am."

"So you owe me," he said, a little too quietly. "Big deal. We're buddies."

He leaned back and closed his eyes for the remainder of the ride up the mountain. Then we climbed out of the gondola, clicked our skis on, and skated over to Walsh's.

"Sarah said if I saw you to drag you up for dinner."

"I can do that."

He smiled. I was relieved.

"But can you do this?"

Tim took off down Walsh's Gully, linking an elegant string of half circles. I closed the other half of the circles about a ski length behind, shadowing him turn for turn; our string of figure-eights perfect.

Chapter Fifty-Seven

Sarah was showing me her latest painting while Tim set the table in their charmingly cramped cabin, its hand-hewn logs swollen with recollections and discarded icons, classic books and rock 'n' roll vinyl. I could smell something delicious that was no doubt homegrown and healthy. I was starving. The painting was oil on canvas of a crippled horse gazing out from a pasture in an urban ghetto. Next to the horse was a dead priest with a red HIV+ stamp on his forehead and a giant porcelain drinking fountain labeled "Whites Only." The work of art looked as if Hieronymus Bosch had repainted Andrew Wyeth's *Christina's World* but was in a bad mood when he did.

"How did you come up with the subject?" I said.

"I think happy thoughts, Jakey," Sarah said. "But you know that."

Sarah's breath was a concoction of alcohol and Listerine.

"That's a heck of a new buggy you parked out front, Jake," Tim said. "You knock over a bank?"

"I got a show in syndication, and I wanted to spend the residuals before the IRS gets ahold of them," I said, lying as easily as I ever had to my best friend.

I offered up a bowl, and Tim began to ladle me some miso soup. What was left of my ring finger stuck out like a sore thumb.

"Oh my God, Jake," Sarah said. "When did you do that?"

"What?" I said.

"Your *finger*?"

I held up my finger and studied it as if for the first time.

"Oh, that," I said. "Stuck it where it didn't belong, I guess."

"And where was that?" Tim said, a little more than simply curious.

"Radiator fan belt, it's why I got rid of that Corvette," I said, still succumbing to deceit's enticing charm. "But I'm not planning on getting married again, so who needs a ring finger."

"If you do, you can use mine," Sarah said.

There was a weird silence, and then Tim laughed a little too hard.

"Hon, we should've had Jake up here a long time ago," Tim said. "He's a blast."

"I think this is the exact right time, Tim," Sarah said, chilling the room.

"I love California rolls," I said, awkwardly chopsticking a roll. "Did you make these, Sarah?"

"Sarah makes everything up here," Tim said, "except they're *Colorado* rolls. They have trout in them instead of salmon."

"I make everything up here except love," Sarah said.

"Now, honey," Tim said. "Jake didn't come way up here to hear all that poo."

"Talk to me like an adult, Tim," Sarah said.

The couple that was made for each other might have been getting a factory recall.

"Uh oh, somebody needs a nap," Tim said.

Sarah got up and poured herself a glass of gin from a bottle hidden behind a large dictionary on a bookshelf. I fidgeted.

"When did you start drinking again, Sarah?" I asked.

"When Tim started getting high again," Sarah said, and sat down.

"One time," Tim said.

"That we know of," Sarah said.

Sarah took a big drink of gin.

"Do you know Tinker Mellon?" she asked.

"*Tinker* Mel-lon?" I said, slingshotting my Colorado roll across the room. "What does she do?"

"Fucks my husband, for one."

"I was high," Tim said.

"And she's in high school," Sarah said.

"It was a mistake."

"I'll say," Sarah said.

"I'm sorry," Tim said.

"You will be."

We finished dinner in silence and then Tim walked me out to the Hummer.

"Think she'll get over that?" Tim said.

"I hope so," I said.

"I blew it, didn't I?"

"Probably not—you guys have a lot of years invested. Sarah's a smart girl."

"When she's not drinking."

"We're all smarter when we're not drinking."

Tim pointed to the bullet holes gashed into the Hummer II's roof.

"What the heck happened to your new car?"

"I hit a bird," I said, to Tim's doubtful look, "then swerved and hit a road sign."

I got into the Hummer and buzzed down the window. Tim leaned toward me.

"I need you to help me out, Jake."

"Sure."

"It's a big favor."

"Is it legal?"

"You didn't use to ask me that."

"With age comes wisdom."

"I need someone to house-sit our place," Tim said, too slowly. "I want to take Sarah down to Mexico for a month or so and see if we can get back on the right track."

"House-sit? Up here?"

"Can you do it?"

I had the feeling Tim wanted to ask me something else but had changed his mind.

"We don't have any locks," he said. "And we got a lot of cool stuff."

Tim fingered the gash in the roof. I think he knew they were bullet holes.

"What do you say?"

It really wasn't that big a favor.

"I'd be glad to house-sit, Tim," I said, and started up the Hummer.

"Hey, you never answered Sarah," Tim said. "Do you know Tinker?"

"She sells drugs," I said. "I know everybody in town who sells drugs."

Tim stared at me for a little longer than I wanted him to.

"Watch your fingers," he said.

"I will."

Chapter Fifty-Eight

I met Jensen at the post office after my run, and we headed over for lunch at the Ajax Tavern at the base of Aspen Mountain, one of the few places on earth where you can shell out twelve bucks for a side order of French fries.

"I had dinner at the Lackeys' last night," I said.

"Oh, yeah?" Jensen said. "How was that?"

"Weird. There's a little noise in their machinery."

"I'm familiar with the sound," he said.

"I'm going to house-sit up there."

I could tell that Jensen didn't like that, but he didn't say anything.

"The perfect couple's going to Mexico to see if they can work things out," I said. "Apparently Tim has taken a ride or two on Tinker."

"Small town."

"They're all small when you get caught," I said.

But I would have bet that Jensen had probably never been

caught at anything, beyond soaping windows or keeping a tad-
pole in his pocket. It made me proud.

"You're going to be up there alone?" he said.

"I'll have Winston."

"Winston can't shoot a gun."

"Winston doesn't have to."

The hostess at the Ajax Tavern was a tall, dark-eyed cosmo-
politan Croat who looked like a Bosnian terrorist who imported
handbags.

"Can we sit in Tinker's section?" I said with a slight Euro-
trash accent I had picked up in Beverly Hills and used as needed.

From my brilliant surveillance, I had learned that the little over-
achiever worked the mid-shift Monday, Wednesday, and Friday.
It was Wednesday. Actually, I had gotten this intelligence from
Lynda. Even though Little Ricky was under house arrest in Boulder,
my flat-mate was still obsessed with her archrival's every move.

"Tinker is working no more here," the Croat said, Euro-
trashing me back.

We sat at the bar. I ordered the French fries and a portobello
mushroom burger with grated Parmesan cheese on an egg-white
egg roll. Jensen went for the twenty-seven-dollar Cobb salad with
minced Montana grayling.

"Where's Youssef?" I asked the bartender.

He was a Japanese kid who weighed about six pounds.

"Youie moved on, man," he said.

His English was perfect but the pitch could have harmonized
with a parakeet.

"You know where *Youie* moved on to, man?" Jensen said.

Jensen was in street clothes, but he still looked like a cop. He
had that all-American quality you hope pilots have when they're
flying you through thunderstorms.

"How would I know that?" the kid chirped.

"Just a guess," Jensen said.

"Are you Youie's dad?"

"No, he's not," I said. "But I'm *his* dad."

"He looks just like you."

"But taller," I said.

Jensen pulled out his FBI ID and flashed it in front of the Asian.

"Cool," the bartender said.

"Thanks," Jensen said. "Did you come here for the music school?"

A big part of the Aspen Summer Music Festival is the school that they run for classical music prodigies.

"Yup," he said.

"What instrument?"

"Xylophone."

"Great instrument," Jensen said.

"If you want to work clown weddings," he said. "It's why I'm tending bar."

"I heard Youssef's a heck of a violinist," I said.

"News to me," he said.

"He's not?" Jensen said.

"Never seen him play," the bartender said.

"Was he a music school student?"

"He was a bartender," the bartender said. "Mostly, anyway."

"What else?" Jensen asked.

"No idea," he said. "All I knew was that he was kosher and always hassled the cooks about how they made his food."

"Jewish?"

"That's funny," the bartender said. "Try Muslim, and a rich one."

"Praise Allah," I said.

"Guy gave me his car, man."

"No shit?" I said.

"No shit."

"Is he coming back?" I said.

"I hope not. It's a nice car."

The portobello mushroom burger was outstanding, but Jensen wasn't impressed with his salad. He thought the Montana grayling tasted more like Kokanee salmon—as if someone could actually know the difference. Jensen paid the tab. We walked down Durant Street, window shopping the ski shop windows.

"Seasonal population is pretty transient in Aspen. People move in and out of town all the time," I said.

"They do."

"You think Tinker took off with Youssef?"

Jensen shrugged. "Maybe he's taking her home to meet the family mullah?"

We stopped in front of Stapleton Sports, and Jensen eyed a pair of bright yellow Atomic slalom skis in the window.

"You have to teach me to ski when I come back."

"Where you going?"

"Home to see the boys, then to Quantico. I'm getting reassigned."

"When?"

I tried not to let Jensen see how bummed I was.

"Right now," he said.

"You're not going to let the city council run the Aspen PD?"

"Nothing is breaking on the case, Dad," he said, "and the Bureau is short-handed."

"When will I see you again?"

"Who knows," he said. "But come visit."

Jensen put his hands on my shoulders and then leaned down and kissed me on my cheek, reminding me that he was a good four inches taller than I am. I rocked forward to the balls of my feet and tried to look him straight in the eye. But I couldn't.

"I'm glad my old man is a good guy," Jensen said.

I watched him walk down the street. Then he stopped and turned. I hoped he was far enough away so he couldn't see that my eyes were filling up.

"You still have my phone, right?"

I nodded.

"Call me."

Chapter Fifty-Nine

I went back to the townhouse and grabbed what I needed for my house-sitting gig. Owen the Aussie massage therapist was sitting on a packed-up duffle bag and drinking a can of Foster's about the size of a hot water heater. Lynda was taking a shower.

"Where are you going?" I asked him.

"Jackson Hole," he said. "Lynda wants me to meet her old man."

"It's that serious, huh?"

"I'm in love with her, I think."

"That's nice," I said. "Is Lynda in love with you?"

Lynda probably was in love with the Aussie. She was at the age where one fell in love about every twenty minutes.

"Said she is," he said, "if I quit drinking."

"Quit," I said.

"I'm from Australia, mate," he said. "We don't have drinking problems down under."

"Must be nice."

"You think I have a problem?"

"I wouldn't know," I said. "But I've been thinking of moving down under so I wouldn't have one."

"Lynda said you quit."

"I did."

"Why?"

"I didn't have enough frequent flyer miles to get to Sydney."

"How'd you do it, mate?"

"I stopped opening my mouth and pouring alcohol into it."

"It was that easy?"

"Easy had nothing to do with it."

Lynda came into the living room wearing a T-shirt. Her hair was bobbed on top of her head and still wet. She looked beautiful but about eight years old.

"Did you ask Jake about how to quit drinking?" she said.

"He just told me," Owen said. "Nothing to it."

Owen tossed the Foster's into the kitchen trash can, nothing but net. But he'd had practice.

I drove up to the Lackeys' cabin, settled in, and slept ten hours straight with Winston curled at my feet. That night it snowed a foot. I skied nonstop all day every day for the next seven days. At night I would stew up homegrown potatoes and beef.

On the eighth night I built a fire in the wood stove and cooked a thin broth. It was time to get down off the mountain and buy more grub, but for some reason Aspen was the last place I wanted to go. I was fancying myself a minimalist, burrowing into my bedroll to finish F. Scott Fitzgerald's unfinished *The Last Tycoon*, a great novel about show business. Maybe I could write an *unfinished* novel. It was the kind of minimal commitment I might be willing to make. Maybe.

I fell asleep and dreamed I was at ABC pitching a series about a fireman. One of the ABC executives was licking my face. But I wasn't at a pitch meeting, and it was Winston who was licking me. I grabbed onto his tail and he led me out the cabin's door. The place was in flames. I puked black soot into the white snow and gagged half-breaths.

"Jesus Christ," I said.

I must have left the wood stove on after cooking my soup and almost my goose. I found two fire extinguishers attached to the outside of the cabin and put out the fire.

"Do I do great work or what?" I asked, as if my heroic malamute could answer.

But Winston was busy sniffing at some snowshoe tracks. Then I realized like a dummy that you can't leave a wood stove on. It runs out of wood. Someone had tried to burn the cabin down—with me in it.

I fired up the Polaris and followed the snowshoe tracks. The tracks ended at the Zaugg Dump.

Chapter Sixty

Herman was hanging from a rope three stories up the side of a gigantic Victorian in Aspen's West End. He was upside down and painting the trim, sweeping the brush in small strokes—like it was a Mac Ten.

"Nice work, Herman," I said.

Herman looked down at me. He was way the hell up there but appeared comfortable. It was a clear day but cold as hell. The work must have been brutal.

"If you can get it," he said.

"Got a minute?"

Herman spidermanned down the side of the Victorian. He looked good. His thinning hair appeared blonder, and he was tan. Herman grabbed a Diet Pepsi out of his lunch cooler and began peeling a banana.

"Want a banana?" he said.

"Thanks."

Herman peeled another one and handed it to me. We both took a bite.

"I'm sorry I called you Bob," he said.

I was surprised he remembered. "Are you making amends?"

"I guess."

Making amends was part of AA's Twelve Step apology program. I used to think that it was groveling, so I never did it. But Herman wasn't groveling.

"How many days?" I said.

"Just got a thirty-day chip."

I smiled.

"How long have I been going bald?" he said.

"Since about 1980."

Herman handed me a Diet Pepsi.

"I need someone to give me a tour of the mines," I said.

"Which ones?"

"I'm not sure."

"Well, you got about forty miles of mines running through these mountains. They go back and forth to Lenado and even that Ashcroft ghost town."

"How about the Zaugg?"

"Zaugg is in a vein that runs all the way to the other side of Taylor Pass," he said, "and then there's bunch of smaller drifts that shoot off of it. What are you looking for?"

"Money and drugs, maybe," I said. "I'm not exactly sure."

"Then count me out."

"It's okay," I said. "I'm working for the FBI now."

"For a TV show?"

"For the real thing," I said. "I'm a special agent."

"And I'm the Duke of Earl," he said.

I told Herman a broad-strokes version of the whole tale as if I was outlining an episode of *The A-Team*.

"That asshole Ernie is *your kid*?" he said. "You should've had a vasectomy."

"He's my kid, but he's not an asshole."

"Guy was always busting my ass."

"Mine, too," I said.

Chapter Sixty-One

It was still dark when I met Herman at the Smuggler Mine portal on the Red Mountain side of town. It was maybe five above zero, but Herman wore only a T-shirt while sorting out our spelunking gear from the jumpseat of a 1978 Porsche Turbo. The Autobahn classic was probably the last thing he had purchased with his race winnings. These days, it looked as if it had been used to test ball-peen hammers.

"I'm missing an AA meeting for this," Herman said.

"Whenever two drunks get together it's a meeting," I said.

Herman handed me a daypack and a football helmet with a flashlight duct-taped to its top. He slipped a small scuba tank onto his back and put on a hardhat with a large flashlight attached to each side. We looked ridiculous.

"I only have one tank," he said. "But we can buddy-breathe if we run out of air."

"We could run out of air?"

"Hey, you ran out of money, didn't you?"

I was wearing my Lowa climbing boots and the Patagonia one-piece with the bloodstains and bullet holes. Herman guzzled from a canteen and handed it to me.

"Since I quit drinking, I'm so thirsty," he said.

"You get over that."

I began to put the Mac Ten and the Teflon pistol into the day-pack.

"No guns," Herman said. "Leave 'em in the car."

"Why?"

"Because they'll ricochet like a video game down there," Herman said. "What the hell kind of special agent are you, anyway?"

Herman clicked on our headlights, and I followed him into the Smuggler mineshaft. It was a large portal, and by the look of the McDonald's wrappers and trash, a tourist attraction. There were a few rusting mining carts, picks and shovels, and dirt and mud. There was also a steel door sealing off any access to the deeper tunnels. Herman swung the axe, hooked the door at its hinges, popped it open, and disappeared into a passageway that was maybe five feet high and four feet wide. A small-gauge rail track was centered in the tunnel. The mineshaft seemed to absorb the light from our flashlights. It was unpleasantly dark.

"Can we get to the Zaugg from here?"

I had decided that accessing the Zaugg from the center of Aspen Mountain in the middle of a ski day might be a little obvious.

"We can get to hell from here," Herman said, like Virgil. He handed me a nylon tether about ten feet long. "Hold on to this."

I looped the tether around my wrist and followed him. I couldn't take a deep breath without choking or a step without banging my helmet against stalactites.

"Money and drugs, huh?" Herman said. "That's why I moved to Aspen in the first place."

"I came for the culture," I said.

It took us about three hours to make the Zaugg shaft, and my lungs felt as if they had filled up with cotton candy along the way. But Herman was enjoying the hell out of himself, telling me the unique histories of the mines.

"Here is where I almost nailed Tinker Mellon," he said. "But I was too whacked."

I could see the chair where Agent Carter had been executed and the old wooden chest where Tim and I had stashed our contraband. The chest was open and empty.

"This the spot you wanted to get to?" Herman asked.

"It's where I wanted to start," I said. "Where does that go?"

I was pointing at what looked like a steel barn door about fifty feet down one of the tunnels. I didn't remember seeing it before. It looked new.

"That could go anywhere," Herman asked.

"I love that place."

It took Herman a couple of minutes to bust open the barn door, and when he did we were almost overcome with the stench of rotting flesh.

"Jesus Christ," he said. "Something's dead in here."

But it didn't stop him, and he disappeared into the shaft. I swallowed back some vomit and tagged along. This tunnel was narrower than the other tunnel, but it was without rail tracks, so the spelunking was a little easier. I was right behind Herman. The smell was horrifying.

"Holy shit," Herman yelled.

He stopped abruptly. But I didn't and tripped over him, flipping face first into something revolting and decomposing stretched across our path. It felt as if I had fallen into a pile of putrid cookie dough, and the smell was so repellent I almost tossed mine. In the beam of my flashlight I could see a lipless white skull with tiny bits of white whirling in insane little circles.

"Jesus Christ, it's a demon!" I said, like a teenage girl at a slasher flick.

I leapt to my feet and off the carcass. It was covered with maggots, and the maggots were moving, feeding in a frenzy on the rotting flesh. My hands were caked in a gruesome stew of rancid tissue and blood.

"It's not a demon," Herman said. "It's a polar bear."

"They don't have polar bears in Colorado, genius."

Herman shined his flashlights on the carcass. It was a bear, probably a black bear. But the feeding maggots made it look white.

"Just an old bear that came down here to die," Herman said.

But I was still rattled, and I gagged.

"You're a very nervous guy," Herman said.

"I've had practice."

The tunnel ceilings got lower, and sometimes we had to duck-walk our way as we journeyed deeper into the shafts. Herman would take a turn down one tunnel and then down another, seemingly without rhyme or reason.

"This isn't good," he said finally.

"What isn't?"

"I think we're lost. But maybe if we can still smell the bear we can follow it back to where we were."

"Is that a standard spelunking technique?" I said. "Dead-bear smelling?"

"Hey, if you have one of your brilliant Hollywood ideas handy, lay it on me."

"There aren't any brilliant Hollywood ideas," I said.

Herman turned the valve on the scuba tank, took a couple of quick breaths and then toked me up.

"Have you seen my wife, Mr. Jones?" I said, songlike.

"I don't have cable."

"It's from an old song," I said, "when the BeeGees all died happy. Before their career did."

"Yeah, well, one of us will probably just kill the other one and eat him."

"For a guy who doesn't have cable, you've seen too many movies."

"I didn't see yours."

"You're not unique."

Then from somewhere way down one of the shafts I could hear Rush Limbaugh's opiated grandiosities. Maybe this was hell. But if Dante was a conservative, I was going to be very disappointed.

"How come his rehab was so easy?" I asked, nodding to the Rushman's echo. "The guy was back behind a microphone before he could pee clean in a cup."

"Because the born-agains are already halfway there," Herman said, "so Jesus doesn't make 'em white-knuckle it like we did."

We crawled on our belly toward Rush's voice and reached the dead end of a tunnel. A portal to a mine stope had been covered over with mud, but we easily dug through and then peered into what can only be described as the kind of hideout recently made popular by Osama bin Laden. It had a bed, a stove and refrigerator, an electric generator, fluorescent lights, and a combination radio cassette player. A rail track dead-ended into the fifty-by-fifty foot cavern. We slid down into it.

Some nut had recorded Rush's blather on tape. I shut off the cassette player and briefly mulled the irony of a man who never listened drugging himself into deafness. Against the far wall, stacked and separated in orderly assortments, were the following:

Four long wooden boxes of M16AR and M16 machine guns.

A half dozen M203 grenade launchers.

An M60 machine gun on a tripod.

An MK19 40mm machine gun.

There were also four M134 mini machine guns, FM 92A Stinger missiles, BGM 71 missiles, and numerous boxes of hand grenades and munitions. I had no idea what this stuff actually was, but it was all conveniently marked and labeled.

"The mother lode," I said.

"A mother fucking load," Herman said.

We heard the rusted squeal of a mining cart rolling down the rail tracks and scrambled up to our opening. Herman and I ducked into the darkness and looked back down into the stope. Chief Rankin entered from one of the tunnels. Two other men were pushing a cart filled with more weaponry. I recognized the two men as the beef jerky general from the militia encampment in Idaho and the Jeep driver who had led me there.

"We won't see you again," the general said.

"That's right," Rankin said.

The two men began walking back down the rail tracks. Chief Rankin pulled out a pistol and shot them at the base of their skulls. Then he pulled out Laura's silver lipstick tube, snorted a blast and recalled a number on his cell phone.

"Noon tomorrow," he said.

Ricky sat down in one of the chairs, closed his eyes and tapped his fingers.

I looked at Herman. He looked at me.

"I can smell the bear," he whispered.

Chapter Sixty-Two

As soon as I could get a decent satellite signal, I called my son. It was 4:30 in the morning but he answered on the first ring. I was exhausted and coughing up black phlegm.

"Are you in trouble, Dad?" Jensen said. "You didn't run over anybody, did you?"

"What the hell kind of question is that?"

"It's a four-in-the-morning kind of question."

"I know what time it is."

I was trying to catch my breath and sound normal.

"Have you been drinking?" Jensen said.

It broke my heart.

"You just need to get here," I said.

It had started snowing heavily, but an FBI Citation risked an all-instrument landing into Aspen four and a half hours later. Jensen and one of the agents who had bitch-slapped Little Ricky down my hallway came over to the townhouse. The agent introduced himself to Herman and me as John Smith. It for sure wasn't

his real name. But Smith was tall and tough, and I was glad he
was on our side. He also had a Mac Ten and wore a grenade belt,
a re-breathing apparatus, and a black titanium helmet equipped
with night vision goggles and a radio. Jensen was geared up about
the same way but without the helmet. He was sitting at the dining
room table with Herman, poring over some maps of old mine
claims and tunnels.

"I think I really need a drink," Herman said for the third time
in ten minutes.

"We can do that," Agent Smith said.

He moved to the liquor cabinet.

"Scotch or vodka?"

"Not a good idea," I said.

Herman looked at me.

"It helps me think," Herman said.

"It turns me into Bob," I said. "Just find the tunnel."

Herman studied the map.

"It hooks up here and zigzags over to Lenado," he said, "by
the old brick factory. But you can't get there from here. Unless
you had something like a helicopter."

"What the hell you think you pay taxes for?" Jensen said.

"I don't pay taxes," Herman said.

Jensen shot me a look.

"Tax cuts for the poor," I said, like a smart-ass. "It's a star-
tling concept."

The FBI chopper set down in the center of what used to be the
dirt-pile town of Lenado; the snow storm was continuing to rage.
Herman was sitting starboard, looking a little too gung ho for my
tastes. Jensen was cool and calm. Smith was dozing. The pilot was
casual but focused. I was probably just flabbergasted by the turns
my life continued to make, but the flabbergastation manifested itself in a series of dry heaves. Either that or I was scared stupid.
We bailed out of the chopper.

"If I don't get out of here now, I won't get out of here," the pilot said.

Jensen thumbed him up and the chopper took off, disappearing into the squall. I put on the football helmet with the flashlight duct-taped to its top. Jensen whacked me on the helmet.

"I don't know what sport you're playing," he said, "but I sure hope you win."

"Me, too."

Jensen broke out some weaponry and handed Herman and me M4 Carbines.

"This is basically just a shortened version of an M16," Jensen said.

"Let me use one of those," Herman said. "The M4's a pea shooter."

He was pointing at a scary-looking weapon with a plastic stock and a short barrel.

"No chance," Jensen said.

"Hey, I'm the reason you guys are even here," Herman said.

"And your country greatly appreciates that," Jensen said.

"It's not my country."

"That's a heavy weapon," Jensen said. "You'd hurt yourself."

"It's an M3 Carl Gustav reusable launcher," said Herman, like he was Colin Powell.

I could see that Jensen was impressed.

"It's a what?" I asked.

"A bazooka that fires antipersonnel and antitank rockets," Herman said.

"Where'd you serve, soldier?" Agent Smith said.

"Swiss Army."

"Like the knife?" I said.

"Switzerland has mandatory military service," Herman said. "I had to do two years before I was put on the ski team."

"Vietnam?" Smith asked.

"Italian border," Herman said. "We kept the body and fender guys from sneaking into Geneva."

"Rough duty," Smith said.

"Yeah, a neutral country with an army that sells souvenirs,"

Herman said. "But it didn't keep me from learning how to shoot."

Herman expertly locked and loaded the M3 Carl Gustav.

"Shit's on," he said in a way that Oliver Stone would have liked.

Herman pointed silently into the snowstorm and then took the lead.

Chapter Sixty-Three

A U-Haul bobtail was backed up to the portal of a large mine. Jensen and Smith slinked up each side of the truck. I tried to stifle another dry heave but ended up gagging instead and instantaneously drawing small arms fire from inside the bobtail's cab. Without wasting a breath Jensen emptied a clip at the front of the truck and everything went quiet again. He looked into the U-Haul and held up two fingers, then reloaded. Smith nodded and waved Herman and me toward the tunnel. When I passed the cab I could see two men bloodied and slumped inside the U-Haul. I recognized the man behind the wheel as a Lebanese immigrant who was part of the snowmaking crew on Aspen Mountain. The man on the passenger side didn't have enough of a face left to recognize. We entered the tunnel.

Jensen wore a helmet that shined a bright beam of light, Smith had his night vision goggles down, and Herman braced the M3. I tagged along behind, thinking about the guy who would no longer be making snow. At the entrances to the drifts that extended from the larger stopes, Jensen and Smith would lean around the corners and fire their machine guns into the darkness.

Herman studied the map and pointed down a small drift that angled off from the main shaft. He led and we followed. We walked maybe a mile into the mine, Indian style behind Herman. He held up his hand and we stopped. Rush Limbaugh's greatest hits were echoing on the cassette player from somewhere way down inside the mineshaft. Jensen shook his head at the right wing pontifications, and I smiled. Smith spit.

"I'd like to tell that guy how much trouble he's causing," Smith said.

"He wouldn't hear you," I said.

A tiny red dot glanced through the darkness and then settled on Smith's forehead as if he was a Hindu bride. The dot was followed by the distant pop of a single gunshot. Agent Smith hiccupped, and then a small circle of blood appeared between his eyebrows as he jerked and fell flat. Jensen dropped to one knee, fired into the darkness and yanked me to the ground. Herman held his M3 at waist level and went charging down the main tunnel. Gunfire was everywhere, but I couldn't tell who was shooting at whom.

"Herman," Jensen yelled. "Take cover!"

But the crazy Swiss just kept firing rockets and sprinting into the darkness. Youssef and four other men appeared out of the black, each of them firing an automatic weapon. They were pushing a mining cart and using it for cover. I let go of my gun, grabbed hold of my knees, and rocked.

"Holy God, Dad," Jensen yelled. "Shoot back."

"Can't we just get out of here?" I said.

I picked up the M4 but couldn't shoot it. This brand of spinelessness wasn't like letting a buddy take the blame for a plagiarized script or bedding a bad actress before she ended up on the cutting room floor. This was whining on the sidelines during an assault on my own flesh and blood.

"Follow me!" Jensen said, rolling across the tunnel floor.

Then my son stopped rolling as a dozen bullets ripped down

the left side of his body. Youssef dragged him into the darkness. I still couldn't move, suddenly consumed with the terror that my cowardly paralysis was payback for how easily I had killed that kid up in Idaho. I wanted more than anything to help Jensen, to charge into the darkness, guns blazing as I tried to save my son. But I didn't, and all I could see were the bullets holes in the young boy's head . . . and instantly I knew I could never let that happen to my boy.

I picked up my gun and ran after my son, bouncing off walls and tunnels, stalactites and dead ends. I kept running until I could neither see nor breathe. The flashlight had been torn from my helmet. It was pitch black. I was lost. I could have cried. But I didn't.

I walked through the darkness like a blind man stepping across a frozen pond. I held my left hand against the rock wall, steering myself down to the main tunnel. If I went left I might find my way to safety and daylight. Maybe I could make it to a highway and flag down some help. My son was somewhere to my right. He might be dead. But I couldn't be sure. I didn't want to leave my grandsons without a dad—better without a grandfather. I turned right. Then I saw light.

The shadows of three men marched down the main tunnel, each swinging a flashlight that made their tall silhouettes appear like a chorus line of pick-up sticks. I pressed against the wall. I could hear Rick Rankin's voice but couldn't make out what he was saying. I reached for the Teflon pistol cradled in the holster at the small of my back and prepared to attack. But someone grabbed me around my neck and covered my mouth, dragging me back into a smaller drift. Rankin and the two men walked past me and then disappeared down the main shaft. I didn't struggle. I didn't have to. A flashlight clicked on and Herman Thayer released me.

"I thought you'd be long gone," he said.

"Me, too."

Herman reloaded my M4 and handed it to me. He held a Mac Ten. It was probably Jensen's.

"Have you seen my son?"

"Not recently," he said simply.

We doubled-timed it through a maze of tight tunnels and shafts. Then Herman stopped, sniffing the air for our decomposing furry friend. He nodded at the aroma.

"Well, how do you like that," Herman said.

"I do," I said.

Chapter Sixty-Four

Herman and I looked through the small opening and down into the stope. Jensen was spread out on the bed, bleeding. Youssef and another man were there with Chief Rankin and the two stick figures from the main shaft, who were now loading the weaponry into mining carts.

"You can't trade him as a hostage," Rankin said, his voice booming in the distance. "Being a frontline soldier is an American fashion statement now."

Herman pointed to his watch, held up two fingers and then pointed back to himself. Then he pointed down to the stope and pointed at me and then to the stope again. I nodded, though I had no idea what he meant. Herman disappeared into the darkness anyway.

There was a knapsack full of money on the ground. Rankin was counting it. I could see Jensen moving, but he was barely conscious. I felt helpless.

Herman Thayer walked straight into the stope and opened fire

on the men loading the cart, killing one of them straightaway. I
surprised myself by heroically sliding into the mix on my belly
with the M4 at the ready. Youssef turned to fire at me with a 9mm
Beretta, but I pruned the alleged violinist's head with a burp of
gunfire. I swung the M4 to Rankin but the gun was either empty
or jammed, and he was able to escape into the mine as the two remaining men were scrambling to trigger their Uzi's. I jumped onto
the back of one of them and snapped his neck with a ferocious jerk
of his head. Herman shot the last man standing in the face.

It was that easy.

I moved to Jensen. He opened his eyes.

"Jesus Christ, don't die," I whispered.

Herman picked up the knapsack full of money and put it on. I
looked at him.

"I'm sick of painting houses," Herman said, holding my gaze.
"I'll split it with you."

"Not with me."

Herman helped me rig my only son into a sling fashioned out
of a blanket from the bed. He had the foot-end of Jensen and began backstepping us toward the main shaft.

"Not that way," I said.

"Why not?"

"Rankin went that way," I said.

We hoisted Jensen through the opening and half dragged him
through the tight, twisting tunnels. It was hard work, but Herman
and I finally got Jensen back to the Zaugg. The former Olympian
stood on my shoulders, unhooked the rope ladder, and climbed
out of the shaft. I tied Jensen to the ladder, scaled it, and then we
hauled my son up. It was barely still light and snowing like hell.
We laid Jensen in the snow.

"I'll go get help," Herman said.

Rick Rankin appeared from the squall and shot Herman
through the chest with his service revolver. My Swiss friend fell
into the fresh snow face first, the bright white quickly turning
bright red. I reached for my M4, but Rankin turned and shot me
twice in the gut. It felt hot.

"You're just a TV guy, Mogul," he said. "You shouldn't have forgotten that."

I pretended I couldn't speak. Rankin kicked the M4 away and then took the knapsack off Herman. I worked my hands toward the Teflon pistol and whispered.

"What?" Rankin said.

I whispered again but made sure he still couldn't hear me. Rankin knelt over me and pointed his service revolver at my head. But I didn't close my eyes.

"And now a word from our sponsors," I said.

"Who?" Rankin said.

"Smith and Wesson," I said.

I emptied six shots into the left side of Rankin's head as if the small pistol was a staple gun. Rankin convulsed and fired a single shot through the top of my football helmet, parting my hair. Then gravity took over and he toppled off of me.

I tried to stand but couldn't. My life was pumping out of my stomach to the beats of my heart, and the blood from the deep ditch in my head flooded my eyes. I probably didn't have long to live. But if Jensen died, it probably wouldn't matter. I half closed my eyes, but somehow I could still see someone skiing toward me through the storm. The style was familiar, the skill unmistakable. It was Tim Lackey. Thank God.

But he didn't look like the Tim I knew. He picked up the knapsack full of money, slipped it on and moved to me.

"It was you?" I said.

"I was only the broker, good buddy," Tim said.

"Help us."

He removed the satellite phone from my pocket.

"You think spending all my money helped me?" Tim said, and skied off.

The *flock-flock* of the FBI helicopter's blades sounded like my old pal the ping-pong ball rebounding off my forehead again but, when I opened my eyes, I could see the middle-aged gal who had saved Winston weeks earlier putting an IV into the back of my hand. I was already in the helicopter. Chief Rankin's body was sprawled on top of a body bag. The large opening on the left side of his head looked vacant, as if everything that had ever lived in it had dried up and fallen out. Two paramedics were ministering to Jensen. They were working quickly but not frantically. Herman Thayer's chest was bandaged, and he was laboring for breath through an oxygen mask. The three of us were still alive.

"Stick to TV, pal," the middle-aged gal said. "They don't use real guns."

"I'm too old for TV, so I'm reinventing myself as a target," I said. "How did you find us?"

"Somebody called in on a secured FBI line. We're still trying to figure out how."

She shot me up with a needle full of something that felt instantly wonderful.

"But whoever it was said to tell you he loved you and that it wasn't the coke talking."

I let out a breath and closed my eyes.

"That was Tim Lackey," I said. "Hell of a skier."

Chapter Sixty-Five

Herman and I were released from Aspen Valley Hospital the day before Thanksgiving. The Swiss hero had a perforated right lung and a broken rib. It had taken ninety jagged stitches to close the wounds in my stomach, and the scar was going to look like someone had pulled a lawn sprinkler out through my belly button. The doctors had also stapled together my cranial canal, and I now had a permanent part on the left side of my head.

"They should've known I didn't have AIDS just by looking at me," Herman said.

We were standing in the hospital lobby, and Herman was looking at his bill.

"Nobody said you had AIDS, Herman," I said. "They just give everybody a blood test before they start cutting."

Both of us had been given the standard-procedure HIV test before the doctors began their handiwork. I was once again pleased with my results. But Herman thought the test was a personal invasion and an insult to his heterosexual reputation.

It cost a hundred bucks," he said. "And what happens when
I want to run for president and they see I had an HIV test? One
thing leads to another, and all of a sudden people are saying I used
to be a promiscuous drunk."

"You have to be born in this country to run for president," I
said. "But it doesn't matter if you were ever a drunk or promiscuous."

He crumpled up his bill.

"Aspen," Herman said, walking out the door. "They test you
for everything."

I entered Jensen's room. His left leg was in traction, and there
was a freshly dressed bullet hole the size of an orange on his right
thigh. The doctors had removed his spleen, and there was a good
chance he would never get full use of his left arm again. I had
spent every day with Jensen since the FBI chopper had landed us
on the hospital's emergency pad. But this was the first day he was
fully awake. Jensen was watching CNN and appeared to be taking notes on a yellow legal pad.

"You watch CNN?" I said.

"I've been personally asked by the State Department to monitor the liberal media for left-wing content," he said, healing faster
physically, apparently, than mentally.

"The liberal media is a myth," I said. "We're lucky *The Washington Post* isn't trying to prove Hillary Clinton killed Vince Foster."

"Ah, Dad? I was *kidding*."

My son had barely regained consciousness, and here I was already going off on a rant. But Jensen smiled at me.

"Oh," I said. "Me, too."

I sat down next to Jensen and he handed me the legal pad.

"These are my final notes on our case," he said. "Even though
everybody is dead, I still have to hypothesize who they were and
what they wanted to accomplish."

"I think you may be the only person in medical history that has
just come out of a coma and can still pronounce *hypothesize*," I
said.

"It has to be a good report. Will you help me write it up?"

"Okay, but if I do, they'll probably want to make you FBI Director."

I scanned the notes. They were neatly printed in black felt-tip pen.

"I'm not staying with the Bureau, Dad."

At first I didn't understand what Jensen meant.

"I'm too shot up," he said.

"You don't have to work in the field."

"Dad, if I end up doing high-school career days, I'll be miserable."

I had to agree with Jensen, and I helped him sip some lemonade through a straw.

"So I asked the City Council to consider me for chief of police."

"You want to stay in Aspen?" I said, obviously thrilled.

"And I want you to think about getting a permit to be a private detective," Jensen said. "We could be a hell of a team."

Jensen was either kidding or still in that coma.

"Has it occurred to my brilliant son that he and his father feed on different sides of the political pigsty?"

"That's the best part. You can work the morally corrupt private sector, and I'll keep it clean and legal on the public side."

"What kind of drugs are they giving you in here?"

"You did a hell of a job, Dad. It must have been all that TV stuff you did."

"I was an instrument of synchronicity and coincidence. Let's not confuse that with what real private investigators do."

But I would have done anything to work with my kid. I wanted to hug him.

"What about the boys?" I asked.

"I want them to move out here with me," he said.

Neither of us said a word about Annie. I sat with my son and held his good hand until he fell asleep, and then I walked back to the townhouse with the yellow legal pad under my arm.

According to Jensen's notes, Chief Rankin had been pilfering contraband from the evidence room for both personal and commercial use. After he scored big by flipping the sextasy to the bent noses in Vegas, Big Rick figured to wheel the two million in cash into many more millions with the purchase of black-market weaponry from a radical Christian militia in northern Idaho he had hooked up with in a Guns & God chatroom. He would then sell the armaments to the highest bidder. But Rankin couldn't do that on eBay. He needed a broker.

When Tim Lackey was in prison, Youssef was his cellmate. The Iranian national was in the can for possessing explosives without a permit while attending Colorado School of Mines on a student visa. He never played the violin. I hoped Tim's adolescent sense of criminal business and a weakness for flamboyant escapade were the only reasons he had gotten sucked into this mess. Tim wasn't a terrorist. He was a slacker. The detailed maps of the Denver Zoo that had been discovered in the glove compartment of the U-Haul truck would have freaked him out. On Thanksgiving Day the zoo is jammed with families, and Youssef probably wasn't planning to free the animals.

If the Persian's plan was obvious and lethally idiotic, it was at least cosmically fitting—if not ironic—that an old TV hack like me had stumbled into it and saved the day. But lethal idiocy is what can happen when bad pomegranate seeds fill up their empty desert days watching Mister T put bombs inside watermelons to blow up the gingerbread bad guys. Television has been syndicating tips on terror ever since Moe first hit Curly over the head with a hammer. Inter-cut that with fear and fanaticism and suddenly Wile E. Coyote has a real gun.

Chapter Sixty-Six

Lynda and Owen had returned from Jackson Hole and were engaged. She was cooking a goose for Thanksgiving. I had left her early that morning in the kitchen with Winston circling at her feet. Jensen was getting out of the hospital on a day pass and was joining us for dinner. Herman said he would be there, too. I was picking up the twins at the airport at three o'clock. Their mom had driven in from San Francisco with her partner. It looked to be an interesting dinner. But I was nervous about meeting the twins.

So nervous, in fact, that I found myself sitting at the back of the seven-forty-five-in-the-morning AA meeting held daily in the basement of the Aspen Community Methodist Church. Owen was sitting in the front row next to Herman. The Australian looked surprised to see me and had tried to get me to laugh by pretending to pick his nose, but Herman hadn't appeared surprised and just waved. I recognized the guy running the meetings as a local guitar player who'd learned how to drink tequila with the Nitty Gritty Dirt Band. I saw a few other old faces from my ski instructor days—apparently it's the liver that goes before the knees. The recovering musician asked anyone who had less than thirty days' sobriety to raise their hands. Owen shot both his hands into the air as if he had just scored a touchdown. I was grateful I didn't have to raise mine.

After the meeting I picked up my mail at the post office and headed over to the gondola. There was a letter postmarked from Puerto Escondido, Mexico. Inside the envelope was the deed to the Lackeys' cabin on the back side of Aspen Mountain and a short note from Sarah informing me that Tim had committed suicide. I hoped it was a lie.

I put my skis in the rack of the first gondola of the day and climbed in. Just before the door closed, another person climbed in and joined me on the hard seat across from mine. It was a young woman. It was Tinker Mellon.

"Awesome day," Tinker said.

"It is."

"Do you live here?"

"I do."

"Man, are we lucky or what?"

"Some of us are luckier than others."

I didn't say it nice. Tinker looked at me.

"Sorry about your stepmom," I said.

"Me, too," she said. "But Laura was so messed up."

"So were you," I said. "I saw the pictures of you and Mr. Dupre."

Tinker took off her ski gloves and examined her fingernails.

"I made some bad choices. It was the drugs," she said.

"Probably," I said.

And I decided to let her off the hook.

"How's basketball?"

"I'm leading in points and rebounds," Tinker said.

"Congratulations," I said. "Are you going to make the Olympic team?"

"You sound like my dad," she said. "I'm not that good."

"Dads are like that," I said.

We didn't say another word to each other.

I skied until two o'clock. My turns were perfect. My legs were strong.

The United Airlines shuttle connecting out of Denver landed. Young Jacob and Jensen were the first ones off the plane and down the stairs, walking courageously between the neat yellow lines that led to the terminal. The boys had nametags pinned to their parkas and they were holding hands. I was waiting with my nose pressed against the glass and wearing a new bright red wool toque over my scar so grandpa wouldn't frighten his grandkids.

"I think you guys are looking for me," I said as they came through the automatic doors."

"No we're not," little Jensen said.

"I think you might be," I said.

"Who says?" Jacob said.

"Me," I said.

"Who are you?" Jensen said.

"Your grandfather."

"We don't have a grandfather," Jacob said.

"You do now," I said.

"What if we don't want one?" Jacob said.

"Yeah, so just leave us alone," Jensen said.

"And anyway, if you're our grandfather, how come you're not with our grandmother?" Jensen continued.

I didn't have an answer and tried to take their hands, but they wouldn't let me.

"That man is your grandfather," a woman said.

I knew the voice and turned to it. Annie Davenport's long red hair was streaked with gray, but her face still looked like it belonged on a Delco Battery calendar.

"Annie," I said simply.

She put a tissue to Jacob's nose and he blew into it.

"Jensen didn't tell me you were going to be here," she said.

Annie didn't appear very happy to see me.

"Is he really our grandfather, Nana?" Jensen said.

"Afraid so," Annie said.

"How come he looks so much older than you?" Jake asked.

"Because he doesn't take care of himself," she said.

Annie looked me up and down and then shook her head. She was beautiful.

"I kept waiting for you to come and get me when you became such a hotshot in Hollywood," Annie said. "Why didn't you?"

"Why didn't you tell me we had a son?"

"I wanted to," she said. "But it didn't seem fair."

"It wasn't."

Annie grabbed the twins and pointed them toward the baggage claim.

"Go wait by where the suitcases come out."

"Why?" Jensen said.

"Because Nana said so, that's why," Annie said.

The boys took off toward the baggage claim.

"Actually, you look pretty good," she said.

"Thanks," I said.

"Botox?"

"Detox."

Annie laughed.

"Are you going to meetings?"

"Absolutely," I said. "First thing this morning, in fact."

She looked at me.

"I loved you very much, Jake. That's why I had Jensen."

"He's a great kid," I said.

"He's our son," she said.

Annie smiled her magnificent smile. It was a smile I had not seen in thirty years.

"May I kiss you?" I said.

"Please."

I kissed Annie. She kissed me back. I felt like I was going to disappear.

I didn't.

Acknowledgments

I do few things alone. Writing isn't one of them. I would like to thank John Wilder, my first mentor, enduring friend, and gifted colleague, for his astute feedback and fearless loyalty. Thanks to Stephen J. Cannell for gambling on me back before I knew what a long shot I was, and for not shooting me when he should have. Much gratitude to Annie Hodgson, whose keen editorial eye and ornery brilliance cleared my early manuscripts of their weeds and debris. I am very grateful to Steve Levine, Kevin Murphy, and Peter Trigg for picking me up and washing me off when I was nearly washed-up and going down; and to Gena Hasburgh, Kathy and Bob Jensen, and my mom and dad, for their chauvinism and blind faith. Big hugs to my sister, Shelly Little, for her potent prayers, and a special thank you to Aspen original, Chris Hanson, for originally asking the book's opening question. Without Luke Janklow's tenacious agenting, *Aspen Pulp* would have never survived; and I will be forever indebted to Sean Desmond for risking his reputation and buying my words. The list goes on, but I won't.